Winter Wonderland

BELINDA JONES

HODDER

First published in 2012 by Hodder & Stoughton
An Hachette UK Company

1

Copyright © Belinda Jones 2012

A CIP catalogue record for this title is available from the British Library.

B-format ISBN 978 0 340 99446 7
A-format ISBN 978 0 340 99864 9

Typeset in Plantin Light by Hewer Text UK Ltd, Edinburgh

Printed and bound by Clays Ltd, St Ives plc

Hodder & Stoughton policy is to use papers that are natural, renewable
and recyclable products and made from wood grown in sustainable
forests. The logging and manufacturing processes are expected to
conform to the environmental regulations of the country of origin.

Hodder & Stoughton Ltd
338 Euston Road
London NW1 3BH

www.hodder.co.uk

Dear Reader,

What a treat it was to get all Christmas-cosy writing this book for you! Enough with the tropical paradises already!

I wasn't expecting to get such a kick tramping around thigh-deep in snow but even when I skidded on the ice and came crashing down on my amply-padded behind I still found myself thinking, 'I'm having the best time ever!' And I hope you will too as you join Krista in the glittering fairytale land of Quebec.

If it were possible to turn the pages while wearing fleece-lined mittens I'd recommend it. Alternatively a pair of mohair socks and a steaming mug of maple syrup tea will serve you well.

Wishing you a festive season filled with crackling fires and an ever-lasting toasty feeling in your heart!

Let the snow-spangled adventures begin!

Your author,

Belinda x

About the author

Following ten years as a magazine journalist and travel editor, Belinda Jones began writing novels inspired by her adventures. She has travelled to over twenty-five countries and hopes to write her way around the world by the time she's done. (Now if only airlines allowed dogs to travel alongside you – at the very least they could dispose of those darn mini pretzels.)

Winter Wonderland is her tenth novel.

Also by Belinda Jones

California Dreamers
Living La Vida Loca
Out of the Blue
The Love Academy
Café Tropicana
The Paradise Room
On the Road to Mr Right
The California Club
I Love Capri
Divas Las Vegas

To the magical Magalie Boutin

(and her fellow Québécois!)

Winter Wonderland

I

I'm lying on a bed of ice. Literally a huge block of king-size ice, sculpted into the form of a hefty four-poster and polished to such a gloss and gleam it more closely resembles glass.

The ceiling and walls that curve around me are made of compacted snow, creating a snug hush, the like of which I have never known. I expel white-breathed awe. This place is magical – even the path to my hideaway led me beneath tinkling ice chandeliers and scroll-topped archways, down corridors seemingly burrowed by polar bears.

I do have to slightly ruin the Ice Princess illusion by revealing that this bed has a conventional mattress but, before you get too comfy-cosy, consider that it's been in the equivalent of a deep freezer for weeks. Those luxurious-looking faux furs splayed on top – the kind that look as if they've been singed on the barbecue – are just for show. My actual bedcovers are a bright orange North Face sleeping bag and a synthetic blanket made of the kind of material typically used to clean sunglasses.

It could be worse. I could be naked, my skin freezer-burned to the bed in a frosty, everlasting kiss. Like some new kind of Bond girl way to die.

The weirdest thing is that I am working right now. This is me in research mode. Albeit horizontal, shivering, *what-was-I-thinking?* research mode.

I'm in Canada, specifically the French-speaking province of Quebec, here to review their annual Winter Carnival. It's the world's largest and repeatedly voted the best. And prettiest. That's all I really know for sure – typically I plan my trips months in advance and get so genned up I could double as a tour guide, but this time we've had to hire a local one for the week because we had a last-minute switch (deciding to save the retro-glamorous ski resort of Cortina d'Ampezzo for next year so we can tie in with the fiftieth anniversary of *The Pink Panther* movie that was filmed there). I literally found out I was coming on this jaunt twenty-four hours ago and, until I checked in, I thought the Hôtel de Glace was going to be a giant ice-cream emporium. You can imagine my disappointment.

If only I'd packed an ice-pick and a bottle of blue curaçao I could be making my own Slushies right now.

Or engraving *Krista Carter Woz Here* in the headboard.

Not that my scrapings could compare to the exquisite etchings that run throughout the hotel. This year's theme is 'First Nation', which is the Canadian equivalent of 'Native American'. My room is called La Coiffe, which roughly translates as The Hairdo, on account of the strong-nosed chief rocking a cockatoo flourish of feathers. There's also a beautiful snow-white (literally!) dove, wings splaying mid-flight.

When I first entered this room I just sat in the perfect stillness and stared at these wall carvings by flickering yellow candlelight.

I may be feeling the cold now but it's nothing compared to the excitement of experiencing something so nerve-tinglingly new. I can't wait to tell our readers all about it.

I write for Va-Va-Vacation!, which is undoubtedly the best, most personally attentive online travel planner in the world. I can say that with utter assurance because I am one of the co-founders, along with Danielle Mitchell who does the design (we used to work on the same magazine back in the day) and Laurie Davis who is one of the few former high-street travel agents who found a way to salvage her career.

We chose the name Va-Va-Vacation! because of its nod to Va-Va-Voom – all sassy-flirty energy with a Fifties flair reflected in our logo. But it wasn't our first choice. Originally we wanted Go Girl! but it was already taken – by a company selling urination devices that allow women to pee while standing up. So good luck to them.

I do the majority of the location guides for the website and make ground level contacts for Laurie to follow up on to arrange discounts for our readers. (Airfares are so scandal-ously high these days we have to try and recoup everywhere we can – not just at the hotels and restaurants but at neigh-bouring boutiques, cocktail bars, art galleries, even nail parlours . . .) We pitch ourselves as the Match.com of the travel industry because all our itineraries are custom-made according to a detailed member profile. Better yet, you always get to speak to a real person (me or Laurie) before the trip (and during if necessary). Our attitude is: Life is too short and travel too expensive to waste a single coffee-stop in a strip-lit chain when you could be basking in a secret court-yard with a waiter who's going to slip you a complimentary macaroon.

Now ordinarily I would go on about our treasure-trove services and all that makes us the ultimate travel companion until you hopped on a train, plane or automobile just to get away from me, but I'm in a bit of a daze. Is it really possible that this morning I was at Heathrow and now I'm in, well, *Narnia*?

I did have a rather different impression on arrival – it honestly felt as if I'd been deposited at the base station for some Arctic expedition. The second I stepped out of the airport taxi I was engulfed in a swirling snowstorm – spiky flakes flying every which way, whisking into my eyes and mouth, up my nose, aggravating me to such a degree I wanted to yell, '*Stop shaking the snowglobe!*'

I signed in at the welcome desk and then went for my introductory talk at the Celsius Pavilion. This wasn't so bad. It was warm, weather-free and they had one of those cool Keurig coffee machines where you slot a little tub into the lid and press down the lever . . . Hot choc for me! Fun!

About twenty-five minutes into the briefing on 'How to sleep at an ice hotel', I started to sense the gravity of this undertaking. Cotton, I learned, is the devil's work. If you sweat it will stay wet and then freeze. As will you. Fortunately I had the presence of mind to pack my highly synthetic thermals and had intended on sleeping fully clothed – coat and all – until the guide insisted I would overheat. That didn't strike me as a pressing concern. He also advised soaking in the hot tubs prior to sleep – the idea being that you raise your body temperature to a steady simmer because, 'The sleeping bag will hold you at the temperature you enter, it will not warm you up.'

The only snag is, I didn't bring a swimsuit. Not the obvious thing to throw in the suitcase alongside your fluffy earmuffs. For a moment I considered substituting my undies, then I saw that a) you have to make a mad dash from the pavilion across the knee-deep snow to get to the tubs which, I should make clear, are alfresco and b) if you forget your hat or let a stray strand dangle, your hair will freeze into icicle fronds.

The bar seemed a much better bet.

Especially since it was home to a blazing, freestanding fireplace. I rushed to its side and held my palms up against the glass casing. Nothing.

'The fire is real but the glass is treated to withhold the heat.'

'*What?*'

'It's just for effect,' my fellow guests explained.

'What a swizz!' I wailed.

'Well, you do realise that if it was real this place would melt.'

'Oh. Yes.'

Even I have to admit, you wouldn't want that.

It is way too miraculous.

Five minutes ago I was in a white wilderness – I walk into the bar and there are lights disco-switching from neon pink to turquoise to emerald green and club music pumping. I couldn't resist giving a rhythmical strut to 'Moves Like Jagger'. It was just so strange to be in a setting where people would normally be in their skimpiest, sleekest outfits and find them bulked up to the max – not one unhooded head in the place.

Many people were drinking tropical mango cocktails but that seemed too much of a stretch for me. We're not in the Caribbean now, folks! So, leaning on the blue-glowing ice bar, I ordered the house specialty – a mix of vodka and Domaine Pinnacle ice cider (a local speciality made from apples picked after the first frost), served in a solid, hand-sized ice cube with a drilled-out middle. Now if I could just get that alcohol to transfer to my lips . . .

'Sip from the narrowest edge,' the barman advised me.

It still felt bizarre and, long after the sweet-tasting alcohol was drained, I couldn't stop sucking on the glass like it was a chunky ice lolly.

From the bar I went on to check out the hotel chapel, scooched down the ice slide, tried to look purposeful as I passed big groups of giggling revellers and then had to admit that, being by myself, I was slightly at a loss for what to do. If only Laurie was here. Danielle is fine, a really fantastic designer, but Laurie is my everything – my best friend, the sister I never had, substitute mum even . . .

When I turned eighteen my real mum pretty much told me, 'I've done my bit, now you're on your own.' She wanted her life back. Apparently I had been cramping her style for too long. Since impregnation, basically.

She gave me a little folder with my birth certificate and a few other documents she thought I might need and I've hardly seen her since.

Which is actually a good thing. It doesn't do much for one's self-esteem to feel like like you're an inconvenience or some kind of never-ending chore.

I don't feel that way with Laurie. She loves to hear every detail of my every day when I'm away on a trip. And when I'm home for that matter. She's a great listener and a great advisor. Mostly because she's done so much emotional 'work' on herself. When she separated from her last '*I'm only trying to control you because I want the best for you*' boyfriend, she decided she wasn't going to get caught out again – no more turning a blind eye to the red flags, no more lessons to learn, no more same issues/different pair of jeans . . . And so she began methodically working her way through the self-help section at her local Waterstones and she's not stopping until she cracks the code – in essence, how to become one of those rare and fortunate people in a genuinely happy relationship.

'I feel like I've got one more shot to get it right,' she told me the last time we had a heart-to-heart over pad thai and lychee martinis. 'I simply can't risk getting into another bad relationship because it's just too darn hard to get out again. I haven't got any more escape acts in me.'

In the meantime she has something better than a mere man – she has Manhattan.

New York City, that is her true passion. And because it's such a popular destination for our readers she does bimonthly updates, using up all her holidays to visit and keep current with club, restaurant and shopping trends. I'm telling you, she could give the concierge at The Gramercy Park Hotel a run for his money.

She also has a particular knack for finding great subjects for our 'Man of the World' slot, which is basically some local hottie quizzed about the highlights of his native city. Laurie adds a different Big Apple Boy on every trip. She says that's all she needs right now – a five-minute street flirtation to put a spring in her step and keep her in the game.

But for me, she wants more.

'We can't let another year go by in which Andrew is the last person you kissed. This has to change. And I think Canada is just the place.'

'You do?'

'Well, they are so famously *nice*, aren't they? I think it's time you kissed a nice man, Krista.'

It would certainly be a novelty.

Let's just say this isn't the coldest bed I've ever lain in. Even before Andrew left there was a palpable chill between us. He used to lie so far over on his side you'd think the phrase 'If you're not living on the edge you're taking up too much room' was his new motto. I would lie there on my back, letting the tears slide down the side of my face and seep into the pillow, wondering how it came to be that my life hurt so much.

The worst of it was remembering how it used to be. In the beginning he was so warm and yielding, wrapping himself around me, holding me so tight, telling me I had given his life purpose. I was precious to him then. His 'only love'. Now he was switched off, shut down and armour-plated.

In some ways I don't blame him for leaving. Technically it was my fault, if beyond my control. There's only one other person who knows the real reason, and that's Laurie. Mostly because I'm still trying to come to terms with it myself. But also because it turns out to be quite the taboo – if you say it out loud in conversation the other person immediately feels wrong-footed and awkward. I guess that's why they invented the phrase 'irreconcilable differences'. What a neat little blanket statement that is.

Blankets! I remember blankets! I start to fidget. At least my feet are toasty – the £28 I blew on mohair socks turns out to be the best money I ever spent. If I could just pull one of them up and over my entire body, I'd be fine.

What is bothering me the most right now is my nose. It's as if all the cold in all of Quebec is concentrated in that small pink triangle. I keep pinching at it, afraid I'm getting frostbite.

Okay. It's time to sleep. Just relax. Hands back down by my sides. Surrender to it . . .

And then something changes. I feel a warm breath pass over my face. A distinct aroma of men's cologne – classic, expensive, with a top note of bergamot. I open my eyes to find a stunning man – seemingly direct from the catwalk of Christian Dior's Winter Collection – looming over me.

I'd say I freeze but that's a given.

'Allow me.' He eases back the hood of my sleeping bag and then begins to gently fan my hair onto the pillow.

Is this room service? Because right now I'd rather have the chocolate on the pillow and the little card with tomorrow's weather report.

He's speaking to me in French which, though profoundly alluring, means I should probably get a translation before Heat-Generating Male Escort shows up on my hotel bill. Especially since he is now reaching under his coat, foraging at groin level.

'*Excusez -moi*,' I jump in.

'*Oui?*' He raises a brow.

'Who *are* you?'

'Gilles.' He says with a sense of 'But of course you know me – everyone knows Gilles'.

'Gilles . . . ?'

'Gilles Pelois.'

Helpful.

He gives me a slightly impatient, 'So now can we get down to it?' look and reaches down his waistband. I try to tear my eyes away but I can't. I'm mildly disappointed to see him pull out a camera.

'You're the photographer?'

'*Evidemment!*'

'I wasn't expecting you until the morning.'

'You didn't get my message?'

'You keep your camera down your trousers?' I counter.

'To keep it warm, so the lens doesn't fog up.'

'Oh,' I say. 'And no, I didn't get any messages. Possibly because I didn't charge my phone . . .'

I hook it up from the base of my sleeping bag and he takes it directly from my hands, pulls off the sleek battery life-extender from his phone and slots mine in. It dings to life.

'Now you can check.'

'It's okay,' I squirm. 'I believe you.' (I know we really wanted this shot – it's the thing everyone wants to know, '*How the hell can you sleep in a hotel made of ice?*') 'I just wish you could've knocked first.'

'On what?'

He has a point. He also has his camera pointed at me.

'At least give me a moment to fix my make-up!' I fluster.

'No-no-no!' He halts me. 'Please. Stay as you are.'

'Really?'

'Trust me. I have a special filter.'

'You mean the lens cap?'

'*Les dames*,' he shakes his head. Which I suppose is the equivalent of a Brit huffing, 'Women!'

'What do you want me to do?' I ask, though my options are limited, straight-jacketed as I am into the sleeping bag.

'Can you bring your arms out for a minute? And turn over onto your stomach. Let your hair fall forward.'

He arranges it so my front layers are partly covering my right eye.

'Now, just look up at me, no need to smile. Just look as if you are awakening from a dream . . .'

'You know this is for a travel website, right?'

'Yes, but we can still make a little er . . .' He searches for the right word.

'Yes?'

'Art!'

'Oh.'

He begins snapping, but when he asks me to blow a good-night kiss at the camera I return to my senses. 'I think I should probably be sitting up with a mug of cocoa.'

'And a woolly hat on your head?' he scoffs.

'Yes!' I roll over and reach into the black storage bag. 'See I have one here with a big pompom!'

His face falls. 'You don't want to look beautiful?'

'Well, it's not really the goal.'

'It's not?' He looks shocked.

'No. It is more of a light-hearted thing.'

'But it is a kind of advertisement, yes?'

'I suppose so, but not like one with a model. *Obviously.* This is about real people. You know, friendly! Having fun.'

He is silent for a moment, as if mentally letting go of any notion of placing individual crystals on each of my eyelashes.

'I am used to photographing fashion models.'

'Well then,' I grimace, 'it's going to be a helluva week for you.'

'Pardon?'

I turn onto my side. 'Reportage? Do you know that term?'

'It is a French word.'

'Oh. So it is.'

'You want me to tell the story of your visit with pictures.'

'Yes, more documentary, less fashion.'

'I need a drink.'

He reaches behind him, burrows in one of the many bags he has brought with him and pulls out an entire bottle of Domaine Pinnacle ice cider.

'I still have my glass from the bar!' I cheer, reaching for it, but it has already frozen to the table. 'Oh!'

'Don't worry.' He sits close beside me. 'We can share.'

'After you,' I say, wanting to make sure he's in on this too. '*Salut!*'

Wow. That was a big glug.

'It won't affect your work?' I ask, a little concerned when I see that it is 12 per cent proof.

'I'll set the camera to auto-focus.'

Suddenly I feel like laughing – this is so surreal. Getting tipsy with a stranger in what is basically a designer igloo.

'Are you willing to experiment a little?' he asks.

'What exactly do you have in mind?' I reply with caution, wondering if my last mega-slug was a good idea.

'We don't have to use these shots for the website, but I had a few ideas before I knew . . .'

'Before you knew what?'

'You know, the style you were looking for.'

'Right . . .'

He goes over to the most voluminous of his bags and pulls out a huge white duvet and a selection of puffy pillows.

'You brought your own bedding?' I splutter.

'I thought it would look like you are sleeping beneath a layer of snow.'

'Is this silk?'

He nods. 'They told me cotton is a bad word here.'

I can't help but chuckle.

'We could use this to contrast the fantasy of sleeping in an ice hotel versus the reality.'

Not an entirely bad idea – more Snow White, less orange Popsicle.

'Travel is a fantasy anyway, isn't it?' he says as he dresses the bed. 'An escape from reality. Or at the very least a new reality.'

'Yes it is,' I sigh, surprised to find myself on the same wavelength.

May I remind you that he speaks with a French accent?

It must be the combination of jet lag, ice cider and Gilles' decidedly unchilly bedside manner because, right now, as I pose for him, I feel like a young Brigitte Bardot, all tousle-haired and winsome. I even have the little gap between my teeth. Which I always hated until I saw the episode of *America's Next Top Model* in which Tyra got one of the beauties to exaggerate her gap, courtesy of a dentist's buzz saw.

Just thinking about it makes me shudder.

'You are cold?'

No sooner has he spoken than his hands are upon my

shoulders, deftly snuggling the sleeping bag back up around my jaw.

'May I generate some friction?'

'Mmm-hmm.'

He pulls my silkworm form against his chest, places his arms around me and rubs vigorously. It is helping, even if it leaves me at a disadvantage – if he chose to kiss me now I wouldn't be able to stop him. But would I even want to? I twist my head so I can take a closer look at him.

'I like your nose.' It's sleekly elegant with the cutest little dip at the tip.

He gives me a quizzical look.

'At least I would be admiring it if I were photographing you. But I'm not. It's the other way around.'

I let my head drop down, both to break eye contact and to hide my blush, but now I'm inadvertently nuzzling his neck.

That's when I notice the pace of the rubbing slowing and the intensity lightening until he is just holding me and smoothing my back.

Despite all the layers between us, this feels incredibly intimate. It's been a while.

But then he sits back and tilts his head in contemplation. I should feel self-conscious, like he can see every flaw, but instead he's looking at me in *that* way – as if he can only see beauty. How do men do that?

'Ready for some more pictures?'

I nod but really I'm not. I have something else in mind. I reach behind my head, kneading the pillow between my fingers.

'Goose down?'

He nods in confirmation.

'Pillow fight?'

His brow furrows, seemingly unsure of my meaning.

But before I can explain, he has grabbed the nearest pillow, swiping at me with one hand, clicking the camera with the other.

'You little tyke!' I exclaim.

Eager to retaliate, I grab my own marshmallowy weapon and start thrashing and lunging, giving him such a clip around the head that I send his fleece hat flying, revealing some seriously mussed-up two-tone hair. He looks as if this could be a problem.

'Wait!' He holds up his hand.

I watch him set up his tripod, switch the camera to automatic and then launch into me again. This time I react with high-pitched squealing and find myself up on my feet, sleeping bag now dropped around my ankles as I get thwacked on the calves, knees and, ultimately, bottom. He's laughing now – possibly at the sight of me in my thermals, but also like someone remembering how much he used to enjoy playing. Before he realised how handsome and cool he was.

We biff and thud and muffle and swing at each other until the air fills with white. Just like snow.

'*C'est magnifique!*' he gasps, snatching at the feathers.

And then he stops and adds a few to my hair, removes the one caught at the side of my mouth and then brushes its silky tip along my bottom lip.

I'm suddenly hyper-aware of the rise and fall of my chest. And our inhale and exhale – exchanging apple-flavoured breath for breath . . . I can't tell if he is assessing me for decorative purposes, framing his next shot, or if he is really moving closer. It's all I can do to stop myself reaching for him. But then his lips are upon mine and the room starts to spin, pirouetting around my head as I succumb to his kisses. Our every move punctuated by the pssht-click of the camera.

'We have to stop!' he pulls away suddenly.

'We do?' I pant. 'Of course we do. Terribly unprofessional. If that's what you mean?'

I can't read his expression. Especially not now that he has turned away from me and is scrabbling to pack up his kit.

'I can't do this.'

Is that an '*I have a girlfriend*' can't do this?

I open my mouth to request clarification but nothing comes out. I just watch dumbly as the tripod is retracted, the bedding squished back into its casing, the camera tucked back down his trousers.

'I will see you in the morning. In Quebec.'

'Okay.' I murmur as I watch him leave.

And then I am alone again.

The hush returns. And the stillness. But I can still feel his imprint on my body, still taste his kiss. And now when I breathe out I can no longer see my breath – because he has warmed the air in here. And me.

'Oh my!' I fall back onto the bed in a swoon, remembering too late that the headboard is made of ice.

2

Throughout the night I kept catching myself thinking, '*Is there a draught in here?*' It's only now that I realise my room is right by the exit. Or '*Sortie*', as they say here. And by exit I don't mean one of those doors with a metal bar you have to lean on to open. I mean a great gaping archway leading directly onto the snow-storm outside. And all that's separating me from the scything winds is my door drape. Which is flapping like a flag.

'Jeez Louise!' I shudder, reaching down into my sleeping bag to check that I can still feel my body. I laugh now at the notion that I would be too hot in my clothes. I long for my fleece now, but it would mean extending an arm from my cocoon and I just can't face it. I have to try and go back to sleep – to will myself to fall unconscious so I can make it to daylight.

But then a new thought arises. I deny it as long as I can but the message is gaining urgency: *I need a wee!*

No, no, you don't. You just think you do.

No, I really, really do.

You do realise what this would entail?

Yes.

And you still want to go?

More than ever.

Who knew that the need to pee overrides all else?

Wish I'd studied the Go Girl! website a little closer now.

I look at my watch. 4.43 a.m. Well, I suppose it could be worse. With the jet lag this was somewhat inevitable. Of course breakfast isn't for another hour and forty-seven minutes. It's then I remember the mini-pouch of peanuts I stuffed in my bag from the plane. Currently in the locker in the main building, along with my suitcase. So now I have two good reasons to brave the cold. And it's not as though it's really going to get any warmer when the sun comes up.

'Right! Here we go. I can do this!'

I sit up and try to claw my way out of the sleeping bag, forgetting in my frenzy that the top toggle is tied too tight to release me. Nooo! I don't want to get trapped half in, half out!

'*She was frozen from the waist up but her legs were still kicking!*' Then I remember the side zip and gasp as the chill rushes over me.

'Wow.' It's actually worse than I remembered. Three times I accidentally rest my ankle on the edge of the bed only to recall that it is made of ice.

I reach for the black waterproof storage bag and pull on my (cold) sweater and my (cold) coat and my (cold) socks and boots. And then I do a vigorous jig as if I might be able to energise some heat molecules.

So this is it. I pause for a moment's appreciation of my room – which come the spring simply won't exist – and then pull back the curtain and step into the corridor. All is silent.

I retrace my steps to the front entrance and find myself gaping at the black snow-flurried sky. Yesterday was a whisk of confetti compared to this onslaught but I can't deny the beauty of the scene – not so much a blanket of snow covering the earth as an overstuffed duvet. I almost don't want to disrupt the crystalline surface with my nubbed boot sole and, when I do take a step, the white engulfs me up to my thigh.

'Woah!'

I look around me. Not a soul. But the Celsius Pavilion and its hallowed bathroom facilities lure me on . . .

'Oop!'

That would be a step there. Not that you can tell: the snow is so deep there's absolutely no indication of what lies beneath. I look back at my footprints/leg indents – already the wind is covering my trail. I give a little shudder and tromp boldly onwards, puffing with eagerness as I reach the toilet.

There were times when my dog could just pee and pee and pee. Now I can relate.

Oohh. I feel better for that.

No sooner am I tucked in, strapped across, buttoned and zipped up than I realise I want to go again.

'I can't believe you did it!' Laurie cheers when I call to tell her that I survived the night.

'Well, half-did it.'

'Listen, anything beyond an hour is a triumph in my book. I don't like lingering too long in the frozen food aisle at Tesco.'

'So you don't think it would be a total cop-out if I left now and got a few hours' kip at the backup hotel?'

'Backup hotel?' she queries.

'It's on the itinerary. Very considerate, actually. For those of us who aren't interested in first-hand knowledge of cryogenics.'

'Are you sure it's going to be an improvement?'

'It's a Hilton.'

'Hilton? Didn't they get our memo about favouring non-chain hotels?'

'Apparently this one has something in particular to commend it. Right now, that would be heating . . . Oh!'

'What?'

'I thought I might have dreamt this but . . .' I pull a feather out from my collar. 'Last night a stunningly handsome man with a French accent came to my room.'

'I thought they might provide a hot-water bottle but that's even better! What did he want?'

'Well, for a few minutes he wanted me.'

And then I tell her the whole story. From initial sniping to pillow fighting to apple-flavour kisses.

'Wow.'

'I know.' I sigh. 'I just wish I was never going to see him again!'

'Huh?'

'Oh you know how quickly last night's bliss becomes morning-after mortification.'

'A story as old as time,' Laurie concurs.

'I've got to spend a whole week working alongside him and I can't bear it if he's all awkward and regretful.'

'I can see how it would have been preferable to have had a week-long flirtation culminating in a night of passion before the flight home,' she concedes. 'Not that I'm complaining, because the fact that you've kissed someone other than your ex-husband is a major breakthrough.'

'That's true.'

'But I thought we decided you were going to hook up with a Canadian Mountie or one of those bendy people from Cirque du Soleil?'

'Well, it turns out that Mounties are a rare breed in Quebec and Cirque du Soleil HQ is in Montreal, which is about three hours west of here.'

'Hmm, might be worth a trip for a side story – most of our readers would be flying into there initially and we could offer a two-centre holiday.'

'Oh I do like a two-centre!'

'Like Manhattan and the Hamptons!' Laurie coos. 'One fine day . . .'

Laurie is convinced that her future husband is waiting for her in the Hamptons. All she needs is an invitation to one of those summer mansion shares and everything will fall into place . . . I'm actually working on a lead for that at the moment but I haven't mentioned it because I don't want to get her too excited in case it comes to nothing. Speaking of which . . .

'What do you make of Gilles' parting words: "*I can't do this!*"'

'Hard to say,' she replies. 'I suppose the obvious interpretation is that there is another woman. Or maybe he's physically incapable of following through . . .'

'Oh dear.'

'I think this is basically one of those "prepare for the worst, expect the best" scenarios.'

'And how does that translate in practical terms?'

'You're going to have to set aside any romantic notions until you are clear on his situation. The last thing you want to do is turn up with an expression that says, "*What was that last night and where do we go from here?*"'

'Even though those would be two perfectly natural queries.'

'You need to detach from the outcome,' she affirms. 'At least for this first meeting. Go neutral. No wariness, no neediness, not even a trace of curiosity.'

'What does that leave me with?'

'Hopefully your dignity.'

I'm not convinced.

'Anyway, you'll know within the first few seconds how it's going to go – either his eyes will light up at the sight of you or he'll get all awkward and avoid your gaze.'

'I suspect the latter.'

'Either way, *you* mustn't be awkward.'

'So basically, act like it never happened?'

'Well, there are basically three ways to go with this.' She proposes. 'One, you could be defiantly upbeat. Nothing to be embarrassed about! You have this effect on men all the time.'

I splutter so hard I look as if I'm giving myself the Heimlich manoeuvre. 'Number two?'

'You have a secret knowingness to you.'

'I don't know,' I cringe. 'Whenever I try to look enigmatic I just end up looking confused. Number three?'

'There's this word . . .' She's silent for a moment, trying to recall it. 'I know! *Beatific!*' She cheers. 'You want to look beatific!'

'Remind me . . .'

'Serene and sort of "above" whatever he throws at you. So if he's all fretful and squirmy you just rise above it all and give him the royal pardon.'

'Doesn't really sound like me, does it?'

'Yes, but he doesn't know that. He doesn't know that you'd typically bend over backwards to accommodate him in any way you can and then immediately set to work finding a cure for whatever ails him. All he has to go on is how you behave in that moment. So if you can pull that off, you're in the clear.'

'Right.' I gulp, wondering if there are any local acting classes held at 5.30 a.m.

'I suppose there is another question,' Laurie adds. 'If he was available, would you be interested?'

'I don't know.' I bite my lip. 'He's not really me. I think he might be a bit "fancy" for my tastes.'

'A bit gourmet?'

I giggle. 'He's used to mingling with the fashion elite.'

'And that may be the greatest thing in your favour.'

And then Laurie's phone alarm intervenes.

'Meeting?'

'Yup, 10.30 a.m. with Madrid tourism.'

'I can't believe it's still so early with you.'

'It's even earlier with you kiddo!' she reminds me. 'So here's what I suggest you do in the short-term – get a hot drink then a cab to the Hilton and get thee to bed.'

'Okay.'

'And do me a favour . . .'

'Anything.'

'Put the Do Not Disturb sign on your door this time.'

Smirking to myself, I tuck my phone in my pocket and head
for the Keurig machine. That's when I spy Another Human
Being, yawning over at Reception in an 'I can't believe I get
the graveyard shift' way.

'Oh hello!'

'*Bonjour!*'

It's too early for me to attempt any French so I simply ask,
'Is it possible to order a taxi?' Though really a horse and
sleigh might be a more appropriate option.

Since the walkway is buried and they haven't had a chance
to clear the pathways yet, Reception dude summons a 4x4 to
take me round to the pick-up point at the Welcome Centre.

I expect the driver to be another insomniac youth, but the
guy has to be in his seventies. Shouldn't he be at home with
a pair of sheepskin slippers and a pipe? I don't know what it
is with old folks these days – they seem more daredevilish
and energetic than people a third of their age.

Not only does he scoop up my hefty case as though it's
filled with candyfloss, apparently he can also read minds
because he says, 'You know we had a ninety-one-year-old
here this week?'

'You're kidding?' I gasp. 'How did he get into his sleeping
bag?'

'Oh he managed fine! I saw the pictures – his kids docu-
mented the whole thing.'

'His kids?'

'Well, when I say kids, they were in their sixties.'

My head rocks back.

'See these cages?' He slows beside a series of large, fenced-off areas, some with stepped concrete structures within. 'This used to be a zoo here.'

'For polar bears?'

'Oh we had everything here – kangaroos, rhinoceros, flamingos . . .'

'What, was this some kind of ski lodge retreat for them?'

He laughs. 'You know it gets up to the nineties in the summer here?'

'That doesn't even seem possible right now.'

'That building you were just in?'

I nod.

'That used to be the ape enclosure.'

I have a little chuckle.

'Obviously they cleaned it up.'

'Oh yes, it was immaculate.'

He tells me that when the zoo closed, the animals were rehoused and the Hôtel de Glace took over the site. That was six years ago and he's worked here every season since.

This is unfathomable to me – to choose to be cold every day for three months of the year? He doesn't even have the heat on in his truck.

'Oh this isn't cold.'

I raise an eyebrow.

'I was in the Canadian armed forces before this, spent six months at the North Pole and that was minus forty degrees and dark twenty-four hours a day.'

Well that certainly puts things in perspective.

'But why did they need soldiers at the North Pole?'

'It was a weather station.'

'They don't have machines that can track that kind of thing?'

'They do now,' he confirms. 'Back then there were two hundred of us on that base.'

'God, I can't even imagine.'

'Oh it was quite something – we used to have ropes strung between the buildings—'

'To feel your way along in the dark?'

'So the winds wouldn't take you. If it was a Condition Two we weren't allowed outside at all.'

'You mean you could literally get blown away into the snowy wasteland, never to be seen again?' I gasp.

'Oh yes, there was nothing out there, no Eskimos, not a single caribou, just snow . . .'

'Well now I feel like a big wuss.'

He smiles. 'You know the best thing about it?'

'There was something good?'

'The bread.'

'The bread?' I repeat.

'All our food would get dropped in by cargo plane and there wasn't room for the hundreds of loaves we needed so they would deliver flour and the cook would make it fresh – oh it was sooo good.'

I blink at him in amazement. Thirty or forty years on it still gives him pleasure to remember that bread! I want to hug him!

'Your taxi is here.'

We've pulled around to the front now, to where my adventure began last night. I feel almost reluctant to leave now; he's made me want to brave it a little longer. What's so great about heat and carpeting anyway? But in I bundle.

The taxi is stiflingly warm and I soon find myself drifting in and out of sleep. There's little to see but white anyway. At one point I notice buildings made of stone and a run of shops denoting civilisation. But it seems a little drab after the neon Jello-shot lighting of the Hôtel de Glace. I close my eyes once more and when I open them again I am at the

Hilton, propelling myself through a revolving door into a vast, modern lobby – all geometric lines and low, squared-off seating.

'You come from the Hôtel de Glace?' the redhead on Reception asks me.

'Is it that obvious?' I ask, wondering if we all get a similarly tweaked look.

She points to the big laminated tag on my coat.

'Oh, that!'

'Did you sleep?'

'In a manner of speaking.'

'Well you will here . . .'

And with that she gives me the key to a room with a pillow-topped kingsize bed and a heating dial that I rack past 30°C so I can quietly oven-bake myself until morning.

'Oh my god, I'm so hot!' I awake in a suffocating sweat and can't get out of my synthetic swaddlings quickly enough.

As I stand there naked, glistening and panting, my phone bleeps a text.

'*Meet me on the 23rd floor at 9 am and don't look out the window!*'

Oh my gosh! He's here! In the building! I quickly cover myself up, as if he can somehow see me.

And then I look at the bedside clock. One hour. One hour to shower, put on my make-up and find a facial expression that convincingly conveys complete ease with myself and the outcome of our upcoming encounter.

Where's a Botox needle when you need one?

3

As our initial meeting is within the confines of the hotel, I can get away with skinny jeans and my favourite fuzzy peach sweater – the one with the outsized, off-the-shoulder collar. We've had such a mild winter back home it's actually quite fun to get into chunky knits.

When my hair goes right, all sleep deprivation is zapped in favour of anticipation. I know I told Laurie that I'd rather not see him again, but that was primarily because he seemed to have got such an intense bout of kisser's remorse. Of course I still don't know which way this is going to go, but his text had a certain playfulness to it that makes me optimistic. With every ding of the lift my excitement heightens . . .

Twenty-three! This is me.

I emerge and look around. Which way now?

'Krista?'

I look up and see a woman in winter-white ski pants. White! Her sand-gold coat is trimmed with real fur, her hair shimmering honey blonde, framing her delicately bronzed, pout-perfect face. She introduces herself as my tour guide, Annique. I can feel my sweater pilling and sagging just looking at her. She is exactly the kind of woman Gilles would like to photograph.

'You got my message!'

'I-I did.' I gulp back the disappointment. It was from *her*. 'Is it just us?'

'For now. Gilles wanted to get some photographs of the Carnival attractions before it opens but he will join us shortly.'

'Okay . . .'

'I thought you might like a little breakfast first, *non?*'

'Oh yes, thank you.'

'We can visit the executive lounge . . .' She slides her card at the door and invites me to enter ahead of her.

Though I expected to only have eyes for the croissants, I am immediately dazzled by the panorama that greets me: a broad icy river expanding out to sea, distant snowy cliffs, an ancient city wall laying a protective arm around a dainty Old Town dominated by a copper-topped castle, all turrets and towers and make-a-wish spires . . .

Looking down all I can see are the footprint traces of the residents, but something tells me they wear bells on their curly-toed shoes, velvet monogrammed tunics and billowing satin capes as they scurry along cobbled streets, sprinkling icing sugar on every available surface.

'Wow,' I breathe.

Yesterday I was the Ice Princess, today I am the Snow Queen, surveying my fairytale kingdom from atop a glass tower.

Annique smiles proudly. 'Welcome to Quebec!'

'Now I know why you chose this hotel' I laugh. 'What a vantage point!'

It certainly sets me straight on why I am here. Never mind any personal shenanigans, this is a dream destination for Va-Va-Vacation! Who wouldn't be enchanted? Already I want everyone to come here, for everyone to feel the wonder I am feeling right now.

'Why don't we take a table by the window and I can point out to you the highlights?'

I am grateful for her direction.

'Over to our left we have the port.' She points to where even the sturdiest of cargo ships appear to be held in an ice-vice – locked into the frozen waters of 'the famous Saint Lawrence River'.

I find myself squinting, trying to discern where the snowy banks end and the icy water begins, though a distant bridge is a clue.

Over yonder a factory puffs smoke as if pumping out fluffy white clouds to decorate the silky blue sky. Winter can be as monochrome as newsprint but here there is a warmth to the vista – the Christmas-card-perfect rows of terraced houses bring rusty red, butterscotch, sage green and duck-egg blue to the scene.

In front of them, what would be a football pitch back in England is home to a game of ice hockey. Little padded figures gliding hither and thither – such graceful motions for such a manly sport. I can almost hear the swish-swishing as they score the ice with their blades, the clash of their wooden sticks. Any minute now a triple salchow . . .

'Is that a real castle?' I point towards the focal point of the city.

'That is Château Frontenac. One of the most photo-graphed buildings in the world. Now a Fairmont hotel. We shall dine there later in the week.'

'What's going on with the roof?' It seems to be curiously bi-coloured.

'They are replacing the old copper with new.'

'Oh but I love that powdery green!'

'Well, have a good look now – it takes about a hundred years to oxidise!'

Before I can get too upset, Annique directs my attention to a yet more prestigious building . . . An elegant quadrant with a tall clock tower sporting an iron crown at its peak and, atop that, the flag of Quebec – clear blue with a white cross and four white fleur-de-lys.

'That is our Parliament.'

'Gosh.' I gasp. 'And the Carnival grounds are right beside that?'

She nods. 'The Carnival is good for the city. For tourism but also for morale. Something to look forward to after Christmas. You can't be pinning all your hopes on summer coming here – it's too long of a wait!' She laughs.

'I think that's such a good idea,' I tell her. 'It's what we all want – something to look forward to.'

'Well, you can complain about the cold weather and hide inside or you can get out and enjoy all the advantages of it – the skiing, snow-shoeing, tobogganing . . . Oh!' She reaches into her bag. 'I must give you this.'

She hands me a tiny snowman figurine or 'effigy', designed to dangle from your coat zipper.

'You need to wear this all the time, so you can come and go as you please at the Carnival.'

I study him closer – he has a floppy red hat, a jazzy waist sash, a big smile and *legs* . . .

'Well, he has to be able to ice-skate and dance . . .' Annique reasons.

'But of course.'

'This is Bonhomme,' she explains. 'He is the ambassador of the Quebec Winter Carnival. You will meet the real version later – he is seven foot tall!'

When she tells me he's been representing the Carnival for fifty-seven years, I ask how they always manage to find a man that tall to wear the suit.

She looks scandalised. 'This is not a man in a costume. Bonhomme is Bonhomme.'

I look around to see if any executive children are eavesdropping – is that why she's being so protective? But no, she is sincere – Bonhomme is Bonhomme. And woe betide anyone who tells you different.

'Is it okay if I take some pictures?' I go from window-panel to window-panel, trying to capture every detail from the old-fashioned globe street lamps to the festive clusters of fir trees until, finally, my gaze comes to rest on Annique.

She really is very nice. And stylish.

'I like your earrings!' I say, noticing the dainty charms hanging from her fine gold hoops.

'*Merci!*'

'And your boots.'

And your metabolism, I think to myself as I take in both her naturally slim physique and the pile of pastries she has amassed.

'We will walk a lot today.' She smiles. 'We need fuel!'

I'm halfway to the breakfast bar when I turn back. 'Mind if I take a snap of your outfit to show my friend?'

She obliges by getting to her feet and striking a Giselle-esque pose.

'Thank you!' I say, sending it directly to Laurie with the caption: 'This is what I'm up against.'

And then I stuff a whole croissant in my mouth, cross my eyes and send that self-portrait with the title, 'Who would you choose?'

Naturally this is precisely when Gilles walks in. I dart behind the glass shelving to give myself a chance to dislodge the croissant and have a discreet coughing fit as the pastry flakes catch in my throat.

All I can see of him is a partial side view. But I have a clear line on Annique. As I busy myself with the coffee machine, I watch her fluff her hair and then rise up to meet him, kissing him on both cheeks. He says something and she reaches up to give him an all too lingering caress of his face.

The coffee cup in my hand starts rattling on its saucer.

They're together. She is the reason that he said, 'I can't do this.'

He's already doing it with her.

Or is he? Am I being paranoid?

Perhaps they are old friends or maybe he had a stray snowflake on his chin.

And then they look in my direction, giving me a little wave. I quickly set down the clattering coffee cup and switch to a more manageable glass of orange juice. Just do it – just waltz back over to the table with a cheery, '*Bonjour!*'

'So of course you know Gilles from last night . . .' Annique places one hand on his back, the other on his forearm, as if presenting a prize on a game show.

'Yes I do.'

'And how was that?' she asks.

'Um . . .' I give him a panicked look.

'The photography went well?'

'Oh yes, very good,' he muffles.

'Lens didn't get too steamed up?'

'Pardon?' I gulp.

'With so much cold air . . .'

I look to Gilles.

'It was fine.'

'I'd love to see the images.'

'Just as soon as I've had a chance to edit them,' Gilles flushes.

Oh this is horrendous! But now I'm even more confused. They obviously didn't spend last night together. Or what was left of it after he was done with me . . .

'Gilles, why don't you get some breakfast and then we can talk about our plans for the day?'

Annique and I watch him head to the buffet, her seemingly admiring the view, me just waiting until he's out of earshot.

'So . . .' I begin. 'Have you two known each other long?'

'*Non*,' she says with a coquettish head tilt. 'Just three days.' And then she adds, '*Trois jours . . .*' with such breathy wonder she may as well be saying, '*Three miraculous sex-filled days . . .*'

I am at a loss for a response.

'We met to discuss this project and then . . .' She gives the classic Gallic shrug. '*Voilà!*'

'*Voilà*,' I repeat.

'I love how passionate he is about his work.'

'Isn't he just . . .'

When Gilles returns to the table I see him hesitate for a second – who should he sit beside? But Annique quickly clears her coat and suggests he take the chair nearest the window, in case he wants to take pictures. Which he does. Conveniently covering his face with the camera for the majority of our meeting.

'And what is that building?' he asks, pointing over to our furthest right.

Annique looks to me, testing my memory.

'That's Parliament,' I tell him.

'I think I just walked past that on the way here.'

'Yes, you see the Carnival lies just beyond it?'

As they reposition themselves for a better look, I retreat inward. In the background I can hear Annique reeling off the list of activities she has planned and though I am ooohing in the appropriate places, I don't hear any of them. All I can think about is getting back to the room to call Laurie.

And then the two of them slip into French, making me feel even more the odd-woman-out. Instead of saying something, I pretend to be oblivious, captivated by the view, which actually isn't too much of a stretch – why, I would like to know, is snow tumbling from just that one roof down there? Wouldn't the wind be catching the whole row? It's then I realise there are two men with shovels – or rakes or brooms or some custom-made combo of the three – systematically brushing and scraping the snow off the edge and sending it cascading down onto the street below. And I thought chimney sweeps had tough working conditions.

Annique notices my stare and tells me that it is a safety precaution, but I have to say the houses look far prettier heaped with snow – while its neighbours have the equivalent of a full head of hair, the cleared one looks as if it got its head shaved with semiblunt clippers, leaving scrappy little patches—

'Okay,' Annique interrupts my inner pontifications. 'Time to go.'

Oh thank goodness.

'So I'll just go back to the room and get into my warm gear and then meet you in the lobby?'

'Perfect.'

I can't get out of there quick enough. But of course they are right behind me and there is an interminable wait for the lift. At one point I hear her give a girlish giggle behind me and I feel sick.

'This is a nightmare!' I wail to Laurie via Skype. 'And look at what I have to wear today!'

'Oh jeez,' she grimaces at my ski pants, and I don't mean the sleek black kind, rather the bulky, extra-padded, 'see you on the piste' version.

'Okay. Take a breath,' she soothes. 'There is clearly no competing with her on a physical level. Besides, when he saw you the first time you were in thermals and a sleeping bag, so really you look positively svelte in comparison.'

'True.'

'Besides . . .'

'Yes?'

'If they really have got something going, then you wouldn't want his philandering pants anyway.'

I sigh. 'You're right.'

'I mean, if he gets itchy feet in a matter of *days* . . .'

'I know, I'm just so . . .' I try to identify exactly what I am feeling. 'Mad. And embarrassed. And indignant!' I sigh. 'And *baffled*.'

'Baffled?'

'Of course it makes perfect sense that two such genetically stunning individuals join forces. There is a certain inevitability to their attraction. It's not that . . .'

'What then?'

I slump on the corner of the bed. 'If Gilles is making "*voilà*" with a goddess like Annique, then why oh why was he kissing me last night?'

4

As I collect up my bag and head for the lift, it strikes me that this is the first non-Andrew man Laurie has coached me on.

I must have been midway through my marriage when I first met her. It wasn't exactly our finest hour. We were attending a fancy manor house wedding in Oxfordshire and I remember Andrew being testy from the first toast. It didn't help that every other couple at our table were Fast-Trackers – one man had just got a great new job paying double his former salary, the woman to his left was pregnant with twins, another couple had just bought their dream home complete with walk-in closets and a trickly stream at the bottom of the garden . . . We might have been able to out-holiday every one of them, but as far as Andrew was concerned we were just shuffling along in the economy passenger lane of life. He didn't like that. He was always very competitive.

Anyway, towards the end of the evening we were on the dance floor – which actually used to be our happy place; it's how we met – when my big toe was skewered by a fake Louboutin.

The perpetrator might as well have taken a corkscrew from the bar and twisted it in, it hurt that much. Andrew was mortified, not at my injury but a) that I was causing a scene with my hopping and yelping and b) I was getting blood on Lord Fetherington-Ashby's carpet on the way back to our table.

'Christ! Who in their right mind dances in bare feet when everyone else is in dagger heels?'

'I think the question is more who in their right mind dances in dagger heels?' I countered. 'Do you have any idea how little support they offer?'

'Normal women, Krista. Normal women wear high heels, not these old lady concoctions,' he taunted, dangling my shoe in front of my face.

'I'll have you know these are professional dance shoes!' I snatched it back from his hand. 'Look, you can bend the sole in half, they are so supple.'

'Is that supposed to be a selling point?'

'It is to me.'

'And what kind of poor excuse is that for a heel? It looks like they stuck a matchbox on the end and sprayed it silver.'

'Forgive me for wanting to be comfortable.'

'It's not about comfort, it's about looking good. Everyone else is suffering, why can't you?'

I blinked back at him. 'You want me to suffer?'

'I just don't understand why you have to be the odd one out!'

'Why can't I be like everyone else?' I stated back to him.

I knew what he was really getting at here. It wasn't about the shoes at all.

But he didn't want to get into *that* so instead he huffed, 'You brought this on yourself – find your own damn plaster.'

At which point he turned and stomped off.

I thought about crying, and potentially embarrassing him all the more, but then a face appeared from under the drapes of the tablecloth.

'Don't mind me!' chirped a wavy-haired brunette with a Sandra-Bullock smile.

Initially I was too taken aback to speak.

'I didn't mean to be eavesdropping but I sneaked under here for a covert piece of wedding cake and then you two came over and I didn't like to crawl out mid-argument so . . .'

'I'm sorry you had to hear all that nonsense.' I cringed.

'I'm sorry your toe got assaulted. That's a pretty messy situation.'

And she would know – being right at eye level with it.

'Could you pass me a glass of water?'

I reached over to the tabletop and passed one to her.

'And a napkin.'

'There's another slice of cake here, hasn't been touched—'

'No, no, I'm fine.'

She then dipped the napkin in the water and started to dab away the excess blood. I flinched a couple of times so she held an ice cube in place to numb it. Then she tore at the napkin with her teeth.

'Careful!' I exclaimed.

'Don't worry, I've got fangs like a Rottweiler.'

She took the narrower strip and bound my toe and then asked me to hand her one of the cocktail sticks to secure it.

'Looks like one of those pigs-in-a-blanket hors d'oeuvres!' I giggled.

At which point she emerged fully from the table and rather surprised me with a perfectly normal figure. I suppose I thought from the secret cake-eating she might be rather voluptuous, but not at all.

'If you don't mind me asking – do you have some kind of eating disorder?'

'Yes I do,' she nodded gravely. 'His name is Eric.'

'Eric?'

'My boyfriend. Soon to be ex. But it's not always as easy to get out of a relationship as it is to get into them, is it? I keep hoping he'll give me an ultimatum – "It's me or the cake!"'

and then I'd choose the cake, obviously, and lead a very happy cream-frosted life.'

I gave a little chuckle.

And then she sighed and reached for what was formerly my wine glass. 'They're always so nice in the beginning, aren't they? Back when they loved you just the way you are.'

'Or the way they *think* you are.'

She gave me a sideways glance. 'Do you know what helps me get through Eric's rants?'

'What?' I was keen to know.

'Buddha.'

I felt a smidgeon of concern as she twisted her mint chiffon frock around to face me, praying – somewhat ironically I realise now – please don't let her be a religious nut!

'So this guy comes up to Buddha and he's full of vitriol,' she began, 'nothing nice to say, going on and on at Buddha, complaining about everything he does wrong, everything that irritates him, really letting him have it. And so Buddha, who is completely unfazed, by the way, says, "Let me ask you a question – if you bought a gift and gave it to someone and they didn't accept it, who would the gift belong to?"

'"Well, to me I suppose," he replied. "Since I paid for it."

'And so Buddha said, "I don't accept the insults you bring to me. I am returning them to you. The gift now belongs to you. Every bit of it."'

My jaw dropped. 'I love it! That's brilliant!'

'Isn't it?'

'Brilliant!' I raved.

'What's brilliant?' I looked up to find Andrew glaring impatiently.

'Just this funny story that . . .' I stop. 'I'm sorry, I didn't get your name.'

'Laurie,' she said, reaching for my hand.

'Krista,' I said, shaking hers. 'This is Andrew.'

'Pleased to meet you,' she said, getting to her feet.

'Yowwwww!' Andrew squealed like a pig, jumping back from her.

'Oh I'm sorry! Did I tread on your foot?' She hoiked up her hem to reveal the deadliest of spikes. 'Good thing you're wearing proper shoes or that would've really hurt!'

And with a covert wink at me, she left.

I still have what was left of that napkin – first I offered it to Andrew to dab away his tears and then, on the way home in the car, I used it to hide my immovable grin.

I didn't see her again for nearly two months. Which is ridiculous when you think that little more than a pane of glass separated us every morning – her travel agency was on my route to work and I used to get off the bus a stop early so I could walk past and daydream about the special offers in the window – typically to a Greek island. It didn't matter which one – anything was preferable to going into the office for me at that point. The magazine I was working for had cut the travel section altogether in favour of more weight-loss before and afters – you too can shed seven stone with just three life-threatening surgeries and a lifetime's supply of watercress soup!

And then this one day I'd actually stopped to take a snap of an ad for a beachside studio in this little fishing village, thinking the sunshine and simplicity could be just what Andrew and I needed to fall in love again, and there was this face on the other side of the glass sticking up a bargain deal for Sharm el Sheikh.

Our eyes widened in recognition, she beckoned me inside and offered me a seat and the opportunity to be late for work.

I took both.

'They're still together, you know?' She updated me on the newlyweds as she handed me a cup of real leaf tea.

'Wow. No one thought they'd see the end of the honeymoon, let alone two whole months!'

'I know, just goes to show . . .'

'You never know.'

'You never do,' she giggled.

'Are you still with . . . Eric was it?'

'Nope!'

'You did it?' I cheered.

'Well, let's just say it's done.'

'Oh. I'm so pleased for you, however it happened! I mean, obviously it's upsetting, I'm sure but—'

'It's the right thing.'

'Yes.'

'What about you?'

'Still with Andrew.' I nodded. 'He's not all bad, really. We've got this situation that is making things a bit tense. Well, a lot tense. I think we just need to get to the acceptance stage and then we'll be fine.'

And then my mobile buzzed a message from my boss and I had to leave so we decided to continue our chat over lunch.

But there was always so much more to say, so we ended up meeting almost every day, talking about man stuff at first and then our mutual adoration of all things travel. That's when we got the idea for Va-Va-Vacation! It was one of those, 'What I'd really like to do is . . .' conversations that leads to, 'Well, why don't you?' And then, 'Why don't *we?*'

At first we thought it would be more of a fun sideline than a full-time job, and it was certainly extremely helpful that we both had an alternative source of income for those initial months, setting up and working through exactly what we were hoping to achieve.

Things really started coming together when we got Danielle on board. You are nothing these days without a sharp, savvy website design, and she's just brilliant at triggering that 'I want to be *there!*' response. So many travel websites are too text-heavy on their Home page, I feel. Images transport you in an instant, which is why we decided to invest heavily in photography – our own unique take rather than the generic stock shots you see used over and over. We wanted everything to feel fresh – the look, our approach, the design of our itineraries. For us it's all about: how do you want to *feel* when you get there?

Exhilarated? Serene? Amazed? Carefree? Pampered? Sophisticated? Cultured? Earthy? Sexy? All of the above?

We can make that happen!

I'm all about the sensory experience – the sound of Spanish castanets, the sight of a whale tail breaching in Alaska, the taste of real Italian spaghetti sauce, the feel of Kashmirian cashmere, the smell of the durian fruit of Thailand – so pungently foul that you are forbidden to bring it into the posher hotels.

Laurie, on the other hand, loves the logistics – putting together flights and transfers like a puzzle, all to minimise your time in transit (not just airport layovers but sitting in taxis in rush hour watching the meter tick away your cocktail money) and maximise your time in your chosen location. And she loves to haggle – not with street vendors but hotel managers.

'Come on, Ferdinand – what would you rather have: ten empty *casitas* valued at three hundred pounds a night or ten full ones with guests paying a hundred? And you know they'll end up eating at your restaurant – no one can beat your tortillas!'

She's a really fast worker too – I only have to mention we've had a lot of interest in Ireland lately and I find myself in Dublin with a Guinness moustache. It's like having a fairy godmother with Airmiles. The fact that she had amassed so very many over the years was a huge, huge help to our initial budgeting. (Even though the airlines find other ways to jack up the cost of your 'free' flight.)

None of us is pulling a huge salary but it really doesn't matter. As Danielle says, she's got to be the only person in Britain making minimum wage who got to Morecambe and the Maldives last year. (And I should add that Morecambe is where her granny lives, not a Va-Va-Vacation! destination.) We give her nearly all the beach destinations to review because that's what she lives for. No one is more experienced at sunbathing with a hangover than Danielle. And she always finds the ultimate sheltered cove, the yummiest picnic lunches and even rates the local waiters according to their flirtiness vs attractiveness ratio.

One of our more popular features is the What I Packed/ What I Wore section, where we photograph the contents of our suitcase like those little cut-out wardrobes for a paper doll and then put a big red tick by the items that got the most wear.

Already I'm wishing I'd brought a second set of thermals and noting that those fluffy Dr Zhivago hats look like a wet cat on your head when the snow melts and soggifies the faux fur. I'll also be reminding our readers to pack their sunglasses – as cold as it is, that snow is squint-inducingly bright.

In essence we are your travel guinea pigs – going ahead to a destination to make all the mistakes you won't have to. We're always upfront about the downsides to a destination. And not just the poverty in India or how much you'll have to pay for a beer in Reykjavik. I remember Laurie asking me about the worst part of my trip to Salzburg and I said, 'Having to call Andrew every night.'

I'd have these zingy, inspiring days – totally loved *The Sound of Music* Tour! – and then the second I heard his voice

I'd feel this weight descending on me, this crushing realisation that he wasn't really paying attention or interested, that no part of him was wishing he was sitting beside me in the coffee house sharing my apple strudel.

It wasn't long after this trip that he concluded we 'wanted different things', but the truth was we both wanted one thing above all else and only one of us could have it.

I sigh.

I mustn't dwell on this now. No one here knows anything about my relationship history. As far as they're concerned I could be delighted about being single again! Yes, I had to let go of a thousand hopes and dreams but now I'm back to that state where anything is possible. Anything!

Which brings me back to the mysterious Monsieur Gilles . . .

5

Unfortunately it is not possible to garner any more clues from Gilles' facial expressions, since all that is visible now is his nose.

The remainder of his face is hidden beneath his hat, sunglasses and chin-covering scarf. If it wasn't for his camera I wouldn't even be able to tell him apart from the rest of the Carnival-goers.

Annique informs me that Quebec was founded on fur trading, but today I think the most desirable commodity would be Puffa fabric by the yard. We're all at it, be it waist-, knee- or ankle-length. Wet-look or matte. Tubular or belted. Of course the kids look the cutest in their bright pinks and yellows, like squishy Jelly Babies come to life. I notice that the majority of the under-twos are being pulled along by their parents on a shiny plastic sled. I can't believe how blasé they are – arms lolling out to the side, some of them even sleeping! I want to shake them and say, 'Do you have any idea how cold it is?'

But no one – of any age – is complaining, or even wincing: they are all taking it in their stride.

'Woah!' I experience an ungainly skid on a covert ice patch, prompting Annique to link arms with me, and then Gilles.

One big, happy threesome.

At one point Gilles scoots ahead and then turns back and starts snapping us. He says he's getting the Parliament building in the background but I suspect he's supplementing his

'My Conquests' album. I certainly won't be using any of these shots for the website – in my padded romper and pompom ensemble I look like an outsized toddler waddling along next to her model mummy.

I expel a white-vapoured sigh.

I still can't wrap my head around this. What was he thinking? Did he forget about Annique and only remember partway through the kiss? It's just so ridiculous. I mean, he knows he has to spend the week with the pair of us. Am I being an enabler saying nothing? Not that I care about making him squirm, but Annique does seem remarkably sweet for someone so pretty and I wouldn't want to upset her. Then again, isn't that all the more reason to warn her before her besottedness deepens?

'We arrive!' She cheers as we pass under a fluttery rainbow arch and enter the Carnival proper, set upon 250 acres of historic parkland known as the Plains of Abraham.

It has the feel of a fairground, complete with big wheel, and so many attractions that my attention is ricocheting every which way. There are all the traditional winter ways to go way too fast (cue much squealing from those hurtling down the 400ft ice slide) as well as more genteel approaches like the jingle bell sleigh rides. And then I spy the can't-quite-believe-your-eyes art . . .

'You want to begin with the snow sculptures?' Annique notes my interest.

'Sounds good to me.'

Gilles remains infuriatingly passive. He's barely said a word this whole time and as soon as we reach the sculptures he drops out of our eye-line, kneeling in the snow supposedly trying to get the right angle of sun filtering through one of the gravity-defying loops.

I have to say these meltable artworks are incredible

– everything from chess-piece horses to ball-balancing seals to a set of dentures biting into an apple core, each having begun life as a giant cube of snow.

Annique tells me that the winner a few years back was a pair of hands twiddling a Rubik's Cube but her favourite was Moby Dick – an open book with a harpoonist rising from the left side and a whale disappearing into the right, pages flaring like waves. Mind-boggling.

I see some artists are using fluorescent spray paint to mark their design prior to the first incision, using implements ranging from a two-person saw, metal teeth chomping through the snow, to wooden blocks bound in chicken wire to exfoliate and smooth the rough edges. Then there's the more traditional chisels for the detail work. I could watch them all day.

'Krista?'

'Yes?' I turn to face her.

'How about we have you pretending to work on one of these creations?' Annique suggests. 'Which do you prefer?'

I do a quick survey. 'That's easy – the polar bear.'

'I prefer the more abstract designs,' Gilles points to a geometric structure akin to an early learning toy.

'The polar bear has a more poignant message – global warming threatening his habitat and his future.'

'I just think visually—'

'Polar bear,' I override him. I indulged his 'vision' last night and look where that got me. From now on I'm thinking only of what is best for the website.

To that end Annique is quite the asset. The artist – Brandon from Toronto – happily hands over his tools to me. As I try to position myself, I can see why so many of them have shed a top layer of clothing: it's not easy to angle your arms with so much padding.

'To me!' Gilles wants me to make eye contact, with his lens at least.

'I like the icy stare,' Annique coos. 'Matches the snow sculptures, no?'

I didn't even realise my eyes were narrowing. Perhaps I'll try something more cheerful . . .

'Oh no!' Annique recoils.

'No?'

'That big smile with a dagger in your hand . . .'

'Psycho-killer?'

She nods.

'Perhaps it's best if I just pretend to be chipping away and you capture me "*reportage*" style,' I tell Gilles.

Frankly I don't even want to look in his direction. I can't believe he's still not saying anything about last night, especially now that we have a moment while Annique is engaged with the sculptor.

'Try and look like you're really sculpting.'

'My acting isn't convincing enough for you?'

The dig goes over his head.

'You need to lean closer. Make stronger motions.'

Everything Gilles says is annoying me now.

'You are looking more like a dentist than an artist.'

That's it! I reach back and thwack the chisel. Too hard. It spears into the thick neck section and, with a devastating creak followed by a powdery thud, the head falls into the snow.

Oh my god, I just decapitated a polar bear!

Gilles is equally frozen in horror.

'What do we do, what do we do?' I hiss-panic.

Gilles steps in to obscure the sculptor's view. 'Can we stick it back on?'

'With what?' I despair. 'You can't glue frozen water.'

And that's when we hear Brandon from Toronto emit a gurgle of anguish.

'*What did you do?*'

My blood runs cold. I can hardly bring myself to turn and face him.

'We're so sorry,' Gilles and I begin, overlapping apologies. 'It was a terrible accident. We didn't mean to even touch it. It was so perfect. This is awful. Perhaps we could show the judges the photos of before—'

'Before you cut him up?'

Oh god.

'We'll do anything to make it up to you, *anything* . . .'

'Anything?'

'Anything.' We solemnly swear.

His gaze flicks to the side. 'I would like a dinner date.'

'That's very flattering,' Annique demurs.

'Not with you. With him.' He motions to Gilles.

'Oh.' I bite back a smile. 'Wow, you're really on a roll.'

'Well?' Brandon's eyes are bright with expectation.

'That seems reasonable,' I speak for Gilles.

'I don't know.' He squirms.

'It's the least we can do, Gilles. And who better to understand a fellow artist's pain?' I take a step closer. 'Besides, it's not like you have to kiss him.'

'Though that would be nice,' the sculptor adds.

'Shall we say eight p.m. at Auberge Saint-Antoine?' Annique is already adjusting the schedule. 'And why don't we make it a party – would you like to bring a few friends, Brandon?'

'Wonderful!' he confirms, already relishing their prospective envy.

Neatly done Annique – sparing us from litigation and protecting Gilles in one slick move.

As my colleagues head onwards, merging into the crowds, I feel compelled to backtrack to Brandon. 'I just wanted to say sorry one more time.'

'Actually,' he confides. 'It is better this way. More dramatic.'

'Really?'

'Listen – already people are stopping and saying, "*Oh no, look what happened to the poor polar bear!*" which is exactly the reaction I was going for. Before they just thought he looked cute.'

Suddenly I am viewing my situation with Gilles in a whole new light. Perhaps the awful realisation he has something going with Annique is actually a blessing in disguise – the Universe is choosing to let me know nice and early on that he's not The One. As opposed to letting me waste eight years of my life. Besides, I never did get the chance to retaliate against Andrew's pitiless behaviour, so perhaps Gilles is a surrogate male for me to torment? I know I should be more evolved than this, but that actually sounds like a lot of fun.

Now I can't wait to catch them up.

6

'What next?' Gilles asks when I rejoin them.

'Something as far from the snow sculptures as possible,' I suggest. I can tell we're making the other artists nervous.

'I have just the thing,' Annique looks minxish. 'The Tornado.'

'Sounds relaxing,' I mumble as we follow her bite-size bottom up and up a steep slope.

'That is the raft.' She points to a robust yellow inflatable last seen on the Colorado rapids. 'The circular one is the Tornado, because it rotates as it descends.'

And what a descent.

'They really pick up speed on the way down the hill, don't they?' I croak.

'Oh yes. Great fun!'

I hesitate. 'I'm not a hundred per cent sure about this.'

'Nothing bad will happen, we can all go together – it takes eight people.'

'Well then I'd like the other five to include a priest and a paramedic.'

'Oh Krista!' Annique tuts. 'You will love it!'

I decide to give it a shot. Now if I could just get in.

With all my swaddlings I can barely lift my leg high enough to get up and over; I have to be assisted and thus enter the group with an unladylike squeak of rubber.

'*Excusez-moi*,' I blush.

Wanting to feel secure, I reach out to grab the outer straps, only to have my hands smacked away.

'Those are what the guys use to spin us.'

'Well, what do I hold onto?'

Annique takes one hand and urges Gilles to take charge of the other.

'I need both hands for the camera,' he excuses himself.

'Grab his knee!' Annique hoots.

'Oh no, I'll be fine!' I say, but then the second we are in motion I find myself grabbing him way too high on the thigh and nothing can persuade me to loosen my grip. 'Oh my god, oh my god!'

I can't believe how fast we are spinning; it's just as dizzying as a fairground Wurlitzer, only with the added sensation of plummeting to your death.

While the others whoop with childish glee, my scream is pure high-pitched terror; but then a funny thing happens – as I clamber out I find myself saying, 'I actually quite enjoyed that.'

'Want to go again?' Annique pips.

'You may have to.' Gilles looks less than enthralled as he reviews the pictures on his camera. 'These are very close.'

He shows me a particularly graphic shot of my fillings.

'Should've gone for porcelain,' I tut myself.

'I think it is best I shoot you from here with the long lens.'

'Okay,' I say as I contemplate the trek back to the top – my own personal Everest.

'Wait,' Annique places her suede-gloved hand on my arm. 'Let me ask if one of these guys can take you up.'

She approaches a pair of snowmobilers, assigned the task of vrooming the inflatables back up for the next trip. Now that looks like a fun way to travel.

'So, they can't take you on the snowmobile without a helmet, but you could sit in the raft and they will pull you up.'

Of course. Anything that makes me look mildly foolish – the only person getting dragged up a hill as everyone else whooshes down.

As I get into position and we begin to move, I feel like one of the kiddiwinks being pulled along by their parents, only on a grander scale – these machines are pretty fierce. I hadn't fully registered just how close to a motorcycle they are; they had always seemed more like plastic playthings to me, but they're chunky and mean and noisy.

'Turn to face me,' Gilles calls after me. 'Arms up!'

Yeah right! I think to myself. I'm holding on for dear life. Up and up we go at an ever-more unnatural angle. To my left, groups are swirling by, squealing and waving their hands in the air. Perhaps I could do one quick, 'Woo-hoo!' at the camera? He'd better get this, I think as I twist around and attempt a wave back at Annique. Of course I choose the precise moment that we hit a bump and out I come, performing an inelegant backward roll and then tumbling messily through the snow, wondering if I will become a human snowball by the time I reach the bottom.

Only I don't keep rolling, I snag on something – a branch perhaps? Wow. I catch my breath. That was pretty hairy. Best try to get to my feet – I don't want to get run over by the next snowmobile shuttle or some off-track tobogganer. But it's not quite as simple as that – the snow here is too deep. I lose my footing, unbalance, and fall back with a hefty *Doomf!*

For a moment there is peace. I am in a white cocoon, a snowy grave pit. All I can see is the pale silken blue of the sky above me. I wonder if I've broken anything, but as I test for movement in my limbs I inadvertently invite a tumble of snow upon myself. Oh no. What now? Stay still and freeze, or attempt to get upright and risk causing my own personal avalanche? The snow is easily above head height, so even if I could get to my feet, how exactly would I claw my way out?

'Help!' I cry, and then realise I should probably call out in French, though '*Aidez-moi!*' sounds so weak. Surely Gilles and Annique saw what happened and are on their way? I hope there's not too much of a fuss. I don't want to get anyone in trouble for trying to spare me the hike up the hill.

It's then I see the face of an angel – a white fluffy angel with black eyes and a black nose. He peers down on me with a look of bemusement as much as anything.

How exactly do I convey to him that I need rescuing? The only word I can think of is '*chien*' and, of course, Lassie. I do hope he has something in common with his collie counterpart because he's taken a good look at me and then turned and left.

I wait for a clue as to what to do next but I can't hear anything – the upper world, the one I used to be a part of, is now muffled by snow. But it's okay. I'm not going to panic. The snowmobiler would have realised his cargo is missing by now. Any minute—

'*Ça va?*'

A new face appears on the brim of my pit. His hair is a wind-ruffled chestnut, his skin tone a natural outdoorsy tan, and I'm not sure if he has a goatee so much as those soft whiskers that casually frame the mouth and line the jawline. He's the kind of guy I picture sitting beside a campfire in a well-worn check shirt, beer in one hand and a tattered novel in the other.

But for now he's in a padded parka looking down at me.

'I fell in the snow and now I can't get out.' I state the obvious.

He takes a step closer and a clomp of snow drops and bursts upon my chest. He raises his hands – '*Pardon!*' And then studies me for a moment before disappearing.

Am I to become the town spectacle? Seconds from now will the opening of my pit be trimmed with curious faces mistaking me for another piece of Carnival art.

But instead he returns with a rope.

'Take this and hold on tight.'

I wrap it around my hand but don't fancy his chances of being able to haul me out.

'You should probably cover your face.'

'Sorry?'

'Use your scarf to wrap your face, in case there is anything sharp in the snow. And keep your eyes closed.'

This is sounding more hazardous by the minute.

'Ready?' he says.

'What do you want me to do?' I ask, wondering if I should be trying to scrabble up the bank of snow with my feet, attempting to gain traction where there most likely is none.

'Don't resist, just let the rope do the work.'

I wonder if I should tell him my weight, let him know what he's up against, but before I can speak I hear him cry, '*Allez, allez!*' and suddenly I am in motion, yanked upwards, arms wrenching at their sockets, roughly ploughing face-first through the snow.

And then everything stops.

I feel him turn me onto my back and gently lower the scarf so my mouth is free.

'Can I open my eyes?' I ask.

'Yes.'

As I do so, he slides his sunglasses back onto his head and I see he has two different coloured eyes – one warm hazel, the other milky blue.

Perhaps I'm a little concussed because I hear myself asking, 'Are you part-husky?'

He smiles a little and then nods beyond my head. 'Well, I do consider these my family.'

There, staring back at me with lolling pink tongues and similarly random eye colours are six puffing husky dogs.

'My sled team.'

'My heroes!' I breathe. 'And what about the Samoyed?'

'You know Samoyeds?' He looks surprised.

'It's my dream dog – all that heavenly white fluff . . .'

He whistles and the dog angel appears. 'This is Sibérie.'

'As in Siberia?'

He nods. 'He's a little old so he can't pull any more.'

I sit up to greet him, amazed at how deeply my hand disappears into his luxurious fur.

'He's just beautiful! They all are!'

And then my gaze returns to his face. Now that I am adjusting to his bewitching eyes, I see something in them beyond the colour – something I can't quite place but something that triggers a yearning in me . . .

I have a million questions but we're being closed in on by Gilles and Annique on one side and the snowmobilers on the other. Before I can even properly thank him for saving me, he has me back onto my feet and is asking my name.

'Krista,' I tell him.

He steps closer. 'Krista, please stay away from the snow-mobiles. They are too dangerous.'

His words have such an intensity, I find myself promising I will never go near one again. (And if he asked me to give up chocolate right now I'd probably do that too.)

'*Mon dieu!*' Annique exclaims, rushing to my side. 'I was so afraid! I saw you fall and then disappear!'

'I'm fine, really, just a little disorientated.'

'Madame! Are you well?'

'*Oui!*' I assure the snowmobiler. 'It was my fault – I should never have let go.' And with that I turn to Gilles. 'So, did you at least get a good picture of me falling?'

'I-I . . .' he falters.

I take that as a no.

'Never mind. Could you get a picture of the team that saved me?' I turn back but they are gone. All of them – six huskies, one elderly Samoyed and my rugged rescuer – totally and utterly *disparu!*

7

I spin around. 'D-did you see—'

'*Oui, oui,*' Annique confirms their existence. 'That was L'homme Loup.'

'Lom Loop?' I frown.

She spells out the French words for Wolfman for me. Then, while Gilles gives one of the snowmobilers a guided tour of his camera functions, Annique tells me that people say that the reason he wins the Carnival's dog-sledding race every year is that his team are interbred with wolves. 'Either way, he is very *sympathique* with the canine. They run faster for him, it seems.'

'I'd love to get a picture of him. For the website.'

'Yes, but this is not possible now. He only runs the first morning of dog-sledding here at the Carnival. Now he goes home.'

'Does he have a dog-sledding business?'

'*Oui.*'

'Well, could we book a ride there?'

'That is over on the Île d'Orléans, but we can go five minutes up the hill and do pictures with the team here.'

She motions for me to follow her.

So that's that? We just move on as if nothing has happened? I take it neither Gilles nor Annique has a mortal fear of being buried alive.

I follow them in silence, repeatedly looking around for

signs of the Wolfman. If I was atop the Hilton I'm sure I could track his progress, but here I'm at a loss.

'Here we are.' Annique steps aside so I can survey the dog-sledding attraction.

'Oh.' I look on in dismay. Nothing against mutts, I've had them my whole life, but these scrappy, skinny dogs with their mottled brown and cream coats simply cannot compare with the stark monochromatic beauty of the huskies. The track itself is a wonky oval, advertised as a ten-minute ride, but I clock it at under a minute and a half. You're on, you're off and they're loading the next.

This is not what I want my first dog-sledding experience to be.

'I think we should wait and go to a real-deal establish-ment,' I say. 'Somewhere in a more natural setting.'

It just doesn't seem so authentic when there's a 1970s tower block with a revolving restaurant on the horizon.

'We can arrange that,' Annique obliges me. 'But I don't think Jacques will agree . . .'

'Jacques?'

'The Wolfman,' she replies. 'Jacques Dufour.'

I'm strangely thrilled to know his real name. It feels like another step closer to finding him again.

'I don't think he courts publicity,' Annique continues.

'Is he . . . shy?' I ask.

'Private. And this year he has withdrawn.'

'From the world?' I ask, picturing him living in a remote, snow-crusted cave with his dogs.

'From the race.'

'Why?'

'I don't know. I just heard yesterday. I was surprised to see him here at all.'

'Okay, so maybe that won't work,' I faux-concede, 'but I

don't think I'm ready to take the ride right now, I'm still rather shaken up from the fall, you do understand?'

'Of course.' Annique consults her To-Do list. 'I suppose the luge is out of the question?'

'As in barrelling down an ice tunnel on a plastic tray for a ride so bone-rattling your teeth get rearranged along the way?'

'Okay, no luge,' she confirms. 'No toboggan, no ski joring.'

I'm about to ask what ski joring is when she says these three magic words: *'Cabane à Sucre?'*

'If that translates as sugar shack, I'm in.'

Again I wish Laurie was here. She's always looking for new ways to sate her sweet tooth. Danielle and I have put on a stone since we started working in an office with an official Teatime. But I have to say, it's such a nice tradition and great stress-reliever. I always used to burrow through the working day, barely coming up for air, but Laurie insists we take that break together – sort of the working girls' equivalent of a family sharing their evening meal. Without the pressure to 'finish your greens'. Unless she's brought along something with pistachio frosting.

Danielle's actually more of a Mr Kipling Country Slice girl, and I love anything splurging fresh cream, but Laurie has us both drooling like dogs the first morning she's back from a trip to New York bearing cupcakes from Magnolia Bakery. She actually has to bind the cardboard box in Sellotape so she doesn't get tempted to claw it open on the flight, and there's always a mad hacking and slashing with the office scissors to get to them. I smile. She's probably just tidying away today's crumbs now – I take out my phone and tap a sneaky response to her most recent 'How's it going?' text.

'Gilles is old news.' I am deliberately blasé in my report. 'Now I'm onto Jacques!'

'Jacques and Gilles – you're kidding?' She taps straight back.

I laugh out loud – I hadn't thought of that. Especially appropriate since I just went up a hill then came tumbling down.

'He has the eyes of a husky dog,' I tell her.

'How does the husky feel about that?' she teases.

I'm eager to chat more to her but Annique is ready to introduce me to the wonderful world of maple taffy.

'Lose a filling for me!' Laurie signs off.

The process begins with me paying three dollars to a lady in a little wooden cabin and in return she hands me a wooden ice-lolly stick. That's it. A bare stick.

'I feel like I'm missing something . . .'

Annique tinkles a laugh.

'Seriously, what happens now?'

'Now you make your own,' she says, pointing to a table of fresh snow where a man with a big ladle is running a thick line of liquid maple syrup . . .

I still can't predict the next step.

'Attach the syrup to your stick,' Annique instructs me. 'Now roll.'

'Roll?'

'Twist it around.'

I do so, if rather ineptly.

'You can tap it in the snow to set it.'

This could easily be a 'hilarious' challenge on a daytime talk show, designed to humiliate the presenter.

'Ooooh!' The taste surprises me as I convey the mis-shapen blob to my mouth. Like golden syrup with an icy frosting. In fact the ice sprinklings taste wonderfully refresh-ing. I dip it back in for an extra layer.

Meanwhile Gilles is trying to position me so that the shack is behind me for the picture.

I can't quite bring myself to look his way as I attempt to control the droopings of the still-molten treat with my tongue – the last thing I want is for him to think I'm trying to be provocative or enticing. I try instead to hold the taffy pop out to the camera but he insists I lick it. Oh jeez. Now I've gone and dropped a great sticky globule on my coat.

'Nooo!' As I go to grab it away I only serve to contaminate my gloves and spread it further across my chest. 'Darnit!'

Annique tries to wipe the mess with a tissue, which in turn adds a layer of feathery white tufts.

'This does not look good,' Gilles frowns into his camera.

'You want to run back to the hotel and change?' Annique offers.

'Actually,' I say twisting at an imaginary shoulder injury, 'maybe I should soak in the tub for a while, write up some notes . . .'

I see Annique cast a furtive glance at Gilles – no doubt imagining what they could do with the bonus time.

'I mean, I have all week to take in the Carnival attractions . . .'

'But we still meet this evening, yes?' she enquires.

'Dinner with the snow sculptor?' I say as I hand Gilles the sticky end of the lollipop. 'I wouldn't miss it for the world.'

I go directly back to the hotel, put my gunky items in for cleaning, change into dry socks and tidy my snow-spattered face. I daren't sit down and risk losing momentum so I quickly grab my alternate coat (black Puffa), add a teal woollen scarf and matching mittens and head directly to speak with the concierge.

'*Oui,* madame?'

I place both hands on his desk to show I mean business, although the mittens do somewhat undermine my authority.

'There is a dog-sledding company in the Île d'Orléans. It is run by Jacques Dufour aka L'homme Loup.' My eyebrow cocks of its own accord.

'*Oui.*'

Oh my god, he knows it.

'Do you happen to know how to get there?' I hope my voice didn't just go up too high.

A brief tap of computer keys and he's handing me a print-out of a map.

The directions couldn't be any more French – Boulevard René Lévesque to Avenue Honoré Mercier, then take the ramp to Sainte-Anne-de-Beaupré . . .

I continue reading as I step into the revolving door, only to find Gilles in the opposing compartment.

Oh no, oh no!

I push forward and try to make a bid for the taxi, but he's too quick, scooting out of a side door and cutting in front of me. 'Krista wait! I need to talk to you.'

'Not now, Gilles. I'm in a hurry.'

'Where are you going?' he protests. 'I thought you came back to rest?'

'Change of plan,' I say as I dodge past him and into the back of the cab.

'What's going on?' he says, holding back the door.

I give a casual shrug as I yank the door closed. 'I need to see a man about a dog . . .'

8

Is this a rebound reaction to Gilles? Am I trying to attach myself to someone else so I don't feel quite so humiliated by our situation? Why else would I feel so compelled to find this stranger? Maybe it's not him at all. Maybe I just want to be around those beautiful dogs. I mean, wouldn't they look wonderful in a picture?

'So why aren't you waiting to go with the photographer?' My devil's advocate enquires.

'Because I need to ask permission first and I think the most effective way to convince him that we are legitimate is in person.'

'And that's all there is to it?'

Well, I suppose it doesn't hurt that he's the complete opposite to the ultra-groomed Gilles – The Wolfman wouldn't even know the term 'manscaping'. Sometimes I think that it's all very well being aware of trends and zeitgeists, but there's something even more appealing about a man who is oblivious to it all . . .

I sigh. There is of course a simpler theory: there are just some people in life that we are drawn to. The initial meeting may be fleeting, but it's enough to make you want to follow that feeling and see where it leads.

It was interesting with Andrew because we were literally 'attached' from the first moment we met. The dance floor was so crowded that you couldn't let the jostling faze you, it was just a question of seething with the masses. But then Andrew's watch snagged in my mesh top and we tried to disengage but there really wasn't the room so we ended up going the other way and he pulled me into him and we were sweatily bonded until the lights came up. It seemed like fate had tied a ribbon around us. Finally a man who stuck around! Prior to him I would excitedly tell the girls at work, 'I've met someone!' and by the next week it would turn into another non-starter. So I stopped telling them after a while, not wanting to be the girl who cried wolf. Though of course today I might get to do that for real!

I can't quite believe I'm doing this. Maybe part of it is simply that I can! I certainly haven't been in a position to pursue an attraction in a long time.

'Not since last night,' Laurie points out when I call her from the taxi.

'That was different,' I protest. 'Gilles just landed in my lap!'

'Whereas this guy is mysteriously out of reach?'

I huff down the phone.

Best I don't tell her about the distant sadness in Jacques' eyes or she will accuse me of being on one of my salvation missions. Which I'm not. I don't think. He just intrigues me, that's all . . .

'Have you thought about what you're going to do when you get there?'

'Not really,' I confess.

'Excellent, that's what I like to hear.'

'Oh don't!'

'No, seriously. Your itineraries don't leave a lot of room for going rogue. This is good. Experimental.'

'Right.'

'Anyway . . .' Laurie excuses herself from the conversation, reminding me that she has her cousin's birthday party to go to and is staying over in Sutton. 'Update me first thing tomorrow.'

'Will do.'

I look out of the window. Since calling Laurie, the taxi has transitioned from city streets to the freeway and now we're on a bridge rearing up and over the Saint Lawrence River, getting a bird's-eye view of the snow-drifted waters below. It's such an unusual sight – Sahara-style sand dunes seemingly made of whipped marshmallows – it makes me feel as though I am witness to an entirely new and fantastical landscape.

'Île D'Orléans!' the driver gruffs as we connect to the island.

We pass one lovely wooden home after the next, each set deep in thick Christmas cake icing. The leafless trees might look bleak and bare in another setting, but here they resemble the feathery accent twigs a florist might use in a bouquet.

I lean my head on the window glass. Everything seems so pristine in the crisp sunshine, definitely less city slush, more untrodden ground here – pretty much ruining any chance of me passing off this visit with a casual, 'I was just in the neighbourhood!'

But I can't turn back now, I'm too mesmerised . . .

It's then the driver pulls over to have a word with a fellow cabbie and I see a family loading into their car with another one of those Jelly Baby children. There's a lot of tottering around trying to capture said Jelly Baby and when the mum does finally scoop her up, it's all kisses and giggles and I feel like I'm going to be sick.

I want that so much and I'm never going to have that. Why-why-why? Why so many of my friends not me? I close my eyes, trying to compose myself, trying to push away these thoughts that plague me. Why couldn't I have a baby? If I had been able to, then Andrew wouldn't have left me. I'm still a little in shock that he did that. Though I could sense the change in the way he looked at me almost straight away – as though I no longer had that mystical other dimension to me. I was not physically capable of bringing a new being into the world. What you see is what you get. End of the line. And it's not enough. Not for him. And not for me.

The driver says something to me in French. It probably isn't, '*Don't think like that, you have so much to offer!*' but I pretend it is.

He continues for less than a mile and then slows, turns the car around, inhales as if to muster his nerve, revs the engine and roars up a snowy slope.

'Oh my!' This is quite an incline, I think, as we claw our way up the unpaved track: it could certainly double as a ski slope on the way down.

'You have very good tyres!' I comment.

'I am a very good driver,' he corrects me.

'Yes, you are.'

And I appreciate the extra adrenalin boost.

For a while I can't see anything but snow, but then we mount the brow of the hill and I spy a barn, a couple of boxy buildings and one idyllic stone farmhouse, which we stop beside.

'What does that mean?' I ask, pointing to a sign bearing the word '*ACCUEIL*'.

'Welcome. Or Reception,' he shrugs. 'It's where you need to go.'

His radio crackles with a message.

'You want to stay here?' he asks.

'Um . . .'

Is it wise to be stranding myself in this way? I look around for further signs of life and see a man doing a backflip out of the top floor of the barn.

My jaw drops. 'Did you see that?' I lurch to the window.

'Did I see . . . ?'

'A man just . . .' I stop. I must surely be seeing things. The barn has to be twenty feet high. Perhaps it was a bird or a piece of rubbish caught on the wind – some kind of peripheral vision illusion.

'Madame?'

'*Oui?*'

'*Tu reste ici?*'

It's then I catch a glimpse of Jacques leading a group down a pathway and my heart-leap dares me to say, 'Yes, yes, it's fine. *Merci!*'

I hurriedly pay the fare and then inch over to the dark red front door of the farmhouse. Before I lift the latch, I hesitate, unsure of quite what I might be walking into.

Then again, what's the alternative? Standing here until I become a porch-side ice sculpture? In I go!

I step down into a large room lined with cold-weather gear, all clompy boots and bulky jackets, and a vast flagstone hearth housing the kind of fire that makes your face glow yellow and your cheeks flush if you so much as look at it.

'*Bonjour! Comment est-ce que je peux vous aider?*'

I look to my left and see a petite girl with a headful of springy curls, partially restrained by a fleece beanie, sitting at a large old wooden desk.

'Er, English?' I prompt.

'You are here for the three p.m. ride?'

'Possibly . . .' I hedge my bets.

She looks confused. 'You have a reservation?'

'I don't. Actually, I was hoping to speak with Jacques . . .'

'He is about to leave with the group.'

'Oh.'

'You can join?'

'You mean go dog-sledding?'

She looks ever more puzzled. 'That is what we do here.'

'Like *now*?'

She nods. 'It is fifty dollars for an hour.'

I picture myself swathed in cashmere blankets as Jacques stands behind me, swooshing us through the sparkling snow and into the sunset.

'I'll do it!' I say, scrabbling for my purse.

'Sebastien! *Tu es libre?*' She addresses the lean young man who has just skulked in. He is wearing kingfisher blue, just like my phantom back-flipper.

He concedes a grunt, letting me know that I have just stolen his break.

'He will take you.'

I hope she means up to meet Jacques. As lovely as I'm sure the Wolfman's rear view is, I don't particularly want to be staring at it for the next hour, unable to interact.

Then again, perhaps they have some onboard communication system? 'Sled One this is Sled Five, do you read me?'

The Reception girl gets to her feet and leans over the desk to assess my outfit. 'You seem okay, you want to borrow any extra clothing?'

I politely decline the additional bulk. I'm roasting right now – all that sun streaming in the window of the taxi and now the fire: the chill will actually be welcome.

'Ready?' Sebastien enquires, motioning towards the door. 'You lead the way.'

I falter. 'This is my first time here . . .'

'You'll know where to go.'

I retrace my steps to where the taxi driver dropped me and then survey the landscape. If I was going on vision alone I would be stumped, but the frenzy of yelping, barking and howling is something of a giveaway. All I have to do is head in the direction of the dog chorus.

'They sound like they're raring to go . . .'

'Always,' Sebastien confirms, giving his peroxide blond tufts a good rub before replacing his hat.

I glance sideways at him. I must surely have been imagining it but I have to ask: 'I didn't just see you doing a back-flip out of the barn, did I?'

His jaw immediately tenses.

'It was . . .' I don't even finish my sentence because what must be a hundred huskies have just come into view.

They are evenly spaced across the field, like a flourishing canine crop, each with their own small wooden hut and a stake bearing their name – Flanders is alert, curious, looking our way, his neighbour preoccupied with digging a big pit in the snow to lie in, just to be extra cosy. I am surprised how relaxed they seem – and so happy to say hello, sharing their luxurious fur with my now bare hand. I stumble from one to the other, marvelling at how different each coat is – finely tufted grey, shaggy black with a white muzzle, several with Friesian cow splotches and a multitude of Zorros and Caped Crusaders!

I laugh as one pure white one jumps up and puts his paws on my shoulders.

'You want a full body hug?' I am quick to oblige.

'Oh they're all so lovely!' I say, as I look around me – dogs, dogs, dogs, as far as the eye can see. But no people.

'Where are the others?'

Sebastien nods beyond the plains to the forest ahead. 'They have already left.'

'Can we catch them?' I try to stave off my dismay.

'You want to play chase?' He looks amused. 'We can do that.'

Without much ado he harnesses a team of six dogs and bids me sit in the sled, which is lower and flimsier than I imagined – little more than a few pieces of balsa wood and matting.

'Keep hold of this,' Sebastien says as he hands me the rope that had previously been anchoring our ensemble.

'Will do,' I say, wondering if I'm sitting right, with my legs stuck straight out in front of me like a propped-up doll. But before I can ask, we're off.

It's a juddering, rickety start, and within approximately five seconds I'm freezing – I hadn't counted on the slashing chill of the wind, or the distinct lack of cashmere blankets, or ratty old tartan ones for that matter. Now I wished I'd taken them up on their lumberjack attire. I can feel my body stiffening with each thrum of the dogs' paws.

But their gait is so neat, the fluffy plumage of their tails swishing so jauntily, that I can't help but smile. Then, as we mount the hill, I sense the dogs slowing with the strain.

'I hope I'm not too heavy,' I worry.

No reply.

I look behind me and – Jumping Jehoshaphat! – it's happening again: either my mind is playing tricks on me or Sebastien is some kind of extreme gymnast. The only parts of him in the right position are his hands, gripping the bar. Other than that, instead of having his feet firmly planted on the rubberised foot panels, they are pointed skyward – his body erect and upside down as if he's performing one of those parallel bar routines in the Olympics.

'What the . . .' I blink. 'Aren't you supposed to be driving?'

'They know this route.'

I face forward again. I can't believe I got the kamikaze musher! I daren't turn around again for fear of finding him gone altogether or, worse, performing some elaborate ribbon routine with the dog harnesses.

Entering the forest, concern is replaced with enchantment – each spiky branch is balancing several inches of twinkling snow and the pine trees are frosted to perfection: just beautiful!

'*Allez, allez!*' Sebastien urges the dogs to increase their pace.

And then I catch sight of the group. We're actually gaining on them.

'Woah . . .'

'We're stopping?'

'They have stopped.'

I squint ahead and see Jacques removing a dog from his pack.

'What's going on?'

'He's rearranging his team. One of the dogs must be slowing up the rest.'

I see him speaking to each musher and then he notices Sebastien and cheers, '*Parfait!*'

(As in, 'Perfect!' I'm guessing, as opposed to the sundae-like dessert.)

As he approaches I feel my nerves prickling. Somehow he has reached celebrity status in my mind. I'm torn between hoping he doesn't recognise me and wanting him to gasp, 'It's you!'

But he's too engrossed in exchanging the dogs to notice the identity of the cushiony blob on the sled. Until, at the very last moment, he turns back, head tilted.

'*La fille qui est tombée dans la neige.*'

It sounds so romantic! Perhaps that could be my First Nation name? Girl Who Falls in Snow!

I want to breathe, '*C'est moi!*', but that would sound almost boastful, so I settle for a rather more pedestrian, 'Hello!'

His head tilts to the side. 'What are you doing here?'

'I-I wanted to thank you. For saving me.'

He shrugs. 'I'm sure your friends would have done the same.'

'Actually, they're not my friends, they're work colleagues.' I attempt to segue into Part Two of my reason for being here.

'You were working?'

'Yes. It was part of my job—'

'As a stuntwoman?' he cuts in, casting a glance at Sebastien.

'Oh no!' I gasp, both at his mis-analysis and the thought of him trying to fix me up with this nutcase. 'Nothing so daring.'

Before I can explain further, the dogs start whining and complaining: '*Jeez! What's the hold up? Can we get a move on here?*'

'We have to go,' Jacques affirms.

'Yes, *allez allez!*' I say, cringing as I realise I have essentially just mushed a musher.

The icy wind is welcome on my hot cheeks. How did that go? I'm not really sure. It's possible I look a tad stalker-esque. If only I had a chance to explain why I'm here . . .

'So, you have already met Jacques?' Sebastien asks, somewhat accusingly.

'Earlier today,' I reply.

'And where was that?'

'At the Carnival,' I say in a small voice.

I wish this sled came with a rear-view mirror because I'm sensing some hostility.

'Careful!' I cry, as we jolt up a bank, tipping a lapful of snow over me. I'm getting nervous now. We seem to be going too fast and then too slow, dragging back until we lose sight of the others.

Now he's stopped altogether.

'Er . . .'

'I need you to get out and come stand on the brake.'

I do as he says, all but raising my hands in the air, very aware that it's just me and him in the woods with six dogs, which I'm not entirely sure would count as witnesses in a court of law.

He ties the rope to a nearby tree and then asks if I want to take any pictures. I pose self-consciously as he snaps with my cameraphone. It's really Jacques I want to ask about doing a proper shoot. Suddenly all I can think about is getting back to base.

'Okay, now it's your turn.'

'For what?'

'To drive.'

'You want me to drive the sled?'

He nods. 'Of course. It is part of the experience.'

I look over at the dogs, taking their break in assorted manners – snuffling in the snow, taking chomps of the flavourless Slurpee, lying down to cool off their bellies and, in the case of one fidgety fellow, maintaining the starting block position. I take a breath and head towards the frontrunners.

'Where are you going?'

'To introduce myself to the dogs.'

'What for?'

'I can't expect them to run for me if we haven't even met.'

Sebastien rolls his eyes. 'You could be Michael Vick and they'd still run for you.'

'Michael Vick?'

'If you don't already know then you don't want to.'

'But—'

'American football player,' Sebastien sounds testy. 'Went to prison for his part in a dog-fighting ring. And it wasn't just dog-on-dog action,' Sebastien continues. 'They were found guilty of hanging, drowning, electrocuting and shooting dogs.'

I feel faint with anger. 'Please tell me he's still there. In prison.'

'Nope. He served less than two years.'

'What?'

'And when he came out, the Philadelphia Eagles signed him up and then the NFL named him Comeback Player of the Year.'

'That's sick,' I spit, not quite knowing what to do with this information.

'Wouldn't you like to set the dogs on him?' Sebastien looks equally disgusted.

'I'd tear him apart with my own bare hands.'

Sebastien nods. 'Me too.'

We talk for a while about the ridiculous amount of money American footballers get paid and how we'd like to take Vick's entire salary and donate it to pitbull charities while having him spend his free time tied to a chain in a rainy backyard where he'd be fed a diet of canned dog food.

'The really nasty, smelly stuff,' I decide.

For a second or two we bristle in silence and then Sebastien walks to the front of the team.

'This is Jupiter. He's the lead dog.' He scratches his brow and then raises the chin of the one next to him. 'This is his brother, Orion.'

It takes me a moment to realise he is indulging my whim. Then I hurry forward and greet them, first with a gently proffered mitten and then a full head rumple, finding them surprisingly affectionate. While Sebastien tells me that the middle dogs are also referred to as 'in swing' and the rear 'at wheel', I form a crush on the dog Jacques traded, name of Maddy.

'Do you have a favourite?' I ask Sebastien.

He looks at me as if to say, 'If you're testing to see if I'm human, I'm not going to bite.'

'Come on, it's time for you to drive.'

He walks me back to the sled and gives me the basics:

'So you hold here,' he taps the wooden handlebar. 'Feet here on the rubber grips and this is the brake.' He sets a toe where I have my feet on a metal bar with ragged teeth. 'If one foot is not enough, use two.'

'So jump on it?'

He looks mildly concerned. 'One foot will be enough. And try and keep the line taut at all times. That's important.' He claps his hands. 'Okay?'

'That's it?'

'That's it.'

'Wow. Well that's the quickest driving lesson I ever had.' I look at the dogs and then back at him. 'Are they just going to take off?'

'As soon as you release the brake.'

'And if I get whiplash, fall back and you leave without me?'

'I will stop the sled.'

I'm about to ask how he could possibly do that when I remember he is part-contortionist. Like right now, he is using the tree to perform a particularly extensive leg stretch.

'Are you even aware that your foot is up by your ear?' I marvel.

'Old habit,' he coughs, quickly bringing it back down to earth.

'I don't know why you don't just go back to Cirque du Soleil where you belong!' I tease.

'Who told you?' he snaps.

'Told me what?'

'About Cirque?'

I study his face. 'You were in Cirque du Soleil?'

He goes to storm off but realises he is in no position to do so.

'Are you serious?' I ask, fascinated.

(Personally I think Cirque du Soleil should be categorised as one of the Wonders of the World. If they have a show in any of our featured cities we always book tickets for our clients because we can guarantee it will be one of the highlights of their trip.)

'It's no big deal,' Sebastien tries to play it down.

'On the contrary I think it's remarkable! I mean, what an honour. And what talent you must have – way beyond what I have seen today.'

He looks huffy. 'I don't want to talk about it.'

'Okay, okay.' I back down, though I couldn't be any more intrigued – I mean why would he leave? And what was it like to run off and join the circus in the first place? What act was he a part of? What show? What kind of costume? Did he travel? Are their parties really as outrageous as I've heard? What stories he must have!

But now is not the time. I've got mushing to do . . .

9

Talk about transitioning from observer to participant. The passenger is to become the driver. Whether she likes it or not.

I still can't believe this is all on me. And without L plates. Now if I could only get up the nerve to release the brake . . .

Ultimately it's the dogs that persuade me – knowing that every extra second I hold back is pure torment for them.

'*Set us free, set us free!*' They plead with their whole beings. And so I do.

I'm tense at first, gripping too tightly, body hunched, terrified of tipping up every time we take a curve or the dogs veer onto un-compacted snow. But then we're out of the woods, quite literally, swishing through open fields of snow, and suddenly this feels like the most glorious sensation in the world. I can't help it, I let out a wild whoop of joy!

'This is amazing!'

I don't know why, but I'm not cold at all now, just exhilarated. I feel connected to the dogs and the landscape and the vastness of the sky. Forgetting Sebastien is even present, I lean back as if I'm water-skiing, even take one hand off. This is a breeze! I feel open and free and happy! Honest-to-goodness happy!

But then the front two dogs start nipping at each other, bickering and snapping. What am I supposed to do now?

Sebastien reprimands them but they don't stop so he calls for me to brake.

First I squeeze the handle bar as though I'm on a bike, then I tap a non-existent pedal like I'm in a car. Darnit! Only when Sebastien throws out his feet and starts rucking up snow with his heels do I remember the jagged metal bar between my feet.

'S-sorry,' I puff as we finally grind to a halt.

'That's okay, you're doing fine.'

'Oh no! Orion's pooping!'

I feel I should avert my eyes.

'Why now, why mid-run?' I ask.

Sebastien shrugs, 'When you've got to go . . .'

Where's Gilles with his fashion lens now, I think to myself. No doubt examining Annique's aperture. Oh dear. That sounded even worse than I intended.

'Okay, go again.'

Soon I'm back to bliss. I could do this all the way to Alaska! What's that race they have there – the Iditarod? I seem to remember it being over a week long. I wonder what that's like? Endurance test or Zen meditation? Do you see the other sledders or is it just you and infinite white?

I'm in a long-haul mindset now but what seems like minutes later my time is up. I experience a brief moment of panic as the dogs charge right through the camp, but of course it's all part of the plan and we come to rest at the exact point at which we left an hour ago. I'm still in a state of euphoria as I step off the sled. Sebastien, by contrast, seems to have dug deeper in his sulk.

'All right?' he grudgingly checks on me.

'Well, I can't feel my feet any more but apart from that . . .'

'There's hot chocolate inside,' he says, and then immediately starts speaking French with one of the other guys.

Well I guess that's me dismissed. I desperately want to shake paws with every single dog at the camp, to linger in this fantastical environment as long as possible, but I do have a pressing need to thaw out. My face is taut and stinging and my toes have bunched up into frozen claws. Not that I really care. All the same, hot chocolate does sound like heaven right now.

'How was it?' the girl on Reception asks as I step through the door.

'Fantastic – I loved it! Those dogs are so good-natured!'

'And Sebastien?' She sounds a little more wary.

'Well,' I search for the right words. 'He's quite the character.'

'Mmmm.'

And then I venture: 'He seems very protective of Jacques . . .'

She nods. 'Normally it's the other way around, *non*?'

'How do you mean?'

'You know, the older brother is the protector.'

'They're brothers?' I am genuinely surprised. 'They don't look at all alike.'

'Different mothers.'

'Ohhh.' I shuffle closer to her desk and lower my voice. 'So was he really in Cirque du Soleil?'

'He told you?' She looks amazed.

'Not exactly. I sort of guessed.'

'He can't really hide it. It's in his body, every muscle, every way he moves. Everything to him is something to jump off or swing on or leap over.'

'Why did he leave? He doesn't seem to have an injury.'

I sense her pull back. 'He made a different choice.'

I want to ask more but the next group has arrived and she needs to check them in.

'Er, the *salle de bain*?' I quickly request directions to the loo.

More fool me for asking in French, because she replies in kind and all I catch is *à gauche* . . .

Somewhere on the left . . . I turn down the corridor and open the first door I come to. Darkness. I feel for the light switch and find myself in a small office crammed with all manner of dog-sledding trophies and memorabilia, including several photographs of Jacques with an all-Samoyed team, their white fur looking rice-pudding cream against the blue hue of the snow. He seems to have competed in a mix of races from sprints to long-distance, and in so many locations . . . I see plaques for the Caledonian Classic in British Columbia, the Can-Am Crown in Maine, the Copper Dog 150 in Michigan . . . Then I gasp – the legendary Iditarod! He did it! One thousand miles with a frosty beard. *Wow*. It makes me wonder – what kind of man would seek to challenge himself that way? A lone wolf, some might say . . .

It's then I acknowledge the other distinct feature of the room – sympathy cards. Dozens of them lining the shelves and desktop, a couple tucked behind picture frames. Are these for dogs that have passed, I wonder? I'm just about to step towards a picture of Jacques with his arm around someone when I sense a presence behind me.

'Jacques!' I jump at the sight of the man himself. 'I didn't mean to be snooping. I was looking for the loo.'

'Next door down.'

'Oh. Okay. Thank you.' I'm mortified but force myself to turn back to him. 'That's an impressive selection of awards . . .'

He looks mildly embarrassed. 'My dad did the decorating in there.'

'He must be very proud.'

'At one time.'

Oh. I give an awkward smile and head into the Ladies. Turns out I don't need to go at all now but I'm glad for the chance to regain my composure. That was a little uncomfortable. And what did he mean, 'At one time . . .' What would have changed? Could it have anything to do with those bereavement cards? It's not the dad who's dead is it? Darn! Why did I open that door? I wonder if I should just leave quietly before I upset anyone else?

As I step out of the loo, I catch sight of the group chatting animatedly in the backroom lounge, hot chocolate in hand. I'm about to look away and return to the front Reception when I notice Jacques holding out a mug for me. At least I think it's for me – I look behind me to be sure. No one else around. When I look back he nods as if to say, 'Yes you, madam, you with the pink nose.'

'Th-thank you,' I gratefully accept the steamy beverage.

'Can't go without your treat.'

'Gosh, I've already had that – the ride was amazing.'

He smiles. 'Sebastien said you were a natural.'

'*He did?*'

'You sound surprised.'

I pull a face.

'You can say it. We all know what he's like.'

'No, he's fine. He seemed irritated with me for the most part.'

'At the moment he's irritated full stop.'

And what's your story? I want to ask. What is the shadow in your eyes? But instead I make so bold as to ask him whether he would consider letting us promote his business on our website and, if so, would he allow me to return tomorrow, with a photographer . . .

He thinks for a minute, asks a few more questions, looks me over one more time and then says, 'I don't see why not. But it would have to be early, before the first group – eight a.m.?'

'No problem,' I tell him.

And then his face softens. 'We have some puppies here I could show you tomorrow, if you like.'

'Husky puppies?' My eyes light up.

He nods. 'Sixteen of them.'

Now my eyes widen – this is too good to be true!

'In fact,' he beckons me around a corner, out of sight of the group, 'I have one right here . . .' And with that he unzips his jacket and a fluffy-downy sleepy-head pops out.

My besotted gurgle quickly turns to concern. 'What happened to his face?' Little scars and scratches intersperse his teddy-bear features.

'His mother turned on him, we don't know why. So I'm taking care of him now.'

And then the little puppy looks up at me and I gasp, 'He has your eyes!'

'Crazy huh? It's actually quite common in huskies, to have different-coloured irises.'

'Less so in humans,' I say, though I'm really basing this on celebrities I know with different-coloured eyes, namely Kate Bosworth and David Bowie. And actually I think David Bowie's is more a case of one permanently dilated pupil.

I'm mid-mind-ramble when a surge of tingly warmth races throughout my body – my fingertips, which until now have been giving feather-like strokes to the puppy's ears and wispy cheeks, just made contact with Jacques' hand. For a millisecond the three of us were connected – skin on skin on fur – and it felt incredible. Like a family.

'I need to get another dog,' I say, stepping back and taking a breath.

'How many do you have?' Jacques asks.

'None at the moment, that's the problem.'

He gives me a knowing look. 'They are the best.'

'What about you,' I ask, 'exactly how many do you have here?'

'Full grown?' His chest puffs and then he blurts, 'Ninety-eight.'

'Ninety-eight?' I reel. 'That's a lot. And you know all their names?'

'Every one.'

I sigh – I could listen to him reeling off name after name after name and it would sound like poetry to me right now.

'Do you count them at night instead of sheep?'

'That's actually a good idea!' He smiles, but then looks a little wistful, as if he really might have trouble sleeping.

But why would that be? And isn't there a Mrs Dufour to soothe him into a slumber? I know later, when I dissect all this with Laurie, she will ask if he flirted with me and I will have to answer no and she will suggest that he may already have a girlfriend he is quietly devoted to. And yet . . . I'm not particularly getting that vibe either. If I was to guess at anything, I would say he's opted out of such things. Perhaps he too is recovering from some kind of heartbreak. Oh no! Maybe it's his wife or girlfriend who died!

'Jacques!' It's the Reception girl calling through to let him know that a) his next group is ready and b) the shuttle is here to take the others back to the city.

I know this because he translates for me *and* offers me a seat on the shuttle, which I gratefully accept.

'So,' he says, zipping up his precious fur-ball. '*À demain?*'

'Until tomorrow!' I smile, glad that my stomach-flip is not visible to the naked eye.

Or is it?

Sebastien gives me a rather intrusive look as he gives me a hand up onto the minibus. He also doesn't let go of my arm when he should.

Is he angling for a tip?

'You can't save him you know,' he says, his natural petulance mixing with sadness now, burrowing the words into my brain.

'Save him from what?' I want to ask. '*You?*' But he's stepped back and the doors have suctioned closed between us.

I sit down with a thud.

What was that all about? Why did he look so haunted when he said that? Was he trying to tell me that I'm not the first girl to want to 'fix' Jacques, and that all others have failed, to the extent of their own demise? Was that really my intention anyway? Of course I'd salve his wound with cooling aloe gel if I could, but mostly I just wanted to know more about him. But is that how it begins?

For a while I feel huffy and judged, and not a little concerned, but then I think of my private viewing of the puppy, how close we were standing, and the fact that I have been invited back tomorrow, and pretty soon my drunken smile returns. Shrugging down in the seat so that my Puffa hood becomes a substitute pillow, I find myself conjuring images of Jacques and me lying on a patchwork of blankets before a vigorous fire, the puppy tumbling between us, moving through various stages of dog-hood as we look dotingly on . . .

Oh *demain, demain*. Why does there even have to be a *ce soir*?

10

I arrange to meet everyone at the restaurant, saying that I want
to meander through the Old Town (which I do), but really it's
more about avoiding any potential alone-time with Gilles. I
don't know what he wanted to talk about before I bolted in the
taxi – a petit apology, *peut-être?* – but now I'd really prefer he
said nothing at all because, honestly, what can I say in response?
Even thinking about our kiss at the Hôtel de Glace makes me
cringe now and, besides, it already seems like a lifetime ago.

Even if it was just last night.

I return to my place of contemplation in front of my wardrobe. How exactly does one dress for a swish establishment
when you have to brave snow and subzero temperatures to
get there? Do the Québécois pack a small overnight bag
every time they go to dinner, switching into their LBD and
strappy stilettos in the revolving door? Or do they forgo
vamp glamour in favour of polo necks and snowflake-motif
sweaters? And, most importantly, can skinny jeans really live
up to their name when you have a rucked pair of long johns
underneath?

I sigh heavily.

And then I spy my silver camisole with the matte sequins.
How about if I layered that with my sheer cashmere cardi?
That would work at the dinner table. Along with my pale
grey scarf if it looks too dressy. I zip a fleece over the top,
which I can remove with my Puffa coat. Black gloves and

boots. Now I have to go and ruin everything with a hat that will simultaneously flatten the front of my hair and create wispy static-electricity elevations at the crown.

Perhaps I'll just brave it without.

I'm two steps out of the front door when I come scuttling back in.

'Frosty the snowman!' I gasp.

It is both colder than I imagined – instant brain-freeze! – and more slippy; trickier to see the slicks of treacherous ice amid the streaky reflections of the street lamps. I run back to the room for my warmest hat and then go in search of some kind of walking stick or ski pole at the gift shop.

What I walk out with is a red plastic cane topped with a white Bonhomme head. I'm not sure how much good it will do me, but it certainly seems to be the accessory *du jour* – I notice that everyone heading in the direction of the Carnival has one. The weird thing is they keep unscrewing Bohomme's head and sipping from the cane.

I find out why at the first bar I pass: they have filled their canes with Caribou – the cocktail, that is, not the vast-antlered reindeer. It tastes just like mulled wine, is also served warm, and after a couple of slugs I'm feeling no pain. I even do a few token baton twirls as I enter the fabled walled city.

If ever there was a place that looked like it had been designed as a set for a movie, this is it. There's not one building that jars the charm or makes you think, 'Now why did they have to go and ruin it all with that eyesore?' Every rooftop, every awning, every window display is evocatively characterful and pleasing to the eye. Even the souvenir shops look appealing, with rugged-knit hats and scarves in the Canadian flag combination of red and white.

Fairylights wink and glow at every turn – I remember Annique saying that they keep up their Christmas decorations until the snow subsides in March; another excellent way to keep the mood festive and avoid the post-Christmas slump.

She also said you can't get lost in Quebec Old Town, but I beg to differ – the place is a wiggly, up-hill/down-dale maze. The one place I have no problem locating is the Château Frontenac. It really is huge. According to my directions, the Auberge Saint-Antoine is just a seven-minute walk from here, though that may be in the summer when you don't have to inch along like you're trying to break in a new pair of legs. It's strange how much you take for granted being able to safely plant one foot in front of the other. I'm looking so tentative at the top of one ice-gleamed slope that an elderly lady, eighty if she's a day, offers me her arm to help me across the street. I kid you not.

Pausing again beside a park where the benches are three-quarters buried in snow, I take another look at my map.

I think I'm just supposed to hug the curve of this road all the way down to Lower Town and then turn left.

Not that I'm in any particular hurry to get there any more, I've entered that lovely blurry alcohol haze that makes everything a wonder to behold. I mean, look at this vast *trompe l'oeil* of the city – it has to be five storeys high with all the seasons represented (snow to autumn foliage to blossoms to sunny streets), as well as different time periods (a horse and carriage alongside a mum pushing a pram). I peer closer at the depiction of a bookshop window, studying each painted title and then Google some of the writers' names and find that every one comes up as a local author. Nice touch.

I decide to take a slight detour to get a better snap of the artwork, and that's when I see an alluring and strangely familiar sight – a ye-olde square of wooden-shuttered houses set around a simple, single-spired, dove-grey church. There's a giant Christmas tree in the centre of the courtyard and I stand beside it, facing the church and wondering, out loud apparently, where I've seen it before.

'*Catch Me If You Can.*'

I spin around. Where did that voice come from?

'You recall the scene in the movie where Tom Hanks finally catches up with Leonardo DiCaprio at the printing press in France?'

'Of course!' I gasp.

'It was shot right here.'

Already wide-eyed, I nearly repeat my earlier fallback into the snow as a certain figure steps out from the shadows . . .

I can't believe it! *It's Bonhomme!*

I look around – not another soul. That can't be right! Where's his Pied Piper-esque following? Shouldn't he at least have an escort or a handler with him?

I reach out and prod him in the belly.

'Help yourself.'

'Oh! I just wanted to see if you were real!'

'As opposed to a Caribou hallucination?'

'Isn't it marvellous stuff?' I raise my cane. 'It's my new favourite drink.' And then I tilt my head. 'Are you lost?'

'No,' he replies. 'Are you?'

'As a matter of fact I am.' I brighten. 'You must know this city pretty well. Do you give directions?'

I'd say he smiles in response but that's a given with his mouth set in a fixed black grin.

'Where do you need to go?' he asks.

'Auberge Saint-Antoine,' I reply.

'Someone has expensive taste.'

'Not me.'

'A date?'

'No, no. Well, not mine – we're setting up a gay sculptor

with a straight photographer. We did something very bad to his polar bear,' I wince. 'It's a long story.'

Bonhomme places his bulky white arm around my shoulder. 'All you have to do is go back up to the top of this road . . .'

'By the *trompe l'oeil*.'

'If that's how you want to pronounce it. Then go right and then left at Restaurant L'Initiale – which does great stuffed quail by the way – and then you'll see Rue Saint-Antoine a bit further down on your right.'

I clasp my hands together like a swooning heroine. 'Oh Bonhomme! How can I ever thank you!'

'Would you like to take off your clothes?'

I blink back at him. 'It's got to be minus twenty!'

'Not right now. In two days' time.'

'Is there some kind of heat wave coming?'

'Two days from now we have the Bain de Neige at the Carnival.'

'Please tell me that does not translate as Snow Bath.'

'Oh but it does. Great fun. I'd like to see you there. In your bikini.'

I feel a little uneasy. Should Bonhomme really be talking this way?

'All I'm going to be wearing is a red hat.'

'That's practically all you're wearing now,' I observe. 'Well, that and this waist sash, which you do wear rather high, if you don't mind me saying.'

'You want me to reposition it?'

'No, no!' I snort. 'Who am I to restyle a fifty-seven-year-old icon?'

'Well, let's at least see how it looks. Turn away while I untie it.'

I turn back to face the church. 'Why do I feel you're getting up to mischief?'

'With these mittens?'

My laughter soon turns into a piercing scream.

'You did not just do that!'

The not-so-little rascal just stuffed a handful of freezing snow down the back of my neck!

I scoop up an armful, looking for an opening in his costume to return the favour.

'This isn't fair – you're all sealed up!' I protest.

'Look over there!'

He gets me again, this time with a snowball in the kidney region.

'Right! That's it!'

I scrabble on the ground and start pelting him with everything I can get my hands on.

I can't believe I'm having a snowball fight with a snowman!

While he darts behind the tree, I start building a stack of ammo. I want to be ready to bombard him when he reappears.

'Madame?'

I spin around and find three policemen staring down at me.

I drop the newest clomp of snow like it's a brick I'm about to throw through a jeweller's window.

'S-sorry, is that not allowed? I didn't mean to mess up the snow.'

'Have you seen a man dressed as Bonhomme?'

'Sshhh!' I giggle. 'You're never supposed to acknowledge that there is a man inside. Bonhomme is real!'

'Madame, this is serious. We had a report of a sighting of him in this area.'

Is this some Carnival caper I don't know about? Is there a hidden camera in that bust of Louis XIV? Are these policeman really actors?

'Madame?'

'He's behind the tree!'

They hurtle to the other side.

Rien! Nothing!

What is it with men disappearing in my life? I've clearly missed my calling as a magician's assistant.

'But you did see him?'

'Yes.'

'And you speak with him?'

'I did,' I confirm. 'I was lost, he gave me directions . . .'

'And that's it?'

'Um.'

'He didn't say anything else? Anything that could help us locate him?'

'I think he's going to be at the Bain de Neige event.'

'Figures.'

A radio bleeps and conveys a message – there's been a sighting down by the ferry . . .

The head policeman gives me his card. 'If you remember anything else, please call us.'

I nod and watch them leave in a state of disbelief. Did all that really happen? I stand and watch the snowflakes softly falling, catching a few on the fingertips of my gloves. And then I take a picture of the church, to prove that at least *I* was really here.

A few minutes later I arrive at Auberge Saint-Antoine.

I'll say one thing – fake Bonhomme gives excellent directions.

'Here she is!' Annique jumps to her feet to greet me. 'Let me show you where you can hang your coat.'

The hotel is incredibly chic. I do like how the rich do cosy: starting with a refined colour palette – what I would describe as cranberry, crème anglaise, and soft taupe – and then adding an eccentric detail or two, in this case moose silhouette cushions and a heavy iron chain in lieu of coals in the fireplace. The bar itself has a mix of high-backed leather banquettes, clear Perspex chairs and cushiony window seats. But what secures a prime place on the website is the fact that the area is book-ended by two inviting insets with their own fireplace, shelves of books and board games and a snug sofa, just like your own bijou apartment – order a bottle of wine and a cheeseboard, drag across the velvet drape and you're set for the night.

Annique explains that we are in fact ordering off the bar menu as a few friends will be joining us later. The more relaxed setting suits me fine, and the more people that aren't Gilles, the better.

'Annique?' I halt her before she heads back down the stairs.

'Yes?'

'Is Bonhomme in trouble with the law?'

'Of course not!' she tinkles. 'He's the most honourable, wholesome, delightful— '

'Yes, yes, I know, he's a national treasure.'

'Why do you ask?'

I take a breath. 'I just saw the police chasing him.'

'Oh!' She looks stricken. 'So it's true.'

'What is?'

'I heard a rumour that there is an impostor on the loose.'

'No!'

She lowers her voice. 'They call him Malhomme.'

'Mal as in bad?' I seek clarification. 'Like Bonhomme's bad-guy alter ego?'

'Yes.' She clicks her tongue. 'This is not a good situation.'

'What do you know about it?'

'Just that he is singling out the tourists – of course the locals know him too well to be fooled.'

'So, for example, someone gawping at the church in Place Royale . . .'

'You didn't speak to him?' she gasps.

'I did.'

'What did he say?'

'Well, he was kind of . . . *flirty*.'

'This must not happen.' She looks genuinely upset. 'Bonhomme's reputation is sacred.'

'You know I once saw a guy in a Mickey Mouse costume taking a cigarette break . . .'

She gives me a dark look.

'Of course this is much worse.'

Annique begins chewing at her perfect French-Canadian manicure.

'I didn't mean to be such a downer,' I apologise.

'No, no. But I think we must report this incident.'

'Well, I've already told the police everything.'

'Everything? Every word. This is very important.'

I look over at Gilles sitting awkwardly with Brandon.

'You know you're quite right. There is more to tell. Let's do it right now.'

I'm not sure if the fact that the impostor is a fan of the stuffed quail at Restaurant L'Initiale will crack the case, but you never know.

I'm still really none the wiser about what this so-called Malhomme is up to. The police don't want salacious stories getting out so they prefer not to give any further details. Fair enough. All we really know is that he is not behaving in a way that is ambassador-appropriate.

'Ooh Brandon, what are you drinking?' I ask as we return to the bar, admiring his pink cocktail served in a slender antler-motif flute.

'French-Canadian Kiss,' he beams. 'Want one?'

'No thanks,' I reply, adding for Gilles' ears only. 'I find it leaves a nasty aftertaste.'

I study the menu and then order a Jalapeño Margarita, just to show how tough I am.

'We've ordered a selection of appetisers.' Annique invites me to dip in. 'And there's a fondue on the way.'

'Yummy! Thank you.' I turn back to Brandon. 'So how did the rest of the competition go?'

'Well, I didn't win but I did get the best prize!' He looks googly-eyed at Gilles.

'Have you two had your picture taken together yet?'

'No,' he says, coyly.

'Allow me!' I take his phone and start snapping away. 'Come on, cuddle up nice and close. That's adorable!'

'By the way, Krista,' Gilles interrupts. 'I think we need to set aside some time tomorrow to go through the photos for the website.'

'No rush,' I chirp. 'I won't be posting until I've viewed the whole lot, so I can get a good balance of images. Unless you're concerned you're not getting the shots . . .'

'Oh no. The quality is there.'

'Good to know. And the dog-sledding should be great. You did get my message about that, Annique?'

'Yes, but I don't know how you did it!'

'Did what?' Gilles looks confused.

'Persuade the Wolfman to let us shoot at his home.'

'Oooh, the Wolfman. I think you've just given me the concept for my new snow sculpture!' Brandon enthuses. 'Is he as sexy as he sounds?'

'Well, he does happen to have sixteen husky puppies . . .'

'Goodness,' Brandon fans himself with a napkin and then playfully nudges his date. 'You may have a little competition there, Gilles . . . !'

'Oh! Here's Simone and Yves!' Annique beckons her friends over.

They begin asking me how I like it so far, where I'm staying . . .

I explain that I managed half a night at the Hôtel de Glace, I'm currently at the Hilton and on Wednesday I'm switching to—

'Auberge Place D'Armes,' Annique helps me out.

'Oh that's so cute!' Simone raves. 'And you have to try their dessert with the banana cognac flambée – *c'est magnifique!*'

Before long everyone has slipped into speaking French, which actually suits me fine as I am now enjoying an all-consuming relationship with the fondue. I'm just about to propose to the crusty French bread when Annique elbows me.

'Do you see the man staring at you from the bar?'

I peek up at the debonair gent with the sandy hair and Aaron Eckhart's cleft chin and give a little snort. 'Bless you Annique, but if he's staring at anyone it's you.'

'No, no. I am not mistaken. I can tell the difference. Let's invite him over.'

'What? No!' I flush.

'You don't want a little romance in Quebec?'

I catch Gilles' eye.

'I've already had my fill.'

'Oh, you mustn't let one sleazy encounter put you off.'

Gilles looks alarmed – *she knows? Annique knows?* I can see his mind whirring: is that what they were discussing earlier, so very intently? Is that why they disappeared?

'It wasn't just the sleaziness,' I sigh, milking it. 'It's just the big lie, you know. But I'll say something – the guy has a lot of nerve.'

And then Annique spoils everything by leaning in and telling the others that I met Malhomme.

'Tell us! Tell us!' They clamour for a re-enactment but I don't have the energy to relive it all again so I excuse myself to go to the Ladies' room.

I admire the modern design and utilise the fragrant liquid soap and lotion, delaying as long as I can, and then slowly make my way back. Aware that my walk is giving away just how tipsy I am, I pause at every other glass display case, pretending to be fascinated by the sets of ancient keys and broken pottery discovered on an archaeological dig on this very site. Apparently the Price family who own this property began their life in Quebec as a Welsh logging company. Didn't they do well?

I'm over at the top of the stairs now, gripping tight and preparing to lower myself back down to the bar, when I see the Staring Man coming up towards me. I feel instantly self-conscious, hotter than ever and utterly unable to move. He really does have the most penetrative stare.

As he draws level he leans close enough for me to feel his breath upon my neck and whispers, 'See you at the Snow Bath!'

That voice! *It's him!*

I turn around but he's already out the door.

I'm torn – do I chase after him? Who am I kidding, I can barely walk these streets and I'd have to get my coat and he knows every alley and cut-through . . .

I place my hand over my pounding heart. Is this something else to tell the police? I could give a fairly decent description of him. As could Annique. But what if I'm wrong?

Though I know I'm not. He gave me the very same feeling.

But why would he be doing this? He looked so well dressed, sitting there, drinking his champagne. Is he some kind of bored playboy, I wonder?

'Krista? Are you all right?' Annique has come to rescue me.

'I do feel a little woozy.'

'You've only had one drink,' Gilles scoffs as I lower myself onto the chair.

'Well, I did have a cane-full of Caribou on the way here . . .'

'Arrrrgggghhh!' they all chorus in a display of tortured empathy.

'You do know what is in that?' Brandon asks.

'It's just mulled wine, isn't it?'

'Tastes like mulled wine but in fact it's a lethal combination of brandy, vodka, sherry and port!'

Oh jeez.

'Add the fact that you've come into the warm from the freezing cold . . .'

'. . . suddenly the alcohol is moving around your bloodstream a lot quicker.'

'God, I remember the time I . . .'

And so it goes, each person with their own Caribou horror story. When they have concluded, I announce, 'I think I need to go back to the hotel.'

'I'll take you,' Gilles leaps to his feet.

'No need,' I push him back down. Rather too firmly, perhaps. 'If you could just get me a taxi, Annique?'

'*Bien sûr!*'

The taxi thankfully takes just a couple of minutes. I can't wait to get into bed, though I probably would have held off on the dreaming if I'd known it was going to involve riding the Tornado with six cocktail-supping huskies while trying to hang onto a pot of scalding fondue.

11

'Now I know why they call that drink Caribou.'

'And why is that?' Laurie asks.

'Because I look like a total moose.'

I've got her on speakerphone in the bathroom while I assess the morning-after payback in the mirror.

'I'm sure it's not that bad.'

'Switch to Skype and I'll show you.'

'Woah!' She reels. 'Well, that certainly gives new meaning to "getting caned".'

'Oh don't! A thimble-full would've done the trick. It was like the world's longest shot.'

'More important than ever to get the outfit right – what are you planning on wearing?'

'Well it's not like you can go for a plunging neckline in this weather. It's either my black coat—'

'Oh you don't want to wear black today,' Laurie shudders. 'That'll just accentuate the shadows.'

'And actually I wore that last time. Ivory it is.'

I just hope Annique isn't in white today or I'm going to look like a big cream puff next to her Mini Milk popsicle.

'Which scarf?' I hold up the orange ombre knit versus the plain grey fleece and then bend down to pick up the glove options. 'Oh lord!'

'What is it?'

'Just another wave of nausea.'

'You'd probably feel better if you were sick.'

'I wish. It keeps threatening to come up but no joy so far.'

'Is that Krista?' A new voice chips in – it's Danielle leaning in behind Laurie. 'Gosh this is a really bad picture.'

'Actually it's a good picture – I just look this bad right now.'

'So you told her?' Danielle grimaces.

'Told me what?'

Laurie clearly pinches Danielle because she jumps back hissing, 'I thought it might help her get closure.'

'Hello! Tell me what?'

'Oh, it's just boring website stuff. Potential redesign. Nothing you need to worry about until you get back.'

'Or you could tell me the truth.'

Laurie looks uneasy.

'What did she mean, get closure?' I persist. 'Is this to do with Andrew?'

She sighs heavily. 'I don't think this is the right time to talk about this.'

Uh oh, I'm starting to get that twisty feeling in my stomach. I swallow back the anxiety and force a breeziness to my voice . . .

'Let's face it,' I begin, 'I couldn't feel any worse than I do already, so really it's the ideal time.'

'True.'

'And I'd rather know now when I've got lots of fun new things to distract me.'

'Mmm-hmm.'

'I'll just obsess all day if you don't tell me.'

Laurie clasps her hands together on the desk, taking on the look of a newsreader in a time of crisis. 'It's not good.'

'What, has he got some girl half my age pregnant?'

Laurie looks as if she might cry.

'He hasn't!'

'She's nineteen. Delivers sandwiches to his office.'

'Oh god!' I scramble to the bathroom and up it all comes – the Caribou, the fondue, the pain.

When I'm done I slump beside the toilet and let the sobs take over, hands rubbing at my face, clawing at my hair. I can't stand this! I can't stand to feel this way – so *disposable*. I couldn't provide the appropriate service and so he's on to the next, and now they've got this whole life to live together and, and . . . the sobs overtake me again.

'Oh Krista,' I hear Laurie's concerned voice from the phone. 'This is why I didn't tell you.'

I crawl back over, covering my face with the fleece scarf. 'I'm sorry Laurie. I don't mean for you to witness all this.'

'Don't be silly. I'm glad I can be here. I just wish Danielle hadn't put her big foot in it.'

'No, it's better I know,' I lie, trying to pull myself together, but all I can think of is Andrew with his hand proudly on her stomach, picking out little booties and a dragonfly mobile for above the cot. It almost seems like the girl herself doesn't matter. I don't wonder about what she looks like or their compatibility – the fact that she is to be the mother of his child is enough. She couldn't find a higher pedestal to be placed upon. And it was so easy for her, so effortless . . .

'I feel so bad . . .' Laurie sighs.

'Don't. Honestly,' I insist. 'It was bound to happen. I mean, that's what he wanted.'

'It just doesn't seem fair that he gets it. You wanted it too! And you would have made a wonderful mum.'

'No I wouldn't,' I shake my head. And the tears begin to flow again. 'I should go.'

'Wait!' Laurie protests. 'What are you going to do?'

The thought of having to get up and dressed and go

dog-sledding with Gilles scrutinising my every move through his prying lens is just too much to bear.

'Maybe I'll just have a sick day.'

'But you're only there a week, you don't want to waste a whole day feeling bad!' She leans closer into the camera. 'I know that bed looks good right now.'

'It really does.'

'But all that awaits you is more misery, going over and over something you've already cried enough tears about.'

Enough tears. How do you know when it's enough, I want to ask her. Why does there always feel as if there's more?

But instead I say, 'You're right.'

'If you stay in bed, nothing will change. If you get up, you could have an amazing day. Besides, what was the one thing that always used to make you feel better?'

'Being with my dog.'

'And how many dogs does this Jacques have?'

'Ninety-eight.'

'Well, then wouldn't you like to feel ninety-eight times better than you do right now?'

'I would!' I smile.

'Okay. So here's what you do: you pull on a hat and go down to breakfast looking like something from a zombie movie, you eat the closest thing they have to a greasy spoon breakfast, you come back up, get in the shower and let all thoughts of his unmentionable self go down the plughole, got it?'

'Got it!' My breathing has calmed now. That was a good pep talk.

'And take one of those Vitamin C sachets.'

'I will.'

'You can turn this around and still have a good day, I know you can.'

'Thank you,' I say, most sincerely.

'Okay. Text me your progress. Love you!'

'Love you too!'

For a good minute I clasp my phone to my chest, feeling extremely grateful to have a friend like Laurie. And then I get up and do exactly as she prescribed, fortifying myself with two helpings of the breakfast potatoes, detoxifying with green tea (in lieu of PG) and then drowning my sorrows (and my French toast) in maple syrup.

I'm about to take my final golden-river bite when an email pops up on my phone. It's from Laurie, entitled: *Check this out!*

It opens with a photograph of a bronze statue of a husky dog with a stripe of snow along his back. It looks vaguely familiar.

Krista!! her email begins. *Do you remember this picture from my Christmas shopping trip to New York?*

New York, I frown to myself.

I took it in Central Park. I just thought it was a cool statue perched on a rock, but then I was looking at the pictures you sent me of your sled-dogs and something about the curl of the tail reminded me . . . and it turns out this is a world-famous husky called Balto!!

On the way back to my room I read about how, back in January of 1925, there was a deadly diphtheria epidemic in Alaska, threatening to wipe out the children of a city called Nome. The nearest medicine was a thousand miles away in Anchorage and none of the trains ran that far north, and the only available plane was grounded due to a frozen engine. Their only hope was a sled-dog relay . . .

'You're kidding!' I gasp as I fumble for my room key.

More than twenty dog-sled teams co-ordinated to run and run through blizzards and subzero temperatures, giving their all, almost as if they understood the urgency and importance of their mission.

I feel a little choked up at their determination, imagining all those pounding paws and lolling tongues.

On the first of February the package was loaded on to the final team and Balto boldly led them across fifty-three treacherous miles – in near whiteout conditions, almost entirely in the dark – to where the world's press were waiting to greet them and declare him a national hero!

Go Balto!

Just ten months later this statue was erected in honour of the mission in Central Park and, remember that the Iditarod race you mentioned the other day? That was devised to commemorate this very journey!

I'm reeling now.

The point is, it's another sign, Laurie concludes, *we're all linked, you and me and huskies and New York and Jacques and sled-racing! You are where you are supposed to be! All you have to do now is keep moving forward!*

She's right. It's time to leave the past behind! What's done is done. Andrew's happiness or good fortune has nothing to do with me, I tell myself as I let the shower pummel my face. His life is his, mine is mine. I am a woman on a mission. Not quite a life-saving serum mission, but I have my own purpose, my own path. I also have the best best friend – how can you not love someone who gives you a pep talk and then follows it up with a secondary super-boost. See how lucky I am?

Once dressed I feel ever more psyched and ready for the day, even comfortable now with the implied jollity of my ombre scarf. Right up until the moment that I walk out from the lift and see Gilles waiting in the lobby.

*   *   *

My initial reaction is to dart into a nook and carry on with my husky research until Annique shows up, but then I have a change of heart. I simply don't have the energy to be snippy with him today. His 'crime' seems so trivial now – it's not as though he made me any lifelong promises; if anything he was quite clear when he told me, '*I can't do this.*'

'Morning!' I say as I sit beside him.

He looks taken aback. 'Hi!'

'You wanted to talk to me? Yesterday . . .'

'I-I . . .' he stammers, looking defeated before he's begun. 'You must think I'm a total eel.'

'You mean heel?' I frown.

'I still can't believe I made such a mess of things.'

'You haven't – everything's fine with Annique. I haven't said anything and I won't.'

'I meant with you,' he looks earnestly into my bloodshot eyes. 'I've messed things up with you.'

'That's okay,' I shrug. 'Let's just pretend it never happened, shall we?'

'I don't want you to think I behave like that all the time.'

'Just when the temperature drops below zero?'

He purses his lips. 'I have tried to find an explanation in myself, why I would be so unprofessional when we had only just met, but all I can say is that I was lost to our creation, I stopped thinking, I was only acting upon my desire . . .'

'Oh,' I swat away his words, though the notion of being desired couldn't come at a better time. 'I'm not a long-term prospect and Annique is – you made the right choice.'

'Then why doesn't it feel right?'

'It's just guilt and embarrassment messing with your head.'

'Is it?' He looks troubled.

'Yes. You two pin-ups are perfect for each other.'

'Here she is now . . .' He gets to his feet.

I turn around and immediately do a double take. I barely recognise her. Her billowing blowout has become a lop-sided ponytail, those wide glittering eyes are shrunken and crinkled, her glowing skin parched.

'Oh my god!' I rush to her side. 'You've been Caribou-d!'

She gives the smallest of nods.

'What happened?'

'After you left we thought we'd play a drinking game . . .'

I turn back to Gilles. 'How come you look so normal?'

'They dropped me back here on the way to the Grande Allée,' he explains as I guide Annique over to the lobby sofa. 'I wanted to go through my shots so I could show you a few of the best, so you'd know I was doing a good job.'

'Okay, well I'll look at those in the car. For now we need to get Annique a greasy spoon . . .'

Suddenly I don't feel so bad. If anything I feel a newfound bond with Annique and Gilles. It seems oddly virtuous to wish them well and a whole lot safer than having any romantic entanglements myself. Jacques is a far better bet for me because he's emotionally out of reach and therefore I can have my secret crush without any attachment to an outcome. I just like being around him. I like his presence. I like his vibe. I like his eyes. I like watching him with the dogs. I like hearing him speak, and when he speaks directly to me I feel honoured. Special, even. See? Utterly harmless crush.

12

'This place is so different in the snow.' Annique watches the Île d'Orléans flash past the car window. 'I used to come here in the summer – my ex's family has a house here.' She looks wistful. 'Every summer for ten years . . .'

I'd like to ask more about how and why this man became an ex – because really, who would let her go? – but decide it's not polite in front of Gilles.

So instead I decide to wow them with my brand-new husky/sledding knowledge.

'Did you know that huskies' nose colour can change from black to pink during the winter?'

They shake their heads.

'It's a condition called "snow nose"!' I reveal, rather tickled by the name. 'And the original Inuit sleds were made of two lengths of frozen salmon wrapped in animal hides with a few stray bones as cross-bars!'

'*What?*'

'Sometimes they just carved the whole thing out of ice.'

'The whole sled?'

I nod.

'That's another idea for Brandon, I think!'

'How come so many of the dogs have different-coloured eyes?' Gilles wants to know.

'I'm not sure about the why but I know the name for it – heterochromia or bi-eyed.'

'Jacques is bi-eyed,' Annique notes absently.

'Yes he is,' I sigh.

Mostly we drive in silence, conserving our energy. At least one of us trying to quell the butterflies in her stomach.

'And you're sure we are welcome here?' Annique checks as we vroom up the driveway.

'Absolutely,' I insist.

It is therefore unfortunate that the first person we see is Sebastien.

'You again,' is his opening gambit.

'Sebastien!' I feign delight. 'I'd like you to meet my tour guide Annique and photographer Gilles.'

He raises an eyebrow. 'You have entourage?'

'Only when I'm working,' I reply. 'We're doing a piece on this place for a UK travel website. Maybe Jacques mentioned it?'

'Maybe.'

Okay. I can see we're not going to get anywhere with him. 'Is he around?'

He nods over to the main building.

'Great, thanks for your help.'

'*Sacré bleu!* What's his problem?' Annique mutters as we head up the path.

'I think he back-flipped out of the wrong side of the barn this morning.'

'*Comment?*'

'Nothing. He's just a grouch.'

Whereas Jacques, aka the Wolfman, the one who is supposed be snarly and aloof, greets us with a warm smile and handshakes all round.

'This place is great,' Gilles enthuses. 'So picturesque. Mind if I . . .' Already he wants to start taking detail shots of the fireplace and clumpy boots and muddy footprints on the slate floors.

'Help yourself, just not of me, okay?'

What a waste, I think to myself. I know the readers could happily while away a tea break gazing at that face.

'Ready for another ride?' he asks me.

'Can't wait!' I reply. 'I'm just a little concerned that I still have last night's Caribou coursing through my veins.'

He snuffles a laugh. 'Well, I'll arrange a gentle team for you.' He looks over at Annique. 'You too with the Caribou?'

She nods back. 'Do you mind if I stay in here? Every time I move my head the floor starts tilting.'

'No problem. There's hot chocolate out the back, blankets in that trunk, help yourself.'

'So, there's a couple of shots I wanted to get,' Gilles explains to Jacques as we head over to the dogs.

First he'll do some stationary ones with the dog-sled team but what he really wants is to lie in the snow and click away as I dash past.

Jacques nods. 'They typically run the whole circuit so we will maintain a forward motion, but we can stop them en route and give you a chance to get ahead of us again.'

Jacques introduces me to my team. I was hoping to see Maddy again but she is having a day off.

'This one – Sherri – she seems rather shy,' I observe, surprised he has her up front.

'Don't worry – you will see when she starts running, she's a true athlete, very focused.' He rubs her copper-coloured forehead. 'All set?'

'Isn't someone coming with me?'

'I have confidence – Sebastien said you picked it up very quickly.'

'Yes, but I wasn't drunk-driving then.'

'You'll be fine. I'll ride ahead so they have me in their sights.'

'If you're sure?'

'I'm sure.'

I like his certainty. It's been a while since a man believed in me. I hope I don't cock it up.

'Okay, step on.' He holds the sled in place while I join him on the metal bar. This is the closest I've ever stood to him – so close that our coat fabrics are rustling together. It's a good feeling.

'Let me get a little way ahead then release the brake.'

I nod.

'You got it?'

As he steps off I add a second foot, for extra security. Now my nerves are really kicking in. It felt a lot more stable with another body weighing down the sled. I never thought I'd say that I miss Sebastien, but right now I do.

Jacques goes ahead to his sled and in seconds he's off like a rocket.

My team are chomping at the bit, near hysterical with eagerness to play catchup. He raises his arm, signalling for me to follow, but I can't bring myself to step off the brake, fearing the sled is going to jerk too violently.

'*Allez!*' Gilles calls.

Oh why did I step on the brake with two feet – now I have to do a little jump onto the feet grips.

'Now Krista!'

Oh well, here goes nothing!

I jump, misjudge the placement of my right foot, stumble as I foolishly try to stabilise myself on the ground racing beneath me, and within seconds I'm lying face down in the snow, my charges hurtling away from me, heading straight for Gilles.

I see Jacques turn back, brake, then cry out: 'Sebastien!'

He's atop the barn again, squatting like Spiderman on a

skyscraper. Surely he's not going to swoop down from there? Of course he is, like only he can – as the sled passes he lands perfectly in the seat and then throws out his boot-clad feet and digs his heels deep into the snow, calling for the dogs to stop. Which they do.

Gilles is on his feet, cheering. '*C'est incroyable! Bravo!*'

Meanwhile I feel utterly, utterly humiliated. I've let down Jacques, proved Sebastien both right and wrong (yes, I'm nothing but a nuisance and no, I'm not a natural at this at all) *and* messed up the photos.

It takes all my strength to get back up on my feet. I should've stayed in bed after all.

'Are you okay?'

Jacques has jogged back to check on me, leaving Gilles holding his sled in place.

'I'm so sorry,' I begin, unable to look at him.

'You don't think every sledder has taken a tumble?'

'In the first two seconds?'

'I forgot the weight was different for you. You'll be fine now you're prepared.'

'You want me to do it again?'

'Of course. Hush!' he shushes the baying dogs. 'Sebastien has them ready to go for you.'

Great. Now I have to face him.

'Krista.'

There he is saying my name again.

'Don't give up on me.'

I look into his eyes, those incredible, other-worldly eyes, and feel a rush of emotion.

'Okay, okay, I'll do it.'

'Good girl!' he says, tapping me on the bottom in the least offensive way – it can hardly be seen as sexual when it's tucked beneath a multitude of quilting.

He runs on ahead as I tramp over to Sebastien, taking deep breaths, ready for whatever comment he has prepared for me.

'Thank you for stopping the dogs,' I say, matter-of-factly.

'No problem.'

That's it?

'You don't want to say anything else?' I squint at him.

'Like what?'

'Like I should just give up and go home?'

'But then what would I do for entertainment?'

I can't tell if he's teasing *in a nice way*.

'Well. I hate to spoil your fun but this time I'm doing it right.'

He studies me for a second.

'Trade places with me and stand on the brake.'

I do as he says but then I'm taken by surprise as he steps on behind me, reaching around me to hold the bar. His chest is pressed against my back and I can feel his chin pressing into my hat.

'Now let me take over the brake.'

'Okay . . .' I carefully place my feet on the bars.

'Take a breath.'

I inflate my lungs and then slowly exhale.

'Let the dogs do the work, they're the professionals; all you have to do is hold on and look pretty for the camera.'

'*Allez allez!*' he cries as he jumps off the brake, throwing himself back into the snow.

I actually find myself laughing this time. He's obnoxious but he's so darn cool! And I'm doing it! Running the dogs by myself! Look at me go! Suddenly I feel entirely uninhibited and fearless!

'Woooohooooo!'

Oh this is just beautiful!

Again I feel as if I could race forever, but Jacques is motioning for me to start applying the brake.

'Woah, woah.' I grind to a halt. It worked! I stopped in the right place.

I watch him tie his sled rope to a tree and then he comes back to assist me. As soon as my sled is secured he throws open his arms.

'You did it!'

I fall into him with a grateful, palpitating thud.

'I knew you could do it!'

'Thank you for having faith,' I beam back at him. 'And patience. And an acrobatic brother.'

He laughs. 'He's quite something isn't he? We have got to get him back to the Cirque.'

'Why did he ever leave?' I ask, reluctantly stepping out of the hug.

'It has to do with me.' He pats the snow off his gloves. 'Bit of a misunderstanding. Either way, the guy is driving me crazy here.' And then his phone rings. 'Hold on. Yes, we're over just past the river. We'll wait for him to catch up.' He turns back to me. 'Your photographer is on his way.'

'Great,' I say, though of course I really wish he wasn't. 'So, would Cirque du Soleil have him back?'

'In a heartbeat. They put a lot of training into him. He's one of their strongest aerialists.'

'As in those contortionist people who dangle by their wrist or crook of their knee, no safety net?'

He nods. 'Of course he does it all.'

'I can imagine. With attitude.'

'Oh, he's a different person in Montreal. It's too small-town for him here. Makes him grouchy.'

I smile. 'Your English is really good.'

'It was my mother's first language.'

'Ohhh,' I nod, then crouch down beside Sherri who has decided to press her forehead into my leg. 'What lovely dogs you are!' Then I look back at Jacques. 'You know I was thinking about going there, to Montreal, maybe write up a day trip or overnight for the website. Perhaps I could hire Sebastien as my guide?'

'He'd be the best you could get but he won't go.'

'Not even for a day?'

'It would take something more . . .' He stops suddenly as an idea presents itself. 'Maybe something to do with our father . . .'

'He lives there?'

Jacques nods and then points behind me. 'Here he comes.'

Gilles gives us an enthusiastic if slightly exhausted wave. If I'd known he was going to be that quick I wouldn't have spent the whole time talking about Sebastien. I hope I haven't give the wrong impression . . .

'You want to get ahead again?'

'No need,' he pants. 'I got it, look at these . . .'

He holds his camera up for us to see the shots.

'You look so happy!' Jacques laughs at me.

'Well, you know, I was vertical so that was an excellent start.'

He looks as though he wants to ruffle my hair, if it wasn't ensconced in a chunky wool knit.

I'd quite like to ruffle his hair too, truth be told.

'So I was thinking I could take some shots from Krista's perspective, of her team?'

'Of course.' Jacques helps Gilles into the sled.

'And maybe I'll take a couple looking back up at you, Krista?'

'Because I'm sure that's an incredibly flattering angle.'

'Have a little faith!'

'Okay,' Jacques unties the rope and hands it to my passenger. 'You hold this and Krista, same thing, give me a head start and then follow.'

'Will do.'

'Have you ever done this before?' I ask Gilles.

'Never. Woah!' he gasps at our jolting launch. 'It's a little bumpier than I thought.'

'You'll get used to it.'

'Do you want some video?' He offers. 'Might be fun for the website?'

'Actually, that would be great,' I agree, imagining a little inset box with constantly running huskies.

For a few minutes we fall silent, focusing on the rhythmic panting of the dogs, the crunch of snow and creak of sled, then Gilles exclaims:

'Oh *merde!*'

'Literally!' I smirk, as Didier takes a little 'bathroom break'. 'Well, don't film him doing it for goodness' sake!'

'You wanted reportage!'

I groan out loud, then get a little giggly. And then I take a deep breath, inhaling the blue of the sky and the freshness of the snow and I think how glad I am that I didn't stay in bed. Laurie was right! It's amazing how quickly your whole day can turn around . . .

13

When we get back to base, Jacques is already welcoming his first group of the day – a dozen or more enthusiasts – so it's all hands on deck.

'Is there any way you can wait an hour to see the puppies?' he calls over to us.

I look at Gilles.

'I'm fine. Happy to do more pictures.'

I'm sure Annique is in no rush. And me? Of course I'm delighted for any excuse to linger longer.

As I pretend to be pointing out adorable furry faces to Gilles, I edge closer to Jacques so I can eavesdrop on the Q&A he's having with his group, all eager to hear about the perils of competing in the Iditarod, which I learn now is nearly a thousand miles long!

'Certainly it can be dangerous,' Jacques acknowledges. 'Between the stop points no one knows what is going on with the musher and his team out in the wilds; it's not like most sporting activities where you get a play-by-play commentary.'

'Have you ever got lost or had an accident, miles from anywhere?'

'I have had plenty of scrapes but nothing too serious. I think the most dramatic incident was a few years back at the Yukon Quest. The Eagle Summit is the highest and harshest hill and that year, I think it was 2006, the weather was particularly atrocious – the gales were so strong they had blown away the snow exposing the ice and rock, and you can't brake on that. The trail markers were gone – also blown away. The visibility was so poor you couldn't see your own team.' He shakes his head. 'One musher became separated from his dogs – he tried to follow them but their barking was drowned out by the wind.'

'Oh no!' One larger woman looks stricken. 'Did they have any chance of survival?'

'Well, the cold would not have been a problem but the fact that they were still attached to the lines and the sled, that could have proved fatal. But it didn't happen,' he quickly adds. 'So many teams had gone missing and the local trappers on snowmobiles had no luck finding them, so the state troopers called in the military – they sent a Black Hawk helicopter up to the summit and in two hours airlifted six mushers and eighty-eight dogs to safety.'

'Wow!' The entire group is mesmerised, breaking into spontaneous applause.

I'm so relieved – the thought of those poor dogs running and running unattended . . .

'Of course none of the rescued teams could complete the race because if you accept outside help of any kind you are immediately disqualified.'

'Gosh. That's harsh.'

'That's the race,' he shrugs.

'What happens if a dog sustains an injury on the way?' a short chap wants to know.

'You stop, release him from the pack, rest him in the sled bag and drive on with one less dog.'

'Is it true you can use packs of up to sixteen dogs?'

'It is. That's quite a handful though. I like twelve.'

'Are there many women mushers?' a younger girl asks.

'An increasing number,' he replies. 'There was an eighteen-year-old rookie at the last Yukon Quest.'

'Any resistance to their presence?'

'With some of the old-school mushers, of course, like with any field that is still evolving.'

'What do you think? You personally?'

'I think it's great. I have a friend competing at the Carnival race this year – Rosalie Morin-Dore. She and her sister have a very gentle, gradual training approach from puppyhood. We tease them because they talk to their dogs.'

'Does it make them run faster?'

'It may be that or it may be the mix – they prefer husky with some greyhound and pointer. And it's working.'

'So women can be just as good mushers as men?'

'Absolutely,' he says, catching my eye with a smile.

I respond with merely a blink, ever more in awe.

And then it's time for them to take off on their sleds, so Gilles and I retreat to the farmhouse, him eagerly pulling one of the semi-collapsed armchairs closer to the fire.

'You really feel like you've earned the warmth after being out there a while, don't you?' I note.

Gilles nods but can't speak. His hands look particularly wind-burned. Not easy to operate a camera with gloves on.

'*Chocolat chaud?*' I offer.

He releases one last shiver. 'Yes, please.'

By the time I've been to the loo, changed my socks and poured out two steaming mugs, Gilles has nodded off.

'Pssst!' Annique beckons me over to her blanket cocoon in the far corner, gratefully accepting the spare mug.

'Feeling any better?' I ask as she makes room for me.

'Much,' she nods. 'How was your ride?'

I describe the humiliating start leading to a finale high and then she tells me that she's been busy too – absorbing gossip . . .

'Really?' I ask with a flutter of nerves. Will this be something I want to hear?

She checks there is no one else around and then says, 'Did you know Sebastien used to be in Cirque du Soleil?'

'Actually I did, but how do you?'

'Oh, people say a lot of things when they think you're asleep,' she winks. 'I think they forgot I was here.'

'Did they say why he left?' I huddle closer.

'Well, this is strange. He seems to be here on suicide watch.'

My stomach loops with concern. 'Gosh. I mean, I know he's a bit moody—'

'No, no,' she stops me. 'He's the watcher.'

'Well, who's he watching?'

'Jacques.'

'*Jacques!*' I splutter. 'He hardly seems like a man on the verge of a nervous breakdown. I mean, there is a sadness to him, but if you were going to compare the two, I'd say Sebastien is the more unstable.'

'That's what they were complaining about – the new workers couldn't understand why he's even here when he seems so bad-tempered all the time, so Lucy—'

'Lucy?'

'You know the girl with the curly hair on Reception?'

'Yes, yes . . .'

'She was explaining to them that there had been an accident . . .'

In hushed tones, Annique tells me that about a year ago Jacques' best friend had come to visit and they had decided to take the snowmobiles out for the day. The guys had played together since they were little kids, always loved to race, but at one point his friend – whose name was Rémy – skidded way out of control, slammed into a tree and—

'No!' I blurt.

Annique nods. 'He literally died in Jacques' arms.'

'Oh my god,' I close my eyes, blanching at the tragedy. I can't even imagine how that would feel, watching your dearest friend take their last breath with you clinging on, willing them to stay, begging them not to go . . . I feel a great weight upon my chest.

And then I think of the sympathy cards. And how Jacques was so emphatic, cautioning me about the dangers of snowmobiling. I sigh. No wonder Sebastien told me I couldn't 'save' him – how could you save anyone from that depth of grief?

'But did he really think that Jacques would want to take his own life as a result?'

'Well. There was a second accident.'

'*A second?*'

'This time it was Jacques. Something to do with falling inside a frozen lake . . . Everyone at the farm was certain he didn't mean to harm himself, but Sebastien was equally convinced his brother would never make an error like that; he knew the land too well . . .' She shrugs her shoulders. 'Either way. Sebastien quit his job—'

'His dream job.'

She nods. 'Came running here and now he'll barely let Jacques out of his sight.'

'And nothing Jacques can say will persuade him otherwise.'

'No.'

'Wow. That's quite some sacrifice. I mean, considering Jacques is okay.' And then I pause. 'He is okay, isn't he?'

She hesitates.

'What?'

'There's more.'

'More?' I gasp.

'More hot chocolate?' Annique suddenly switches tack.

'Huh?'

Belinda Jones

I look around and see Gilles heading our way. He's bleary-eyed and oblivious to what he is interrupting.

We all reconvene to the kitchenette but I soon withdraw from the conversation. I'm pretending to be writing notes but in reality I am just squiggling on a page.

I keep looking at my watch. The team will be back from the ride in twenty minutes or so. I'd like to know the rest of the story before then so I don't put my foot in anything. I don't know how Jacques can even run these circuits, every day passing the place where he lost his friend. Or perhaps they had gone off track. Flying through uncharted territory. Whooping one minute and then . . .

I shudder.

And I thought I had it bad with Andrew disappearing from my life. It's nothing compared to this.

'Krista . . .'

'Hmm?' I look up at Gilles.

'Are you feeling all right?' He looks concerned.

'I was just thinking of something sad.'

'Don't worry, the puppies will cheer you up,' he says.

But he's wrong . . .

Of course there is an initial rush of rapture – how could there not be? All those fluffy, round-bellied bundles tumbling and tripping and stapling their little puppy teeth into trouser hems and dangling scarves, flossing with loose hair strands. But now my heart is panging so badly for both Jacques and Sebastien, I just want to bury my face in the dogs' wispy fur and have a good cry.

Of course this could also have something to do with this morning's news. Cradling a little being just a few weeks old is inevitably making me think of Andrew and his baby-to-be. Not that babies wriggle as much as puppies, and they don't tend to get involved in synchronised wrestling matches, pinning each other down by clamping their jaws around their opponents' neck. They also don't throw themselves off ledges, eat straw or scratch behind their ears using their foot.

'Towards me,' Gilles instructs as I try in vain to corral one pup with apricot accents to her fur.

'You can tell you've never had children,' he jokes as the puppy twists and flounders until I am now holding her upside down.

Of course he doesn't mean to hurt my feelings.

Then again, why would anyone say such a thing? Who would want to hear that they have no natural aptitude in this arena? Even if it's true. Perhaps because my body can't produce a baby, it doesn't see the need to be able to nurture and care for one. Perhaps even adoption would be unwise. Perhaps I'm better off with animals that are more resilient to being dropped . . .

I turn away on the pretext of trying to rearrange the wriggler, but I can't stop my eyes brimming up and over. How is it possible that my tear ducts have refilled so quickly after this morning's outpouring. Why is there so much left? Why can't I stop it?

'Jinx, are you misbehaving?' Jacques steps in, blocking Gilles' prying lens. 'Here.' He boosts Jinx higher so her furry face is now level with mine, her little puppy tongue quickly lapping away the salty streams.

'How's that?' he asks with the tenderest tone.

'Better,' I nod.

He looks as if there's something more he wants to say but not in present company. I wonder if he has any children of his own?

'Why don't you sit here?' He guides me to the wooden ramp leading to the hutch. 'That way you can hold more than one,' he says, as he heaps Toutou and Sky and Asha onto my lap.

The trio are almost entirely soft beige, but with flecks of black along their lower spine and tail. Toutou has velvet ears that flop forward in little triangles, Sky has milky sapphire eyes and Asha looks as if she slept in her mascara, waking up with rings under her eyes.

'And you have to have Bandit, he has the best eye mask of them all . . .'

He keeps going until I am overrun with loving, nuzzling, leaning, licking puppies, all cramming into the baby-less gap in my heart and filling it up with fuzzy puppy love.

'This is fantastic!' Gilles raves as the remaining pups trot over to join the party, grouping around my feet. 'Just look at the camera and let them do their thing!'

Now these pictures I can't wait to see – I have no idea what mischief they are up to around me.

'Watch out for Biscuit,' Jacques laughs. 'I think he's going to start nibbling on your ear!' And then his phone rings.

He turns back to give me a significant look as he says, 'It's my father.' And then he excuses himself, beckoning Sebastien to take over the puppy supervision.

I try not to even look in his direction as he enters the pen. It will be all too apparent that my attitude towards him has changed. Instead of bombarding him with questions and challenging him, I only want to offer quiet understanding. And a little admiration at his loyalty and devotion to his brother. Even if said brother is, at this very moment, concocting a plan to release him from his Guardian Angel contract.

'Well I can't this week: it's the Carnival, we're booked solid,' Jacques projects loudly as he heads back over. 'I'll have to send Sebastien.'

'What? Send me where?'

'Montreal. Dad needs the old car, his Citroën has finally died and he has to be at the physio by Friday.'

'Well I can't leave.'

'What choice do we have? We can't leave him stranded.'

'It's only three hours away, isn't it?' I chip in.

Sebastien shoots me a look that clearly states, 'This is none of your business.'

But I ignore it . . .

'You could leave first thing in the morning and be back on the train before dark.'

'Do you have some vested interest in this?' he snaps at me.

'Only that I'd like to visit Montreal, and hear about all the hotspots from a native.'

He looks between the two of us, sensing a conspiracy.

'Give me the phone.'

'What?'

He snatches the mobile from Jacques' hand and presses redial.

'Dad?' There's a pause. 'Oh. So it's really broken. You want it on Thursday now?' He sighs heavily. 'All right. All right! I'll see you then. Yes, yes, and the citron-pistachio biscotti, I know, I know.'

He hands the phone back to Jacques.

'Café Olimpico?'

Sebastien jerks his head for a yes and then sighs, 'Well, I suppose it's an opportunity to get some more of my stuff.'

They exchange a few words in French and then Sebastien says he's going to the barn, which seems to be his equivalent of the garden shed.

Jacques waits until he's certain he's out of range and then gives me a high-five. 'Six months I've been trying to get him back there! I know he'll get hooked again once he sees his old haunts. If you could try to prolong his stay as long as possible . . .'

'I'll certainly try.'

'This is great,' he enthuses, gently rubbing at Bandit's belly with the edge of his boot.

'You will be all right while we're gone, won't you?'

He stops what he's doing. 'Why wouldn't I be?'

'I just mean, you won't be short-handed?'

'I'll be fine. There's a guy in the next village I can call upon anytime. No need to worry.'

I wish I could be certain. This is what you get for meddling before you have all the facts. It seemed such a simple solution before – your brother has left his dream job to get under your feet and on your nerves? Let's get him back to Montreal so you can both get on with your lives! But now I know why Sebastien is here, I'm not so sure that I want to be the one to take him away. What if something, god forbid, did happen while we were gone? But no. I'm being silly. It's just one day. And Jacques seems in genuinely good spirits about it all. Besides, there are so many people here to watch over him, all of them know the situation. They wouldn't let anything bad happen.

'Jacques!' Lucy is calling out to him to let him know the next group has arrived. It's time for us to move on.

'I'm sorry I've been so unprofessional today,' Annique apologises when we collect her from the farmhouse.

'Not unprofessional,' I correct her. 'Human.'

She smiles and then gets a twinkle in her eye. 'You know there is one thing I can do even with a hangover . . .'

'What's that?'

'Shop!'

'Ooooh!' Now she's got my interest. 'Not that you can let me buy anything,' I tell her.

'We'll just lick the windows!'

'Eww!'

'That's what we call window shopping.'

'Ohhh!' I laugh. 'Actually, I need to do a shopping section for the website – you know, special Quebec buys?'

'Yes, I remember from your email. I have a list of places to show you.'

'See how professional you are?'

'Oh!' she blushes then looks at her watch. 'We should go! Many of the shops close at five p.m.'

'Just like the good old days back in England,' I smile.

As we make our way to the car, we pass Jacques on the path.

I take a moment to stop and thank him again for being so obliging at such a busy time.

'It was my pleasure.'

And then he hands me a card. 'This is Sebastien's number, so you can make the arrangements for Montreal.'

'Great!' I say, though I am a little dismayed that he hasn't added his own. I don't even know when our next encounter will be. 'Well, I'd better go.'

As I turn to leave he says, 'See you at the Bain de Neige.'

I switch back around. 'What did you say?'

'The Bain de Neige – Gilles said you'll all be there.'

'You're not doing it?'

'No, no. I'm actually helping the police with something.'

'Catching Malhomme?'

He purses his lips. 'All I can say is that I inherited a sniffer dog from a friend of mine and they want me to bring him along to the event.'

I wonder if I should tell him about the Staring Man at Auberge Saint-Antoine? I open my mouth to speak but Annique overrides me with a honking horn. No worries, it can wait until tomorrow. Everything can.

Right now I'm going to set aside all complex concerns and indulge in some all-consuming consumerism . . .

14

We start at Artisans Canada – a pleasing emporium for local crafts, gifts and apparel, all made in Quebec '*avec fierté*' – with pride. They even stock a clothing range by former Cirque du Soleil costume designer Rosie Godbout. Her garments are predominantly black with intricately entwined swatches of colour and, though the voluminous coats are a little eccentric-art-teacher for my readers, I am immediately drawn to the nearby rail of patchwork sweaters in a rather more rustic palette . . .

'These are really unusual,' I say, holding up one asymmetrical top with a man's tie re-purposed as shoulder straps. 'I like the mix of textures and patterns.'

'They also sell them at the Hôtel de Glace,' Annique informs me

'Oh, I didn't see them – I was up and out before the gift shop opened.'

'Krista,' Gilles beckons me. 'Hold this up in front of you.'

He's finally getting my vibe – a T-shirt with a cartoon beaver and the words '*Dam it!*'

We peruse every trinket and tchotchke in the place, but my most highly recommended purchase leads us back to Cirque du Soleil – jewellery by young designer Anne-Marie Chagnon.

The woman behind the glass display tells us that Cirque du Soleil creator and founder Guy Laliberté saw her designs and pretty much declared, 'I want your work in every one of our boutiques around the world.'

She's been creating exclusive collections for them every year for the past ten.

Can you imagine that warp level of success? One minute you're tinkering with your mini blowtorch and a heap of metal alloys, the next you've been *discovered* . . .

I immediately fall for a cool, chunky pewter ring with a geometric slice of honey-coloured glass. This is the first time I have seen my hands displaying anything since I removed my wedding ring. And what a different message it sends, I think as I hold out my right hand to admire it. My wedding set was classic, traditional; this is a whole lot edgier and more independent.

'And the prices are not too much.' Annique shows me the tag which works out at about £50.

I am sorely tempted but this being our first shop, I decide to hold back. For now.

Next is Simons department store – founded in 1840! – which Annique suggests I explore at my leisure, but we peek inside the old-fashioned doors so she can show me the sale they have on gloves, hats and scarves. Definitely the place to come for bright red mittens and stripy beanies with fleece linings.

'I've just realised we're on the Côte de la Fabrique!' I point up at the street sign when we step back outside. 'How appropriate!'

Gilles dutifully snaps the sign and then asks, somewhat plaintively, 'Is anyone getting hungry?'

'Yes, yes,' we girls chorus, with Annique adding, 'Let me just show you one more place – Harricana; it's on the way . . .'

I love the window display – everything looks fluffy, strokeable, and slip-off-your-shoulder sexy. Thick knits, chunky boots and pristine, shiny-shiny furs.

And therein lies the problem. The fur is real.

'No, no, this is different,' Annique insists as I explain that this just isn't cool in England. 'Everything here is recycled.'

'How so?'

'In Quebec everyone's grandmother owned a fur coat, so they collected up all the ones that had been left in storage or rejected in favour of modern fabrics and they created something entirely new. See this?' She reaches for a cropped, collarless jacket and then points to a photograph showing the original long, voluminous form.

'Quite the transformation!' I note, also clocking a selection of furry bags, Yeti leg warmers and nifty capelets.

I must confess that, in my more shivery moments, I have wondered what it would be like to be enrobed in luxurious mink, but ultimately I came to the conclusion that it would be better to persuade the live animal to cosy up around your neck and shoulders, then you could trade off each other's body heat.

As it happens now, I'm too hot. Shopping here comes with an inbuilt time limit – you are blown in through the door with an icy gust, so happy to be greeted with abundant warmth, and then gradually the chill leaves your body and the heat seeps in and then you start to sweat and that's when you've got to get out. Purchase or no purchase.

Of course it's different in a restaurant because you can relax and take off your coat and selective layers, which is what we do at Les Frères de la Côte.

I like this place straight away. An eclectic bistro with ketchup-red walls, multi-era memorabilia and a wine list penned on the mirror behind the bar. The waitresses look as if they've seen it all, but whereas in England they'd sling the menus on the table without even looking in your direction, here even the most jaded face softens into a smile.

'You know, I'm starting to notice a trend . . .' I muse as our particular server heads off to place our order. 'Everyone here in Quebec looks at you like they really see you.'

Annique and Gilles look bemused.

'I mean, they're not glazed or distant; everyone here seems *present*. And they are all so nice.'

I leave it at that, but what I'm really thinking is that this is what life could be like if no one had any hang-ups, just an easy-breezy openness. It's certainly extremely validating when people take the trouble to have a genuine interaction. It makes you feel better about yourself and thus you are more inclined to pay that pleasantness forward . . .

'Oooh, food! *Merci!*'

As Gilles turns a snap of my quiche-salad-fries combo into a work of art, I ask him how he got into photography. Unsurprisingly he tells us that his interest was first piqued when he was working as a model.

'I used to stay on in the studio after the shoot, asking questions, watching and learning; then I started assisting, and one day I got my first commission,' he shrugs. 'It is my love.'

My eyes flick to Annique, who is looking on with admiration.

'Did you ever model?' I ask her.

'One campaign,' she takes a sip of water. 'For my ex's company. That is how we met. My first and last job.'

I wonder if I'm detecting regret in her voice but then she adds. 'But for me, a tour guide is best.'

Better than jetting between Paris, New York and Milan?

'Modelling is a lot of judgement and a lot of introspection. I like to look at the beauty around me, in the buildings, in the landscape. I like to see people's faces light up when they first see my city.'

'Like the view from the Hilton?' I think of my own reaction.

She nods. 'It is a privilege to share this place with visitors.'

I believe in her job satisfaction. And she's certainly a people-person. So naturally charming in her every interaction, chatting and laughing with the waitress when she comes back with the bill.

'We will have our dessert elsewhere,' she whispers for our ears only. 'Something very particular.'

We're about to leave when Gilles excuses himself to go the bathroom. *Finally!*

'Annique,' I hiss, motioning for her to meet me halfway across the table. 'You said there was more to Jacques' story . . . ?'

'Oh yes.' She sighs. 'Apparently one of the hardest things for Jacques was not just losing his best friend but also his second family . . .'

'Second family?'

'Well, now this I heard directly from Lucy.'

'You did better than me,' I note. 'I couldn't get anything out of her the other day.'

'Well turns out she used to work with Mason – my ex – there on the island so . . .'

'. . . a trust was established.'

'Actually, a mutual dislike of my ex.'

'Oh.'

'Anyway. She said that Jacques used to be so close with Rémy's family – the boys had grown up together and Jacques was inside their house every Sunday into adulthood, even when his friend moved to Montreal to join the riot police.'

'Riot police?' I repeat. 'So he survived all manner of clash and conflict only to lose his life joy riding?'

'I think that's what must have blown the mother's mind. She was always worrying about him when he was gone and so when he came home she thought she could exhale for a moment and it really caught her unaware.'

'And she holds Jacques responsible?'

'It sounds that way – immediately after the accident he sold all the snowmobile machines and equipment and tried to give her the money but she would not accept a penny and she has not spoken a word to him since.'

All I can think is, there has to be a way to reconcile them. Maybe if they had a mediator? Or perhaps a neutral party could test the water, see if perhaps time had mellowed her a little and really the rift was nothing more than a habit now.

'It's so sad all round,' Annique sighs. 'Apparently Rémy had just met a new girl too. Life is messed up sometimes.'

'Ready to go?' Gilles is back.

As we make our way out of the restaurant and up Rue Saint-Jean, I pay little attention to the boutiques and focus instead on sending a discreet text to Laurie:

'Totally random but can you try and find the surname of guy named Rémy who died in a snowmobiling accident on the Île d'Orléans about a year ago? He was in the police. Probably aged between 30-40. I'm trying to find his family.'

'Anything for you Sherlock.'

My heart is beating a little faster. I know this is a delicate undertaking and any approach from me could be most unwelcome, but it has to be worth a try. I'd feel so much better leaving for Montreal if I knew the mother had extended the olive branch to Jacques. It would surely mean so much to him.

'*Alors!*' Annique comes to a halt. 'I think the boutiques are a little more chic on Le Petit Champlain but that is in Lower Town and it is nearly four p.m., so what I think is nice right now is to introduce you to a world of maple syrup.'

Before I can question how this qualifies as shopping, Annique shows me every feasible maple product from maple coffee to maple mustard, even maple exfoliators and lip balms.

Like I don't already stuff my face with enough sugary items.

Les Delices de L'Érable – or Maple Delights – is also a gelateria and café, with every cake, sorbet and beverage sweetened with maple syrup.

'Which has fewer calories than honey,' Annique tells me.

'Really?'

'It really helped me to lose weight,' she insists. 'And it has potassium and calcium and magnesium!'

'So, in a roundabout way, it's healthy!' I decide as I point to my pastry of choice and then add a book entitled 'Cooking with Quebec Maple Syrup' for Laurie.

'Upstairs they have a quaint little Maple Syrup Museum.'

'Mmm-hmm,' I say, I mean, how much does anyone really want to know about maple syrup beyond its taste?

But then she adds, 'You know Jacques is part of the co-op that produces maple syrup for Quebec?'

'I did not know that.'

'The work is seasonal so he runs the dog-sledding business in the winter and does maple-syrup tapping in the spring.'

Suddenly I want to know everything there is to know.

'I'll just take a quick look,' I say, heading for the stairs.

I'm up there half an hour.

It turns out that maple syrup was first discovered by the Amerindians who would cut a V-shape in the tree with their tomahawks and then insert concave pieces of bark to collect its sap. Most modern-day tappers use a high-tech tree-tubing system that runs the sap directly back to the sugar shack, but part of me hopes Jacques does it the old-fashioned way – with a wooden spout and a metal bucket and a horse-drawn sled. I can just see myself out in the woods in a jaunty head-square, gingham shirt and denim capris, or perhaps luring

Jacques back home with wafts of orchard fruit pie, served *à la nude* – in bed with two spoons.

When the season is over it would be the summer and we'd go swimming in the lakes and have big sprawling picnics with our friends. Come the autumn we'd drive down to Vermont and stay in rustic-elegant B&Bs and watch the leaves change colour before our very eyes. What a life that would be! Naturally I'd end up writing one of those *Year in Provence*-type books entitled *Miss Maple Syrup Pie* or *Becoming Québécoise* or *I Married the Wolfman*, and it would become a bestseller and we'd offer themed tours and I'd read sample chapters to the person riding in my sled and we'd have a little café serving homemade goods . . .

I try to stop my mind racing but on it goes:

Gilles would do portraits of all the dogs and these would line the walls of the farmhouse reception. For our annual Christmas card he would somehow get all the dogs to look his way just as the camera clicked.

It's all too wonderful and then some contrary part of me says, 'But what if he wants children?'

To which I reply, 'I think he has enough on his hands with the dogs.'

'Are you talking to yourself?' Annique interrupts my wild imaginings.

'Oh! I was just, um, this is all so fascinating!' I bluster. 'I had no idea it takes thirty-two litres of maple sap to make one litre of maple syrup!'

'Amazing isn't it? Here – I bought you a cup of maple syrup tea to try.'

'Oh thank you.'

'I just found out that Gilles has a sweet tooth!' She looks thrilled. 'He's on his third maple mousse!'

And then my phone pings this message:

Rémy Walker. Family live in Wendake about 20 minutes from Old Town Quebec. Mother, Johanna Laframboise, works at restaurant called La Traite.

I look back at Annique, my heart a-flurry. 'You know our plans for tonight?'

'Yes, we watch the parade—'

'I was wondering,' I cut in. 'If Gilles could cover that and you and I might go to dinner. Just the two of us.'

'You had somewhere in mind?'

'La Traite.'

'La Traite?' she repeats. 'At Wendake?'

'Yes, you know it?'

'The food is meant to be exceptional. But this has to be tonight?'

'Actually, yes, the sooner the better. And there's another thing – I would like you to translate for me.'

'Okay.'

'When I speak to Rémy's mother,' I gulp. 'She works there, at the restaurant.'

Now she looks uncomfortable. 'Well, I don't know if that is possible . . .'

'I understand that this may seem like interfering in someone else's business and there is a risk of upsetting two people who have already suffered enough. But I can't help thinking it could start such a positive chain reaction – she gets back in touch with Jacques, that's two people who feel better right there, not cured,' I hasten to add. 'Not absolved of grief but at least a tiny bit comforted, a tiny bit healed. And then Sebastien feels confident that his brother will be all right and he can get back to his life in Montreal . . .'

'It's not that,' Annique replies. 'I just don't know if I am going to be able to translate. Do you know what tribe she is?'

'Tribe?'

'If it's Huron-Wendat I can help you because they speak French, but I don't speak Cree or Iroquois or Algonquin.'

My brow furrows.

'La Traite is part of the First Nations hotel. Everyone who works there is what you would call Indian.'

'So Rémy's mother could be, for example, Mohawk?'

'Yes.'

'Wow.' Now I am hesitant. I feel I need to be more respectful than ever but I'm not sure what this might mean in practical terms. 'Do you think we should still go?'

'Well,' Annique appears to be giving the matter much consideration. 'I have been hearing great things about the maple fondue, I'd love to try it.'

I smile and reach for her hand. 'Thank you. I really appreciate this. Why don't you go home and get a few hours' rest? We could meet again at eight p.m.?'

She looks grateful. 'That would be most welcome.' And then she turns back to me. 'Do you have any idea of what you are going to say to his mother when you see her?'

Now it is my turn to pause. 'No,' I reply in a small voice.

'Well then, I want you to visit this one last shop on your way back to the hotel.'

She writes down the address and hands me the piece of paper. 'It might help get you in the right frame of mind . . .'

15

The drive to Wendake is dark and full of trepidation.

What if I'm doing the wrong thing?

What if my approaching Madame Laframboise prompts some kind of freak-out or meltdown? What if she loses her job because a random stranger caused her to collapse in a heap of tears on the restaurant floor?

'I meant to ask,' Annique interrupts my frettings, 'did you get a chance to visit Le Sachem?'

'I did,' I confirm. 'I think that's the first time I've seen a dream catcher outside of a New Age store.'

I found it almost surreal to be handling authentic moccasins (made from butter-soft suede) and rough woven rugs and Hiawatha dolls with leather-laced braids. My cousin had one of these as a child and I remember thinking she knocked spots off pale, stick-like Barbie with her beautiful big dark eyes and fringed dress.

Even after visiting Harricana earlier in the day, I wasn't prepared for an entire wall of trapper hats – coyote, fox, muskrat, racoon, beaver and pure white rabbit: they had them all. There was even a pair of drop earrings with a fluffy bauble of mink at the end.

But the thing that stopped me in my tracks was the way a parent, a dad, dealt with his toddler when he nearly toppled the stuffed bear.

Instead of yanking his son away and bundling him out of

the shop in an angry huff, he knelt by his side so he was at eye level and then softly said, 'Remember we spoke about this – you must treat everything around you with care and respect.'

'Care and respect,' the child repeated.

My jaw dropped. No wonder everyone here grows up to be so genteel!

All I ever got was the 'If you break anything, it's coming out of your pocket money' speech.

Even in all my imaginings about having a well-mannered child I never thought about introducing the concept of respect before they could even spell it. That's deep.

'Did you buy anything?' Annique asks.

I tell her that if my grandmother was still alive I would have got her one of the little white bear ornaments, seemingly etched from a gritty salt block, with an onyx fish in its mouth. I did buy a box of herbal tea for Laurie because the name gave me a giggle – nothing wrong with *Chief's Delight* or *Warrior's Brew* but *Teepee Dreams?!* – I think the marketing department might want to rethink printing the word 'pee' alongside 'dreams'.

And then I got a selection of the incense sticks for myself. I actually lit the maple one before I left the hotel and wafted it over me in lieu of perfume because apparently Amerindians use it for 'meetings' on account of it producing 'a warm ambience as it purifies negative elements in the air'.

I don't mention this to Annique, though, in case she thinks I've lost the plot.

'Wendake!' Annique confirms our arrival by pointing to a stop sign printed with both French '*Arrêt*' and Huron '*Seten*'.

I had prepared myself for a rundown community offering only the most basic living conditions, but it turns out that the Huron-Wendats are one of the most prosperous First Nation tribes in the country.

'And why is that?' I want to know.

'Well, they were always into trading whereas other tribes' skills, like hunting, have proved less profitable over the years.' And then she turns to me. 'Did you know that the Mohawk have such a good head for heights that they are always the first choice for any skyscraper building projects?'

'I did not,' I smile, fascinated. 'Oh look – they even have a beauty párlour!'

The sign has a Victorian style to it and the wooden building, complete with front porch, is positively chintzy.

But a few feet away is a dramatic waterfall – the Kabir Kouba – plunging over forty feet.

'Let me quickly show you this church.' Annique pulls over to the side of the road. 'Notre-Dame-de-Lorette.'

'Are you sure it's okay for us to go in?' I hesitate before I leave the car.

'It's fine, we are not interrupting a service.'

Inside I'm surprised both by the homeliness of the place and the curious mix of Catholic and First Nation detail – Jesus figurines and ornate incense swingers suspended alongside animal-skin drums and a portrait of a raven-haired woman with a beaded headband. Best of all, there's a pair of snowshoes propped against the altar.

'The Church of the Sacred Snowshoe!' I smile delightedly.

'It's such a fascinating culture, isn't it?' Annique sighs. 'So earthy, so spiritual.'

'You know when I was little, I knew absolutely nothing about the suffering of the people, even with all the cowboy and Indian shows on TV. I always thought the bow and arrow was cooler than a gun. That riding bareback was preferable to driving a rickety old wagon. All I knew for sure was that I wanted long black hair and a fringed skirt and a feather headband. Even now my only real education is *Dances With Wolves*.'

'There is a lot to know. Every tribe is so different.'

'And there's so many of them! There was this song by Adam & The Ants and they listed a whole string of names: Blackfoot, Pawnee, Cheyenne, Crow, Apache, Arapaho . . .' I recall. 'I never even heard of Huron-Wendat before!'

'Do you know where their name comes from?'

I shake my head.

'Well huron is from a French word for wild boar because the European explorers thought their hairstyle resembled its tufty bristles!'

'Really?' I say. 'Can't think why the local beauty parlour didn't adopt that as their motif!'

Annique tinkles a laugh and then takes my arm. 'Come on!'

And so we proceed to the Hotel-Musée Premières Nations, home to Restaurant La Traite, meaning The Treaty.

Let's hope it's a peaceful one . . .

I know there are motels in America with cement tepees for rooms. It isn't that I was expecting that exactly, but I certainly wasn't prepared for a swish boutique establishment straight from the pages of a Hip Hotels coffee-table book.

The lobby is sleek, spacious and smells wonderful, be it fresh pine needles or cedar wood or their own designer incense. We naturally gravitate towards the firepit set beside floor-to-ceiling windows looking out over the moonlit snowscape.

'Ahhhh,' we sigh in unison, infused with a sense of calm well-being.

'Shall we sit for a moment before dinner?' Annique suggests.

The sofas and armchairs are draped with wolf furs. Though personally I prefer my antimacassars without tails and paws, it does feel an honour to be able to see the plush cream/black/amber brushstroke-effect of their coat up close.

'Hors d'oeuvres?'

A young man appears with a wooden platter set with three

perfectly presented options – the first is a spring roll. 'Duck,' he tells us. The little tartlet Annique identifies as elk, but my hand is already reaching for number three, a purplish concoction decorated with a bright yellow flower.

The delicacy is halfway to my mouth when he says the word, 'Seal.'

'Seal?' I look at Annique, wondering if there's some mistake in translation. 'Not the fluffy little sea mammal with coal-black eyes and a smudgy nose? Not that seal!'

She hands me a napkin.

Now my trepidation extends to the menu. With due cause. It comes to something when bison seems like the safe choice.

'I can't do escargot,' I blanch. 'Or eel. Especially since that comes with fiddleheads, whatever that is.'

'It's a fern,' Annique quells my wild imaginings.

'What is wapiti steak?'

'A kind of elk.'

'I think no to the red deer. I wished I liked salmon because I like the sound of the pear liqueur and wild blueberry marmalade . . .'

'I think I'll have the rabbit with the pumpkin puree and arnica jelly,' Annique decides.

'Oh no . . .'

'What?'

My eye has strayed to the desserts where I see '*fondant chocolate au parfum*' – so far so good – but it comes with '*Infusion au thé du Labrador*'.

'Just how exactly do they extract tea from a Labrador?' I wince, fearful of seeing 'Carpaccio of Husky' or 'Samoyed Surprise' on the next page.

Annique tuts at me. 'Labrador is not the dog, it is a northern region of Canada. Where the Inuit live. The tea is herbal. You'll like it.'

'Oh.'

She gets to her feet. 'I think we should go down to the restaurant before you chicken out.'

'Chance would be a fine thing,' I mutter under my breath. I'll never take chicken for granted again.

As we wait to be seated, our eyes scan the room looking for a woman in her fifties to sixties with Laframboise on her nametag.

Suddenly Annique pinches me, 'There she is!' She nods towards a short, neat woman with dark hair.

For a second I think she is headed right for us, but at the last minute she diverts to a more central table and we in turn are assigned a male waiter.

'If it's all right to ask,' I venture as we cross the room, 'which tribe you are?'

'Huron-Wendat,' he replies.

'And this girl?' I point to a passing waitress.

'She is Iroquois.'

'And her?' I enquire, heart juddering as I single out Madame Laframboise.

'Huron-Wendat.'

'Ohhh,' I give a significant look at Annique. We're in. She'll be able to speak French. 'Very interesting, thank you.'

'Enjoy.'

As it happens, we do. Despite my fears, the food is cooked so impeccably and the flavours are so intense, I now find the menu *extraordinary* in a positive way. It doesn't hurt that we have a bottle of the local Cuvée Natashquan Seyval Blanc to wash it down. Well, we needed a hair of the dog, and a way of lingering until Madame Laframboise finishes her shift.

And then, as she is savouring her dessert of maple fondue, Annique says, 'My daughter would love this!'

'I didn't know you were a mum!'

She nods. 'To Coco. She's now five.'

'Coco?' I perk up. 'What a lovely name!'

'You know, I almost was not allowed to call her that . . .'

'Who by?' I frown.

'The government.' Her voice darkens.

'The government?' I repeat, baffled.

'They wrote to me when I registered her birth and they told me that they had no record of any other Coco in the province of Quebec and therefore I was leaving her open to ridicule.'

'But what about Coco Chanel?' I protest. 'She couldn't be any more French!'

'I know! But here I was the first and they told me that unless I could defend my choice of the name, in writing, I would have to change it.'

'Outrageous!' I gasp. 'But you did convince them?'

'I did. So now it is quite the name to live up to!'

'And is she . . . living up to it?'

'Oh yes, she takes after her grandmother on my side – plenty of personality to carry it off!' She reaches into her bag and flips out a photograph.

'She looks so smart!' I grin. And then hope Annique doesn't mistake this for a euphemism for her child being unattractive – it's just that she has one of those particularly alert expressions, as if she knows exactly what is going on and may well be able to outwit all the grown-ups. 'She's very cute,' I add for good measure.

'Of course I agree.' Her pride is unmistakable.

I pause while our waiter tops up our wine and then ask, in all sincerity, 'What's it like, *really*, to have a child?'

She studies me for a moment and then says, 'It's complicated. At least for me, my situation, with Mason . . .'

'The ex?'

'Yes.' She looks immediately burdened. 'That is the hardest part. I don't think he ever really wanted to be a father. He knew how much I wanted to be a mother and he went along with the process but . . . how can I say this? It was not a good fit with the image he has of himself. He likes the finer things in life and children put sticky fingers on those things.'

I give a little smile.

'Children are not glamorous. Everything is reduced to basic human function – pooping and peeing and vomiting. High temperatures, coughs, rashes – all these elements he found . . . irritating, distasteful . . .'

'Oh gosh. So he wasn't very hands-on?'

'Not at all. If he'd had his way I would have kept her hidden until she could intern at his business. Or if she came top of class he could say, "That's my girl, she takes after me!" but we didn't get to that stage. And it wasn't only Coco. He didn't like the change in my appearance. He didn't like the attention away from him. He didn't like the inconvenience of having to book babysitters or attend school meetings . . .'

'Gosh, that must have been so hard for you – not being able to share anything with him, good and bad.'

'I used to get so upset for Coco – that her father wouldn't play with her, wouldn't cuddle her, wouldn't twirl her up in the air and make her feel like a princess . . .'

I nod.

'I spent too much time wishing for him to be different, wishing for him to love her like I did. She delights me every day, surprises me every day – how could he not see what I saw? Feel what I feel?'

'That must have been very lonely.'

She gives a little shrug. 'I think it bonded me with her all the more. We were kindred spirits and he was the grumpy man who came home and spoiled our fun. It is such a relief to be away from him and yet of course we must be in constant contact for the custody.'

'Did he even want to share that?'

'That was the strange part – he fought me for her every step of the way. I think because he knew that she was most precious to me and I would agree to virtually anything to have more time with her.'

'Leverage,' I tut.

She nods. 'So now I must see him once a month and all he does is criticise how I raise her.'

I frown. I can't imagine Annique being anything but a wonderful mother – clever, encouraging, warm, fun – with fantastic shoes to totter around in.

'He is very particular. About everything. He sends me emails commenting on the style of her new clothes or telling me that I need to start taking her to ballet three times a week . . .'

I feel a flare of anger and frustration on Annique's behalf that she should be tied to such negative energy and make a mental note to get her some fir incense sticks. It amazes me that even a woman of Annique's beauty and calibre can wind up with the sticky end of the lollipop. None of us are exempt, it seems.

'I keep wanting to believe in happy endings,' I say. 'But it's so hard. Especially when the ones that get off to the greatest start so often go awry.'

'I would never have predicted I would become a single mother,' Annique acknowledges. 'But I had to leave him for Coco. I did not want her living in an environment where she did not feel wanted. She could be standing right in front of him and he wouldn't even look at her.'

'I think you've been very brave,' I tell her. 'And you definitely made the right choice.'

I pause our conversation to order a glass of the corn beer

– just to try! – while Annique settles for a coffee. And then I cock my head to the side. 'So what about Gilles? Is it very different with him?'

'Well, he's a lot better-looking than Mason,' she laughs. 'But he is hard to read. And another workaholic,' she concedes. 'His photography consumes him.'

'You wouldn't mind coming second?'

'Not to something I can also enjoy. I take pleasure in his work. I think he is an artist. I like the creative people.'

'Maybe you two could "create" a sibling for Coco?'

At this she falters. 'I don't know if this is coincidence, but he has been a little distant since I mentioned her. Of course today I have not seen him alone—'

'Tomorrow will be better,' I assert.

'You think so?'

'I do.' Not least because he has now been relieved of any guilt in my direction and can now focus purely on her. 'By the way, are you entering the Snow Bath?'

'Nooooooo!' she scolds.

'I think you should.'

'Why?'

'With your figure, are you kidding? You'd be the belle of the ball, and you know nothing reignites a man's passion more than to see his lady appreciated by others.'

She thinks for a moment. 'I do have a lucky bikini!'

'Well then!'

'Only if you do it with me.'

'Oh!' I choke. 'I'm strictly on the sidelines on this one.'

'But Krista,' she pouts. 'What is the fun in just watching a party?'

Direct hit to my Achilles heel. But I don't even have a swimming costume.

'I can lend you one,' Annique offers.

'Oh yes, because we're exactly the same size.'

'I have been many sizes in my life, trust me, I have a one-piece that will fit you just right.'

'Well . . .'

'Come on, it could be such fun! We'll have a little liqueur first.'

'How can you even think about liqueurs after last night?'

'This is different. They make it in my birthplace of Isle-aux-Coudres, so I know exactly what is in it and it doesn't hurt you the next day.'

Perhaps it's the corn beer or the camaraderie or the fact that I owe her for giving up a night with Gilles to come meddling with me, but I agree, fool that I am, to prance near-naked alongside a supermodel in the snow.

We talk a little more about Coco but I don't mention my situation because I don't want Annique to feel awkward. For some reason I find it comforting to hear her talk. I think it's because she's so honest. Listening to her, I realise we all have our issues to deal with – nobody's life is perfect. I certainly don't envy her her continued contact with her ex; at least I never have to see Andrew again. There would be no point anyway – the man I married, the man who loved me, is long gone.

I look up. 'Are we the last table?'

Annique grabs my arm, alerting me to the fact that our target is on the move.

Before I can let nerves apprehend me, I hurry to catch her up. 'Madame Laframboise?'

'*Qui*?' she turns to face me.

Her expression is polite, curious, if a little tired, but there is another layer in her eyes, a dark pool of sadness that makes my heart ache just to look at her.

'I wonder if you have just a minute or two to talk to me.' I make my request via Annique. 'My name is Krista Carter. I am a friend of Jacques Dufour.'

She looks instantly conflicted.

'I don't want to upset you,' I speak in my softest tone. 'And I promise I will be brief . . .'

'Is he okay?'

I consider this a good sign, that she is concerned.

'Yes and no,' I reply. 'He has his health but his grief is profound, and I think a big part of his pain is no longer having you in his life.' I pause, waiting for Annique to make her translation. 'I can't even imagine the agony you live with. I don't have children of my own but there can be no greater loss. I understand it would be natural to blame—'

She shakes her head. 'It is not blame.'

She then looks for an available sofa and bids us sit. For a moment she is silent and then she says:

'I cannot look at Jacques without seeing Rémy. They were always together and every time I see Jacques I look for Rémy and find him gone.' Her voice wavers. 'It is too much to bear. To be reminded over and over.'

I nod, desperately wanting to reach for her hand but not wanting to overstep the mark.

'The last time, he came to me with money and all I could think was, "You took my son away from me. I don't want money. I want him back."' She hangs her head in shame. 'And that is not the Huron way.'

'How do you mean?'

'We must not attempt to recall to earth souls who have departed. We have rituals to prevent grief from disrupting our lives. This is how we have been raised. And yet . . .' She heaves a long sigh.

Annique's eyes flick to me. 'I think she is saying that her people have two souls: one goes to a village in the sky when they die, the other waits to be reborn.' Her frown deepens. 'I think she is waiting for Rémy to be reborn.'

At this point, a fellow waitress comes over to check on her. From their interaction, it sounds as if she is her ride home. She gets to her feet and tells us she must leave.

'Just one thing!' I hasten to add. 'Jacques doesn't know I'm here, so if you did ever consider contacting him, that would be your choice. If not, he would never have to know we had this conversation.'

'You mean well.' She touches my face. 'You too must forgive yourself.'

I blink back at her. What does she mean by that?

Her hand drops to my tummy. 'Forgive.'

Something tells me she doesn't mean forgive myself for ordering a second dessert.

Annique and I drive back into Quebec, lost in our own thoughts. All the while, my hand never leaves my belly.

Once back in the room, I light one of the fir incense sticks (calling upon the aspect that heals wounds) and find myself having my own private ceremony.

'I forgive you, my body, for not being able to grow a baby inside of you. I know you would've given it your all if you could. I'm not going to be angry with you any more. No more holding on to the disappointment. I'm not going to blame you. I'm not going to feel faulty or broken or less than. I didn't mean to make you feel like a failure. You have served me in a million other ways. And for every one of those I am grateful. I know there is something that will make sense of all this one day. I will be patient until that day comes. You do your best for me every day and for that I thank you.'

And then I get into bed and close my eyes.

There's something else out there for me, I know there is.

16

The wind is so bitingly cold today I feel I'm being Tasered every time it strikes.

And that's with my usual twenty-seven layers on. It seems unthinkable that I will be performing a striptease with Annique within a matter of hours.

But the first item on today's agenda is transferring to the new hotel in Old Town. I'm sorry to leave my Hilton haven with its beaver-hatted doorman and best-way-to-start-the-day breakfast potatoes. But if this tower gave me a sweeping overview of the magic kingdom, then Auberge Place D'Armes lies snug in its bellybutton.

The building has only twenty-one bedrooms and no lift, but as soon as I climb the steep entrance steps, I feel at home.

'We have a package for you, madame,' the receptionist announces as I give my details.

'Really?' I wonder for a moment if Gilles has printed out some pictures, but the envelope is squishy. I open it right there and then, pulling out a red hat with a pompom bobble on the end.

'Perfect for the Carnival,' the receptionist smiles. 'Just like Bonhomme.'

I get a chill. 'D-did you see who delivered this?'

She shakes her head. 'It was already here when I started my shift.'

Of course it could be Jacques. Not that he knows where I'm staying. But then how would Malhomme? I try to think back to the night at the bar. Is it possible that it came up in conversation with the others and he overhead? I'm too hazy to be sure.

'There's no note?'

I reach my hand back inside the envelope and yes! There is a card. With two words etched on it.

'Oh!' I gasp. 'What does that mean?'

I hand it to the receptionist, hoping it's not too improper.

'Wanna toque?' she reads, pronouncing 'toque' as 'took'.

'Is it bad?'

'No, no – toque is this, the hat.'

My relief is short-lived. I can be certain now this is from Malhomme. Jacques is simply not the innuendo type.

The receptionist hands me the key to Room 7. I check every cupboard and jewel-knobbed drawer before I even take off my coat. All clear. And all cute. My darling attic hideaway has a whitewashed wooden bed with a pale blue patchwork quilt and hand-crafted furniture stencilled with a fleur-de-lys motif. Whereas the whole of one wall at the Hilton was window, here there are just two tiny rectangles filled with snow, except for a peek-a-boo triangle in the top right-hand corner. All I can see are the domes and spires of neighbouring buildings – almost like a display of ornate bottle-stoppers – and that's fine by me.

I am about to start unpacking when there's a knock at the door.

'Yes?' I enquire with caution.

'*C'est moi* – Annique!'

She seems in good spirits as she looks around the room making approving sounds, especially at the modern glass sink in the bathroom that I hadn't even seen yet.

Then she turns to me and says: 'Ta-daaa!' and throws opens her coat, flashing a white bikini with red maple leaf motif. She looks like a cross between a Miss Canada and a modern-day Eve. I don't know if she's applied one of those shimmer-infused lotions or her skin just has a natural luminosity, but her every contour – from cleavage to calf muscle – seems to be highlighted.

'Wow!' I can't help but gawp.

'Is okay?'

'If you've got it, flaunt it!'

She reaches into her bag. 'I have your *maillot de bain*!'

I close my eyes, fearing some kind of cutaway Rihanna number, but instead she pulls out a round-necked Speedo.

'Oh.'

'You said you wanted more coverage.'

That I did. I just don't recall asking for anything from the Chaste & Celibate collection.

'Perhaps I'll sit this one out,' I suggest.

'No, no!' Annique protests. 'I'm sure we can make something work.'

I quickly move my earmuffs from her sight. The last thing I want is fluffy bunny boobs. As she starts going through my suitcase, her first suggestion is to cut my sequin top in half and pull the lower section down to cover my groin.

'Isn't that bit go-go dancer?'

'Let me see your underwear.'

Definitely nothing that passes as swimwear there.

'Besides, I can't have as much flesh on show as you,' I say, exposing my stomach to ram the point home.

'There must be something we can use . . .' She strums her fingers and then pips, 'I've got it! Wait there!'

'Where are you going?'

'To the souvenir shop next door. Won't be long.'

I try to guess what she has in mind, but can't quite see how shot glasses and fridge magnets are going to aid this cause.

'Gosh, that was quick!' She's back already. 'What did you get?'

She pulls three long fringed sashes out of her bag – replicas of the snazzy one Bonhomme wears around his waist. 'We can wrap these around and around you.'

'So basically I'd be going as a Bonhomme groupie?'

'It is very *Carnival* spirit.'

'If you say so.'

She kneels beside me. 'You know this arrowhead pattern has its roots in the Amerindian culture?'

'Really?' I take a closer look at the weave – the bold red, black, white, yellow and royal blue colour-way – and then Annique takes the last sash from my hand, completing an ingenious halterneck design that would make Tim Gunn proud.

'You're good at this,' I marvel. 'And fast!'

'I've had a lot of practice playing dress-up with my daughter.'

As she adds safety-pin reinforcements, I ask how Gilles was with her last night.

'I didn't see him. I thought I would let him miss me and then today—'

'Knock his socks off?'

'All three pairs!' She gets to her feet. 'You look *très jolie*.'

I have to say I don't look too bad. It's actually more flattering than a conventional swimsuit in that the material is thick, the arrow pattern sends the eye in multiple directions and Annique has positioned the ties on my hips so the loose ends fall over the tops of my thighs.

'I wouldn't move around too much, but it should be secure enough for the picture.'

I give her a careful hug. 'Oh by the way . . .'

'*Qui?*'

'Do you remember that guy from the bar the other night, the one that was staring . . .'

'The one with the gold hair, YSL suit and *fossette*?' she says, marking a dimple on her chin.

I smile. 'So you'd recognise him again?'

'Well, it depends what he is wearing . . .'

'What do you mean?'

Does she know?

'We were inside then, so he was less covered up. If I saw him on the street in hat and coat . . .'

'What if he was in his swimwear? Or less . . .'

Her eyes narrow at me.

'I've just got a feeling he's going to show up today,' I shrug. 'So if you see him before I do . . .'

'I'll let you know,' she says, still looking suspicious.

It's a very strange thing walking around wearing next-to-nothing under a Puffa coat. I feel like a winter version of a strip-a-gram – about to peel off my elbow-length wool gloves and twirl them under the nose of some unsuspecting tourist.

My real clothes are stuffed in my bag. I've never longed for my long johns like I am doing right now. I still can't believe I'm going to do this. Not that I'm entirely sure what it is I'm about to do . . .

'So what exactly happens when we get there?' I ask as we enter the Carnival site.

'It's a little chaotic, some people dive into the snow, we have a little dance, we play with Bonhomme . . .'

'So the real Bonhomme is going to be there?'

'Well, we certainly hope it is the real Bonhomme.'

'Yes we do,' I say, checking every passing man for a cleft chin, though the majority are disguised by high collars or scarves.

Would he really have the nerve to show up at such a public event, knowing that everyone is looking for him?

'Patrick! *Bonjour!*' She kisses a handsome stubbly face that is a precision cross between Russell Crowe and Marti Pellow from Wet Wet Wet. Now that's a name I haven't said in a while.

'Patrick is the PR manager for the Carnival. He is the one who arranged all our passes and our registration for this event.'

'And a photo opportunity with Bonhomme!' he grins, bidding me follow him.

'Where's Gilles?' I ask Annique.

'Waiting for us . . .'

Indeed, he has everything prepared; all I have to do is drop my coat and step into the scene he has arranged beside Bonhomme's Ice Palace. Just drop the coat. Unpop the poppers, unzip the zip and let go.

'I can't do it!' I bleat to Annique.

'Yes you can!' She insists.

'Go on, for me!' Bonhomme encourages.

I look back at him. He's certainly very similar to Malhomme, but probably a foot taller and his head has a different texture, akin to a million little polystyrene bubbles. I certainly don't want to be seen to be wasting his precious time, so I scrunch up my eyes, drop my protective layer and step into the frame.

'Our outfits match!' Bonhomme cheers, flipping his sash.

I decide to give him a little test. 'You do wear that quite high, don't you?'

'Perfect position, no?'

'Yes,' I smile. 'It's perfect.'

'Okay!' Gilles calls over. 'Let's get a hug!'

'Ooomf!' I gasp, as Bonhomme nearly squeezes all the cellulite out of me. 'You're really strong!'

'Thank you!'

'Got it!' Gilles calls.

'Can we do a quick one with Annique?'

'Is that okay?' She checks with Patrick.

He nods his approval and then metaphorical socks begin to blow off in every possible direction.

'Y-you look amazing!' Gilles' hands are actually shaking.

Seconds later, the mad dash of the Snow Bath is underway and Annique begins the Winter Carnival version of Bo Derek's run down the beach in the movie *10*. If she's not in slow motion now she will be later as hundreds of spectators zoom their mini-movie in on her frolicking form.

Not having had that liqueur she promised, and not fully grasping why this is considered 'fun', I stand awkwardly on the sidelines as the clinically insane people throw snow in the air like it's dollar bills and generally do everything in their power to get hypothermia.

I hate to be a party pooper but my skin is already zinging scarlet and my teeth are chattering like castanets. I did it and I'm done. But when I backtrack to grab my coat I find it gone.

'You've got to be kidding.'

I spin around. Gilles is nowhere to be seen. He couldn't be carrying all our stuff and taking pictures, so he must have stashed it somewhere.

'Holy mother of . . .' I gasp as the wind slashes at my skin. This is too much. I've got to get out of the cold. I start hurtling towards the nearest firepit when I feel myself yanked back.

'What the . . . ?' I look behind me and find a German shepherd chomped on to the end of my sash, paws dug deep in snow, pulling backwards. 'Oh no, no, no!' I plead, as I feel my lower layers unravelling. 'Stop! Let go!' I try to pull back but his grip only tightens, this time with a low growl. 'Nice doggie, let go of the sash . . .'

'Niko! *Lâche-toi!* Release!'

It's Jacques! My saviour! *Again!*

'You're frozen!' he tuts. 'Where's your coat? Where are your friends?'

'I don't know and I don't know.'

'Well let's call them!'

'My phone is in my coat, I don't know the number . . .'

'Niko stop it!' He reprimands the dog as he stands to full height and puts his paws on my shoulder, seemingly wanting to take a chunk out of my head.

And then it dawns on me. 'I think it might be this . . .' I can't believe I'm actually going to take off another item of clothing, but I pull off my red toque and hand it to Niko – immediately he's snuffling all over it.

Jacques looks confused by my hurried explanation but then quickly snaps into action. 'Here, take my coat,' he says, wrapping it around me (which feels good on so many levels). 'I want you to go and warm up in the bistro here and I'll be back in just a minute. Don't go anywhere.'

For a makeshift food concession this is very nice – modern white chairs set around black-clothed tables, cool lighting and, over at the back, a raised area with lime-coloured sofas and an armchair that is just about to become free . . .

The only snag is that the line for paninis and hot coffee is an unwieldy snake. Not that I have any money on me anyway. Still, Jacques will be back any minute.

'Beaver tail?'

'Excuse me?'

I turn and find the waitress offering me a flattened pastry coated in maple butter icing.

'I wish!' I sigh longingly. 'I didn't order it.'

'The gentleman asked me to send it over.'

'What gentleman?' I ask.

She looks back towards the counter. 'Oh. He was just there . . .'

'Did he have . . .' My finger rises to my chin.

She nods. 'And blond hair.'

'Oh my god,' I gulp, getting to my feet and looking wildly around the room. Why is he doing this? I'm getting really freaked out now. Do I dare even eat this?

I roll my eyes. Why is that even a concern to me? I've got far bigger things to worry about than what to do with a complimentary pastry. Like finding my clothes and figuring out why Malhomme is singling me out.

It really does smell good though – all warm and sweetly fragrant with crispy deep-fried edges.

Just one tiny bite then . . .

17

'What is it with you two?' Jacques asks when he returns with my coat and bag and I bring him up to speed on my encounters with Malhomme – the snowball fight at Place Royale, the Staring Man at Auberge Saint-Antoine, the toque waiting at my new hotel and now this beaver tail. In and of itself, nothing to arrest a man over, but I do seem to be a magnet for his mischief.

'By the way, where's Niko?' I look around us.

'Sebastien has him,' Jacques explains. 'I thought it would be a good idea to get some hot food in your system.'

I look back at the lunch queue.

'Do you have a picture ID with you?' he asks.

'Um . . .'

'Driving licence, passport . . .'

'Just how far are we going?'

He smiles enigmatically. 'Do you?'

I check in my bag. 'I do.'

'Okay, come with me.'

I flinch a little as we step back into the cold.

'Don't worry, five more minutes and all this will be forgotten.'

As we head for the nearest exit, we pass Gilles and Annique sheltering around the back of the hot tubs, apparently opting to skip lunch in favour of devouring each other.

'Oh!' Jacques stumbles in shock. 'I didn't see that coming.'

'Really?' I frown. 'Can you honestly picture a more perfect physical match?'

'It's just . . . I thought he was into you.'

'What?' I hoot. 'No.'

'That's odd, I'm usually right about this stuff.'

'Well . . .'

For a second I consider mentioning our initial frisson at the Hôtel de Glace, but why on earth would I tell him that?

'Well?' He looks expectantly at me.

'Well this time you were wrong!'

Initially I think we're cutting across the Parliament building grounds to go back to the Hilton, but then Jacques diverts up to the front door.

I hang back. 'Do you have a quick ballot to vote on?'

He laughs. 'Come on.'

'We're going inside?'

'Yes.'

'I thought we were going for lunch.'

'We are. Everywhere else will be too busy.'

I'm still waiting for his choice to make sense.

'Are you a part-time politician or something?' Perhaps this is what he does in the autumn?

'Quebec is a democracy, and one of the ways the government likes to demonstrate that is to make their restaurant available to the public.'

'So you can dine next to the Minister of Health?'

'Yes,' he shrugs. 'Why not?'

There's just the small matter of getting through security, which is on a par with the airport.

'Madame, we need you to take off your coat.'

Jacques hangs his head. 'I forgot, you haven't had the chance to change yet.'

The only toilets available at the Carnival were Portaloos

and it simply wasn't possible to dress without trouser legs collecting slushy detritus and scarves falling into the chemical abyss.

'What shall I do?' I fret.

Jacques does his best to explain in French but they are insistent.

'And the food here is really good?' I check.

He nods.

'Okay! Here we go!' I pull off my Puffa and stuff it onto the conveyor belt along with my bag.

'What are they saying?' I blush as I wait the eternity for it to appear on the other side.

'Just how patriotic you are.'

I give a little snort. 'And how diplomatic you are.'

'Here.' He places the coat around me and guides me to the Ladies.

Even when I do get my clothes on, I wonder if I am appropriately dressed for such grand surroundings.

It's all ornately tiled floors, everlasting staircases and jewel-bright stained-glass windows featuring coats of arms with sinewy lions and ermin-trimmed crowns.

And to think that I was angling for a panini on a paper plate.

I notice now that Jacques is wearing a nice blue check shirt under his round neck sweater. He looks almost bookish, which is all the more appealing knowing the rugged man that lies beneath.

Together we ascend the glossy wooden staircase to Le Parlementaire restaurant. The dining room, inspired by the Parisian beaux-arts period, looks more like a ballroom to me – soaring pale blue ceilings, imposing columns of cream and gold, rich blue draperies and glittering chandeliers. I feel as though I should have my hair piled high and embedded with jewels. Reassuringly the maître d' doesn't bat an eyelid at our rather more casual attire. Instead he shows us to a lovely table by the window, impeccably set with navy and ivory china accented with gold fleur-de-lys. I take a seat on the striped velvet chair and then just *marvel*.

I wish I could count this as a date because it would make a great 'first lunch together' story. It's not every menu that opens with a welcome note from the President of the National Assembly.

We order the three-course table d'hôte for just £12 – this is so going on my list of Uniquely Quebec experiences.

The soup, together with a gourmet version of a cheese straw, arrives swiftly, and from my first slurp of puréed country vegetables I can feel my insides thawing out.

'So, were you always an outdoorsy kind of person?' I ask Jacques between spoonfuls, keen to find out more about the kind of man who chooses to work al fresco in the deep midwinter.

He nods as he adds a little pepper. 'My father was very athletic, got us into all kinds of sports; and my mother loved to be in nature whenever she could.'

'And the dogs?'

'That started pretty young,' he smiles and then leans forward. 'We had this neighbour who was not kind to his dog.'

'Oh no.'

'He was always on a chain, always barking. Everyone was afraid of him, said he was old and mean, just like his owner. But I knew he just wanted to be free. And maybe eat something better than scraps from the garbage can. So. When the summer holidays came I would sneak over after the guy left for work and I'd take off his collar and use some garden rope as a leash and I would walk him. Every day.'

'You weren't afraid?'

'I knew he wasn't a bad dog. I'd be crazy too if you chained me up twenty-four hours a day. I was a little kid and he was gentle with me. He wasn't as strong as he looked anyway – he didn't have any muscle tone because he wasn't getting any exercise. But that started to change. We'd walk and walk, then if it was too hot we'd hang out in the garage and I would do my reading and he would sleep with his chin on my foot . . .'

'That's so lovely!' I pang.

'And then one day I went over there and I guess the owner was home from work and I didn't realise . . .'

'Yikes!' I flinch. 'What did he say?'

'He told me that if I took the dog one more time, all the barking and the complaints and the vet bills and the cost of food would be my problem.'

My eyebrows rise. 'Really?'

'Best punishment I ever had!' he grins.

'And your parents were okay with you taking him in?'

He nods. 'Barney was part of the family by then.'

'Barney?' I smile.

'We renamed him. The owner had called him Cujo.'

'God, what's wrong with people?' I despair.

'I know,' he shakes his head. 'I only had him a few years, he *was* old, but he was the sweetest company.'

'And how great that the last years of his life were the best – it's not often that way round.'

Jacques nods and then looks wistful.

I tense slightly, aware that we have paused on the subject of death. He must have lost so many dogs over the years, as well, of course, as Rémy.

'And then the sledding aspect?' I try to move the conversation on.

Jacques' gaze returns to me. 'My dad took me on my sixth birthday. I told him that day, "This is going to be my job when I'm a grown-up. This is what I want to do."'

'And you did!'

'Was it the same way for you and your writing?' he asks.

I think for a moment. 'I can't really remember a time when I wasn't writing. It was just the thing I did that felt most like me.'

'So no confusion over what to do with your life?'

'No.'

'You must be a natural.'

'I don't know about that – I've never found it easy. But I think that's just the way of it. And there are great perks – like now, doing the research, that's the best!' And then my eyes narrow. 'Which brings me to a question . . .'

'Yes?'

'Are you really the Wolfman? Have you tamed wolves?'

He laughs. 'No. I've certainly had dogs that resembled wolves, and who's to say there wasn't a little mix along the line, but typically wolves attack dogs.'

'Ohhh. So it's not true that people have heard wolves howling at your farm?'

He smiles. 'Huskies howl like wolves. They're known for it. It's an easy mistake to make. But nothing I care to correct!' He leans in. 'I kind of like having that reputation. Nobody gives me any trouble.'

'I bet!'

And then we lean back as two piping hot bone-china plates are placed before us – mine with the fresh catch of the day, his with a hazelnut-crusted pork medallion.

'The cutlery here is so nice!' I admire the weight and design of the silver as I take it in my hands. 'There's this café that my friend Laurie and I go to almost every lunchtime and they have the cheapest knives and forks with edges that dig in your hands and leave marks, so we've actually started bringing a set from home!'

'That's quite a testament to their cooking.'

'It's the chips,' I tell him. 'They do the best chips!'

'Have you tried ours yet? The poutine?'

'Poutine?' I frown.

'It is chips that are golden brown—'

'And a little bit soft?' I ask hopefully.

'Yes, the ideal chips, with gravy . . .'

'Okay.'

'And then topped with cheese curds.'

I know I'm not pulling a pretty face now.

'Honestly, it is so good. Will you promise to try it?'

'I did have fries with mayonnaise once in Amsterdam.'

'Is that a yes?'

I hesitate. I don't want to make any false promises to Jacques, but cheese curds? Still, I trust him. 'Okay, I'll do it.'

'They actually have some of the best in Montreal, at La Banquise, if you have time . . .'

I take out my notebook and scribble down the name.

'They have about twenty varieties. Including Poutine Kamikaze if you're feeling daring.'

'I don't have a death wish.' Oh god! There I go again. 'Any other recommendations?'

'Toi, Moi et Café. That's my favourite.'

'You and me?' I translate and then feel my cheeks pinken. I think it's my favourite thing too.

'See if Sebastien can take you there for breakfast.'

We talk a little more about food – him saying how he likes to cook for people, me saying how I like people who cook – and then comes a mini-dessert, or 'sweet taste', as they call it.

'I think this is genius,' I say as I contemplate my one perfect profiterole. 'You don't even have to ponder whether or not you'll order pudding, it just arrives like a gift with your coffee. It's so civilised!'

'I like your definition of civilised!'

'Well, I've never been one for deprivation when it comes to food.'

'You should try the dog-sledding diet,' he grins as he takes a sip of coffee. 'All the girls who come to us arrive so health-conscious, and then they see how many calories get burned with the feeding and the cleaning and the tours and they realise they can eat all the pastries and cakes and second helpings the guys do and they don't put on a pound!'

'Sounds like heaven!' I sigh.

'Have you ever been married?'

For a second I'm thrown. I didn't see that question coming.

'I'm sorry,' Jacques apologises. 'I don't mean to pry.'

'No, no. Um.' I try to collect myself. 'The answer is yes. I was. But I'm not any more.' I squirm a little. 'This is actually quite new for me – it was just official six months ago, so I haven't quite got my story down pat.'

'That's okay. I shouldn't have asked . . .'

'It's fine, really. What about you?'

'Yes,' he confirms.

'Past tense?'

'Past tense for nearly three years now.'

'I'm sorry. It's never pleasant, is it? Divorce. Was it one big thing or lots of little things?'

'One big thing.'

'Me too,' I tell him.

I'm glad we don't go any deeper at this point. I don't want to spoil our lunch. Besides, with so many emotional land-mines to negotiate, is it really such a mystery why marriages end? To me the miracle is that any survive.

And then I tilt my head. 'I thought I read that people in Quebec didn't really get married?'

'It's true. But it runs in our family. My dad has been married twice and now he's looking for wife number three!'

I give a little chuckle. 'That's some kind of optimist. And Sebastien?'

'There's a girl in Montreal, Julie. They split up when he moved back here, but they should be together.'

'I'll add that to my To-Do list for the trip.'

He smiles back at me. 'Wouldn't it be great if life was that simple?'

And then my phone bleeps. 'Sorry!' I cringe, feeling terribly uncouth, as though I've ruined a scene in *Downton Abbey* with my new-fangled technology. 'I meant to turn it off.'

'Go ahead and check it, it could be important.'

It's a text. From Annique.

I look up at Jacques. 'She has one more activity for me back at the Carnival.'

He sighs. 'I need to get back too – check in with Sebastien and Niko.'

Neither of us moves.

And then I find my hand reaching for his across the table. 'Thank you for bringing me here, Jacques. It was such an elegant experience.'

'My pleasure,' he replies, giving me a little head bow.

It's therefore all the more of a contrast when we return to the Carnival and Annique insists I join a game of human table football, or fusball as the Americans call it.

'So, just to be clear, because I haven't been traumatised enough today, you want to strap me to a horizontal pole that slides from side to side and have a ball ricocheting around me.'

'Well, hopefully you will get to kick the ball.'

'Yes, I'm sure I'll get a goal.'

'It's just so much fun,' Annique rallies. 'I know you'll love it.'

'You're not doing it?'

'I played the last two games and now they say I have to let someone else have a go.'

'Really?' I check with Gilles.

'She's extremely competitive.'

'All right,' I sigh. 'But only because I owe you.'

I enter the green boxed-in area, put on an outsize red shirt (to show which unfortunate team has me on their side) and then get buckled and clicked into position on a yellow pole.

'Secure?'

'Yes,' I reply, finding myself all too restricted.

A whistle blows, the ball is in play, cheers and jeers resonate as the two teams flounder and duck and reach and scramble. One young boy loses his footing altogether and finds himself hanging horizontally from his pole like something out of Mission Impossible. Twice I make contact with the ball – just not with an appropriate body part.

Suddenly the ball is at my feet, out of my opponent's reach. This is my chance. I go to give it a hefty kick but my foot slides over it without making contact, at least until the way back when I send it neatly in the opposite direction and score an own goal.

'Bravo!' A voice cheers louder than the rest. A voice I know . . .

There he is! Bold as brass, leaning over the barrier at the far end. His sandy hair may be hidden beneath a hat but I'd recognise that chin anywhere . . .

I twist around, looking for Jacques – is he still within view? Annique is busy talking to Patrick and then I think of Gilles, with his camera . . .

Just as I turn his way the ball hits me in the face. I'm stunned for a moment and then recover.

'Gilles!' I call out to him.

'It's okay, I got it – great shot!'

'No! I need you to photograph . . .' I go to point out Quebec's Most Wanted but of course he's already on the move. I grapple with my buckle but the more I struggle and wriggle, the more trapped I become.

'Need some help with that?' It's him again. Level with me now, taunting me.

It's then I realise I've been calling the wrong name. 'Niko!' I cry. 'Niko, Niko, here boy!' And then I give the whistle I learned when I got my first dog.

He holds my gaze for a second. 'I didn't think you'd do that.' And then he's off.

Shortly followed by Niko and Jacques – they're onto him!

The police are hot on their heels, all very Keystone Kops, skidding hither and thither, then myself (having been freed by Annique) and Gilles.

There's no doubt I am slowing up proceedings, so Annique hails a taxi and we follow the trail all the way down to the ferry port.

'That's twice he's been traced to here,' I note.

'We're going to go across,' Jacques informs me as we join him on the side of the road. 'Do you want to join us?'

'Can we all come?'

Jacques looks to the police chief for approval.

Obviously no man is going to turn down Annique, and Gilles has a potentially useful zoom lens, so the answer is yes.

It doesn't occur to me until the ferry disconnects from the shore and we start moving into the frozen waters that we could be placing ourselves in peril . . .

18

'You know, it's not just the French-Canadian people who are nice,' I tell Laurie. 'They even have nice toilets on their ferries.'

'I do worry about you sometimes.'

'What?'

'Aren't you supposed to be chasing a criminal?'

'Well, criminal is a little harsh. I'd say he's more of a public nuisance.'

'So why the sniffer dog and police posse?' she challenges.

'Well, I don't suppose they have much else on.'

'On account of everyone being too *nice* to break the law?'

'Pretty much.'

Laurie groans and then asks me if I'll be including the Quebec–Lévis ferry ride in the guide.

'As a matter of fact, yes – you get a great new perspective of the city and it's only four pounds for a round trip!'

'Sort of like Quebec's answer to the Staten Island Ferry!'

'Exactly!' I laugh. 'You don't necessarily want to get off at the destination, but it sure does make for a marvellous ride!'

Typically when New York is mentioned, Laurie starts billing and cooing and recalls some other highlight from her most recent trip, but this time she simply says, 'Okay, well thanks for the update—'

'Wait!' I halt her, suddenly concerned that something is off. 'Any news your end?'

'Not yet.'

'*Not yet?*'

'I'll let you know as soon as I know . . .'

I feel a stab of nerves. 'It's nothing bad is it?'

'No, no! Not at all,' she insists. 'Quite the opposite in fact.'

My eyes narrow. 'You want to give me a clue?'

'Not yet.'

'Hmmm. All right. Well, you behave yourself.'

'And you try to *mis*behave with the right person.'

'What's that supposed to mean?' I frown.

'I mean try to stay attracted to the nice guy and not the naughty one.'

I almost take offence for a second. But then I decide to take heed. Laurie is usually pretty savvy about my weaknesses. But if she could see Jacques now, I think, as I head back in his direction, if she could feel what I feel when I look at him, she wouldn't even entertain such a thought.

There is nothing new to report as I rejoin the group. Niko has already had a good head-down, nose-foraging sniff of the ferry, and only supplied one false alarm with a man luring him with his packet of crisps.

The police, however, have their own bait. Me. They want me to stand on the outer deck of the ferry and lean nonchalantly over the barrier.

'So he can have the opportunity to approach you.'

'And tip me over the side?' I suggest.

'You don't have to do it if you don't want to,' Jacques intervenes.

'No, I will. I'll be fine. Where do you want me to stand?'

'Over this way,' the policeman directs me to the closest door. Here I go!

I gasp as the wind whips my breath from me. And then I take a tentative peek over the edge . . .

The water surrounding the ferry looks more like a raggedy half-melted ice rink than a river, giving me a whole new perspective on the sinking of the *Titanic*. Just the thought of taking a dip right now all but stops my heart. I wonder how Jacques survived his fall in the lake? He must have got out pretty quick. Perhaps he climbed aboard an iceberg? These ones don't look substantial enough – more like jagged white lilypads or panes of broken glass, jostling and grinding against each other. It's almost as if they are part of a self-shifting puzzle, with certain pieces forcing and dominating themselves over their flimsier counterparts. Sometimes they just graze them, other times they ruck them up and churn the ice like a blended margarita.

Still no one approaches me. My only human interaction is with a woman stepping out to photograph the Quebec skyline – layer upon layer of artfully arranged buildings, the Château Frontenac raised highest on the Cap Diamant bluff, its pointy turrets now in silhouette.

'Jesus!' She flinches as the wind roughs her up, sending her scuttling back inside.

A minute or two more passes and then it would seem the police have given up because the others come out to join me.

'Come on! Give us the Rose pose!' Gilles cries, lifting his lens.

'It's way too cold to stand with my arms out!' I protest, hugging myself for warmth. 'And don't even think about asking me to climb on the railings. How about a nice shot of me by the vending machine?'

Nobody objects to heading back inside. I get a bumper selection of chocolate bars and hand them out to the police – that's what I remember most from the London riots in 2011: those nice people who made cups of tea for the police. Made me feel proud to be British.

As we compare our candy bar fillings – nougat versus

caramel, peanut versus hazelnut, etc, I start to feel as if I'm on a family outing. This is fun!

'Oh Krista, not again!' Annique tuts as she points out my mess of chocolate smudges.

I roll my eyes. 'I'm just going to wash my hands!'

'Don't go alone,' the police chief cautions me.

'Oh, I don't think he's dangerous.'

Everyone turns and looks at me as if I'm one of those women who correspond with inmates in maximum security prisons.

'But of course I could be wrong,' I correct myself. 'Annique, would you care to join me?'

'Aren't you a little bit worried?' she asks me as I rinse my hands off in the sink. 'He does seem to be singling you out.'

'The only thing that gives me pause is that I set Niko on him,' I say as I switch to the dryer. 'That may have slightly soured the relationship.'

'Maybe,' she smiles. 'I just don't want anything bad to happen to you.'

'Really, you mustn't worry,' I insist. 'If I can survive Delhi Belly and the Mall of America, I can survive it here!'

She sighs. 'I wish I had a friend like you in Quebec.'

I blink back at her. What a lovely thing to say. 'You know I'll be back. I can always tell if a destination is going to be a one-off or another room in my house,' I tell her. 'And honestly, this is one of the most charming places I've been.'

'You should see it in the summer!' She brightens.

'I actually think I'd miss the snow!' I confess, surprising myself.

When we return to the others, we find Gilles in conversation with Jacques.

'So how did you end up with a sniffer dog?' he asks. 'Or did you train him to be that way?'

'Actually he belonged to a friend of mine,' Jacques replies.

'And he gave him up?'

'In a way.'

'I'm always surprised how people can leave their dogs,' Gilles tuts. 'You'd think they'd have an especially close bond in this case. Maybe that's why he looks so sad . . .'

Annique and I exchange a horrified look. But there's nothing we can do to stop him. The damage has been done.

'Excuse me a moment,' Jacques steps away, taking Niko with him.

'Gilles!' Annique swipes at him, explaining his faux pas.

'I didn't know!' he protests. 'Perhaps if you'd told me?'

I leave the two of them bickering and head towards Jacques, who has stepped back outside. But then I hesitate. I don't officially know about Rémy. If I approach him I'm going to be tiptoeing around the conversation and will probably end up making things worse.

I head instead to a spot further down the ship's rail. I want him to at least know that I'm nearby.

The light is just beautiful now, turning all the buildings on the opposite shore gold, the snowy banks reflecting the pink of sunset and the water, by comparison, looking all the more deadly . . . Oh my god! Did I just see . . . ?!

'Jacques!' I call to him.

He looks up, still lost in his thoughts.

'Quick! Come here!'

'What is it?'

'I thought I saw . . .'

'What?'

'It looked like a flipper,' I gush. 'You know, like scuba divers wear? There!' I exclaim. 'Oh!'

I slump back down as a bit of tyre rubber manoeuvres to the surface. 'As if anyone could survive in these waters!'

Jacques smiles kindly and then raises his gaze. 'You know every year we have a Carnival canoe race that goes from bank to bank.'

'They race in these conditions?' I can't believe it.

He nods. 'Château Frontenac sponsors a team.'

'Of penguins?'

'No,' he laughs. 'Real men. In wetsuits.'

'But what if someone fell in?'

'It is possible to survive submersion, for up to five minutes actually.'

'Really?' That seems unfathomable to me right now, though of course the man next to me is living proof.

'The main thing is to control your breathing,' he informs me. 'You'll start hyperventilating from the cold shock, so you need to slow that down to conserve enough energy to drag yourself out. I've known people who've got their upper body out and then let their arms freeze to the ice just to give them a firm grip to extract their lower half.'

'That's crazy!'

'If you do get out, you don't want to stand up straight away as the ice around the hole is weakest. You have to slide on your belly to a stronger spot . . .'

I can't help but shiver at the mere thought of the ice-drenched clothes and no one for miles.

'I actually had a fall last year,' Jacques confesses. 'Not here. In a lake near the farm – totally misjudged the thickness of the ice. But I'm still here.'

'I'm glad that you are,' I hear myself saying.

'I'm glad you're here too,' he smiles back at me, and suddenly I feel as warm as can be!

The chief then announces that they are joining the police team at Lévis, but the rest of us are relieved of our duties. We can stay on the ferry and go back to the original shore.

I feel a pang saying goodbye to Jacques. I leave for Montreal early tomorrow morning and I don't know when I'll see him next. But at least I will be connected to him via my mission. That's some consolation.

As is the *filet mignon avec deux sauces* at Café de la Paix . . .

'It really is the best of both worlds here,' I decide as I mop up the last of my sauce. 'All the splendour and gastronomic delights of France without any of the snobbery!'

Annique laughs.

'I'm serious! You don't know what it's like for British kids going over to France! They make you study the language at school for years, you go to Paris all eager to try out your vocab and they just give you this infuriating blank stare as if to say, "I don't understand a word you are saying, you uncultured fool." And all you said was, "*Un pain au raisin, s'il vous plaît!*"'

'You know they are the same way with us!' Gilles offers.

'What? It's not possible.'

'Oh yes it is. We're not true French to them.'

'You're the super-breed of French! French flair with North American friendliness and cheer!'

Annique and Gilles exchange a smile as I tell them that I also think that Canadians seem a tad more palatable to the cynical Brit who can find Americans rather OTT. 'Canadians seem more understated,' I decide. 'Less showy – more natural, I suppose.'

'Well, thank you for that,' Annique raises her glass.

We all chink. I'm getting a warm feeling again. Partly due to the fact that, even when my dinner plate is removed, it leaves a circle of warmth on the tablecloth. The only thing that persuades me to release my séance-like pose is the arrival of our crème caramel dessert. Light but appropriately slippery, it sets us up nicely for an evening at the Carnival . . .

It's quite a different atmosphere after dark. Sort of like a child-friendly rave with a lightbulb-flashing big wheel at its centre. Music is pounding out of the speakers at the Ice Palace – a Lego-like blue-tinted building fashioned from blocks of frozen water. Still can't quite get my head around that. There is a stage and dancers and Bonhomme doing high kicks and hugging the Carnival president whose name, believe it or not, is Mr Alain Winter. Talk about the right man for the job!

Annique finagles us entry to the disco dome, where the dance music intensifies and people are pumping arms and thrusting hips, but I can't get into moving my body, not least because it would be like working out in thermals and a cashmere polo neck.

'Why don't we go skating under the stars?' Gilles suggests, causing both Annique and myself to swoon for a moment. Me at the concept, at least. Now if only I could skate . . .

'Oh it's easy,' Gilles insists.

'Why do people say that?' I groan. 'Balancing on a knife-edge is not easy. Trying to stop thinking about your hand being sliced open by a passing skater when you fall is not easy.'

Gilles laughs.

'Really? That amuses you?'

'You amuse me.'

I look at Annique, suddenly feeling a little awkward, but she is smiling too.

'Wouldn't it be lovely if you could tell people that you learned to skate in Quebec?'

'Yes, and I'd like to say I learned to surf in Maui and walk like an Egyptian in Cairo, but it doesn't mean it's going to happen. Although actually I did do that last one . . .'

'Well then!'

'Come on!' Gilles sets me in motion. 'Didn't your dad ever take you when you were a little girl?'

I shake my head.

'I guess it's different here – ice hockey being a national obsession. Was he more into cricket?'

'I didn't know my dad,' I say in a small voice.

'Oh,' Gilles looks thrown. 'Sorry.'

'It's okay. I've made up for it in later life. In activities, not dads, obviously. Besides, it was different then. Parents didn't live to entertain their kids, you just went along with whatever they happened to be doing. You didn't feel like the centre of anyone's universe.'

Now Annique is looking sad.

'It was the same for all my friends.'

This doesn't help.

'Oh god, all right!' I despair. 'Teach me to skate!'

'Really?' They both brighten.

'Well I don't suppose I'll ever be more padded!'

'Good girl!' Annique cheers. 'Sit down here and I'll do your boots for you!'

It's a strange thing to well up over, but I do. My Puffa dumpling self squatting on a bench, with Annique kneeling before me like she has probably done hundreds of times with Coco, yanking off my boots, setting them to one side and now lacing up the leather ice skates, just like a mum would.

'Not too tight?'

'Just right,' I tell her. 'Does it count if I sit here in my skates and watch you two?'

'No. Get up.' Gilles is uncharacteristically forthright.

I can't decide if I'm better off holding onto them or trying to find my own balance. Either way I am completely and utterly freaked out.

'You know, I really don't think this is my thing,' I announce after five minutes' flailing and shrieking.

'You just need to fall over,' Gilles advises.

'Yes, that's my goal.'

'No, so that you realise it's not so bad.'

'Listen,' I say, holding up my hands and wiggling my gloved fingers. 'These babies are my livelihood – if I can't type how I can I write?'

'If you break all your fingers, I'll buy you a dictation machine and personally type up your notes, I promise.'

'God, you sporty people are always so persistent!' I complain. 'I don't go around trying to enforce my slovenly, cowardly state on you!'

And then, out of the blue – or should I say out of the black – the sky starts popping and cracking and fizzing with fireworks.

'Look at that!' I gawp upward.

'Come over here, you can see better . . .' Gilles pulls me over to the right.

I can't tear my eyes away from the sky – I love that golden shower effect! The spangles that stay suspended long after the initial burst, the manically whizzing-whistling streaks . . .

'A little further.' Annique moves forward and I follow.

'Just keep going,' Gilles encourages.

Before I even realise it, I have found a rhythm.

'I'm skating! I'm skating!' I gasp, amazed, looking down to see exactly what my feet are up to.

And that's when I fall over. Taking Gilles and Annique with me in a big tumble of limbs.

Oomf-doomf-thwack!

'Hands in the air, hands in the air!' I cry as I right myself.

'What?'

'Everybody put their hands up!'

'It's all right, Krista, everyone still has all their fingers,' Annique tries to calm me.

'And you can still move your legs?'

'I will be able to when you move off them.' Gilles wriggles free of my bulky bottom.

Meanwhile the fireworks crescendo towards their megawatt finale – zapping and clashing and overlapping like a celestial superhero fight: *Kapow! Zowee! Zing! Take that!*

We sit there in a happy heap, looking up at the dazzling explosions, and then it dawns on me; all the places I have been in the world hoping to have a profound thought or revelation – gawping out across the Grand Canyon, standing beside the Ganges river, closing my eyes as the Islamic call to prayer wafts over me in waves of Arabian heat – and here I am having the least earth-shattering thought and it's far and away my favourite:

I really like it here. I really, really do . . .

19

It's still dark when Sebastien comes to collect me at the auberge. I'm so disorientated I almost climb into the boot along with my overnight bag, packed to cover all eventualities.

Though I am somewhat loathe to leave Quebec, I am more than a little curious about meeting Jacques' father, because it will be like discovering another aspect to this man who has quickly become the focus of my day. And perhaps it will clarify the link between two such different brothers, though it may just be the inherited athleticism Jacques referenced when we had lunch at Parliament yesterday. I smile to myself. Parliament indeed! Quebec is a hard act to follow!

It's only when the sun starts to rise and I reach the halfway point in my flask of coffee that I regain my ability to converse. Much to Sebastien's disappointment.

'It's flatter than I was expecting.' I peer out of the window at the endless fields, accented with the occasional barn. 'I think of Canada and I think of the Rockies, all vast lakes and mountains . . .'

'We are the second largest country in the world,' he informs me. 'We have room for a little topographical variety.'

Well that told me!

'Here,' he reaches behind him then hands me a map book. 'Take a look.'

I open it onto the relevant page and he points to Quebec.

'Our province alone is three times the size of France.'

'Eyes on the road!' I urge, though really it seems to be a straight shot all the way to Montreal.

As I look closer, I see our route is speckled with saints – Saint-Celestin, Saint-Hyacinthe, Saint-Lazare-de-Bellechasse . . . Even, rather pleasingly, a Saint-Bernard.

'Now that's my kinda town,' I chuckle as I hold up the map. 'Saint-Pie!'

'It's named for Saint Pius.'

'Oh,' I slump. 'That's not quite so much fun.'

'*Tarte*!'

'Excuse me?!' Oh my goodness, did Sebastien just enter into a little playful banter with me?

Er, no.

'*Tarte*: t-a-r-t-e,' he spells out the word. 'That is French for the kind of pie you like. As in Tarte Tatin.'

'Ohhh.' I'm getting hungry now but continue to distract myself as I can't see my driver wanting to stop. 'What about this place?' I point out a town called Asbestos. 'Does that mean something different in French?'

He shakes his head. 'That town once had the largest asbestos mine in the world.'

'And they wanted to advertise the fact?'

'It was before the dangers were discovered.' Sebastien's fingers strum the steering wheel. 'That community was thriving in the Sixties.'

'It says here that Montreal is twin-towned with Hiroshima,' I note. 'I'm starting to notice a worrying theme . . .'

He is not amused. I decide to lose the jokes and go for a more conventional line of questioning.

'So is Montreal where you grew up?'

'Born and bred.'

'And Jacques?'

'No, he was born in Quebec. He stayed with his mother when my father left.'

'Oh. So you actually didn't grow up in the same house?'

'No.'

'But you're so close now . . .'

'Well, we would have holidays together. He was always very protective of me – being ten years older.'

'And now you're returning the favour?'

'I owe him.'

'You owe him?' I raise a brow.

He gives me a warding-off glance but I ignore it.

'In what way do you owe him?'

'I owe him my life.'

For a second I say nothing. This sounds serious. But then Sebastien has a way of making everything sound dramatic.

'It's because of him I joined Cirque du Soleil.'

'Really?' I brighten. 'So it's a good kind of payback?'

'I lost my way as a teenager. Jacques got me back on track.'

Something tells me that drugs were involved. This would perhaps have been around the time of his parents' divorce. He went off the rails, Jacques put him back on and suddenly his life goes into warp-drive with Cirque du Soleil. Strange that he thinks his debt of gratitude would include giving up the thing he loves the most. Can't he see what a burden that is to Jacques?

Then again, depending on the drugs he took, maybe he doesn't exactly think straight.

'What are you thinking?' Sebastien asks me, suspiciously.

'Just how incredible it is that you got to perform with Cirque du Soleil.'

'Have you ever seen any of their shows?'

'Oh yes. I'm a huge fan. I even applied for a job there once. Just as an usher when they had their big top in London, in Battersea. I thought it would be fantastic – show people to their seats and then stand there, night after night, gawping up at the stage. There's always so much going on, I knew I'd never get bored . . .'

The truth is my own life seemed so dull at the time; I longed to escape into their fantasy world, even vicariously.

'And did you?'

'Well, they said they were having trouble finding English-speakers so they wanted me to work in the box office and answer telephones, but that wasn't quite so appealing.'

'They had trouble finding English-speakers in England?'

'Well, London in particular is such a melting pot, we've become quite the rarity!'

'So which shows did you see?' Sebastien can't help be curious.

I twist around in my seat. 'Where do I begin? In Vegas I saw *Mystère*, *O*, *Zumanity* and *Kà*, which blew my mind. Basically all of them except the Beatles one.'

'Everything except *Love*?'

The comment seems oddly personal so I move swiftly on. '*Saltimbanco*, *Alegría*, *Quidam* . . . And then, not so long ago, I saw the *Michael Jackson Immortal* show.'

'What did you think about that?'

'Well, it was probably the one I was least interested in seeing but it was worth it for the ring routine to "Can You Feel It?"'

'And what was so great about that?'

'It just got me – the music was pumping, it's such a rousing song anyway, and you've got these four guys in their metallic helmets and bare chests with their arms twisting every which way like Action Man figures . . .' For a second it's as if they have appeared before my eyes. 'They're swinging so high, flying through the air at the perfect crescendo moments . . . it just seemed so powerful.'

Sebastien splutters a laugh.

'What?'

'That's what I used to do.'

'No!' I squeal.

'That is a great song.'

'But what does it feel like?' I ask, practically up on my knees now. 'To be out there – part of such a spectacle?'

'Well, obviously you're concentrating on hitting your marks, but when the group does a spinning dismount and you hear the audience gasp, it does give you a thrill.'

'Can you sense it, when you've got them? I mean, there seemed to be a point at which the whole arena was spellbound . . .'

He nods. 'The energy changes, for sure.'

'Oh I can't believe it! I can't believe I'm in a car with someone so cool!'

Sebastien rolls his eyes.

'I mean it. I'm a bit in awe now.'

'Being able to do a backflip doesn't make you a better person.'

'It does in my book,' I tell him. 'Did you ever perform with Julie?'

Immediately his face falls. I've gone too far.

'Perhaps you should get some sleep.' He grunts. 'There is much to see in the city, far to walk. You don't want to be tired when we arrive.'

I think about trying to make things right with him, apologising or changing the subject, but what he seems to want most of all is my silence. Best I leave him in peace with his own thoughts.

Settling back into my seat, I give the landscape another scan: it remains all bare trees and frozen lakes, some stamped with tyre tracks – I try to follow their trail, wondering if the .

car made it back to solid ground, but we're moving too fast . . .

I suppose it wouldn't hurt to get a little more shut-eye . . . Discreetly I remove my scarf and roll it into a substitute pillow so I can rest my head on the juddering window. The next thing I know I'm surrounded by skyscrapers.

I sit up and pay attention. 'Gosh, it really is a lot bigger here.'

Three times bigger than Quebec, Sebastien tells me. And an island. (Surrounded by rivers, as opposed to the sea.)

'There is an area at the heart of the city, a mountain or a hill, either way, five hundred acres with a park and a lake and cemeteries with a million bodies buried.'

'A million?' My eyes bulge as I imagine Cirque du Soleil re-enacting *Thriller* here, what a chorus line that would be!

'It is called Mont Royal,' Sebastien continues, clearly happy to be back on a neutral subject.

'Mont Royal,' I repeat. Why does that sound familiar?

'That is how Montreal got its name.'

'Ohhh!' I smile. 'I didn't know that.'

'If it was summer I would take you there.'

'But it's not.'

'No, it's not,' Sebastien confirms as we watch a pedestrian turn sideways to shoulder her way through the wind as she crosses in front of us.

The light changes and on we go. The first thing he wants to show me is the Old Town. Sounds familiar.

'I was wondering . . .' I try to sound casual. 'For breakfast, I've heard about this place called Toi, Moi et Café?'

'Jacques already made me promise to take you there. But first I want you to see this.'

He pulls over beside a greying cathedral. 'Notre-Dame Basilica.'

Perhaps he senses that I'm not entirely sold because he adds, 'This is where Celine Dion got married.'

Now I'm curious. 'Can we look inside?'

He allows me to step in first, so he can stand to the side and watch my jaw drop.

Gloriana! I don't know that I've experienced a more vibrant, spirit-lifting cathedral. I've seen opulent, I've seen ornate, but this one has an almost Disney-like glow . . .

The dominant colour is blue – a luminous mix of azure and cobalt – with a gold centrepiece that is almost a kingdom unto itself, with its multitude of arches, spires, statuettes and, rather comically, a Hoover abandoned on the carpeted steps leading to the altar.

Even the stained-glass windows seem more colourful – beyond the traditional blood reds and royal blues they feature subtler, prettier shades like blush pink and lilac.

'This is just gorgeous!' I whisper, lured from gem to gem. 'I love how these pillars look like the spines of old books – you know those leather ones with the gold detailing?'

Before Sebastien can reply, his phone bleeps. 'I have to take this.'

'I'll wait here,' I tell him, happy to do so.

Until, that is, a young couple pass me . . .

They are being escorted to the rather more affordable chapel at the back, and suddenly I find myself transported back to my own wedding day. Knees weakening, I stumble to the nearest pew and then turn back, as if I am looking at myself, walking up the aisle . . .

I was so determined not to get caught up in wedding hysteria I went for a very simple dress and then I wondered, just before I stepped out, whether I was short-changing my groom in some way, not giving him a major transformation to gasp at. Was I deliberately trying to play things down? It seemed such a big statement, getting married – so much further to fall. Did some part of me always know it wouldn't work out, or was that just me trying to keep a level head? I couldn't understand how people managed to go cock-a-hoop at a time when divorce seems more likely than seeing your first anniversary. How do you buy into the eternity ideal any more?

But on the day itself, all cynicism went out the window and I found myself on an unexpected high – I had never felt so bonded with another person. As we stood at the altar I could barely differentiate between us and it felt wonderful to go 'all in'. The ultimate free-fall!

And everyone around us just seemed so pleased for us. I hadn't expected that – so much well-wishing. It seemed too good to be true – I get your love and that of everyone around me too?

Who wouldn't want that to last?

Sitting here now, I wonder whether he ever really loved me or whether it was all about the possibility of what I could bring to his life. Not even a month after we first met we started talking about our children – what they would look like, which of our personality traits we'd most wish upon them and how we would bring them up, possibly on a diet of cereal since neither of us could cook. It was such fun – the idea of creating something so deeply personal *together*. Andrew never really liked his job and I think he viewed his future children as his life's work. Well, I hope that works out for him. I hope that baby growing inside the sandwich girl's tummy doesn't feel too much pressure to be his everything. I hope he allows for some mistakes and doesn't cut little Him or Her off if they don't turn out to be perfect.

My eyes prickle. I'm doing it again. Upsetting myself. Rummaging around in a hurtful place, stirring up resentment, just making it worse. I have to stop this. Think a different thought. Set myself in motion . . .

I get to my feet, turning towards the silent prayer room, but then finding myself confronted with a painting of Madonna and child. I expect to feel another stab of pain but there is something so serene about this place that instead I find myself lighting a candle, both for the baby that never was and the one that might yet come into my life. Because that does happen. Sometimes a baby finds a different mother in the world. There's still hope.

And then I move on and light a bright yellow one for Laurie and all her New York City dreams. Another three dollar coins in the donation box, I choose snow white for Jacques, then strawberry red for Mrs Laframboise, and for Sebastien I choose blue.

'If you're going to light every candle in this place, it's going to get expensive.'

I turn and smile at him. 'That one was for you!'

He looks so taken aback I wonder if it's a bit much – the idea of being 'prayed for' – so I tone it down by adding, 'To thank you for bringing me to Montreal.'

'Oh. Okay.' He shrugs. 'A bagel would've done the trick.'

20

Stepping back into the sunny chill of the outside world, Sebastien tells me that he's going to leave the rest of Vieux-Montreal for me to explore at my leisure. But barely two minutes later he's pulling over again, this time beside Place Jacques Cartier – an elongated pedestrian square leading down to the river.

'Guy Laliberté used to perform here as a stilt-walker and fire-breather.'

My head clunks the window. This is where Cirque du Soleil began? I can't help but get a thrill.

'Now you can go around the corner and eat at his restaurant – L'Auberge Saint-Gabriel. We've had some good parties there . . .'

I take out my notebook and write down the name, intending to make that my dinner spot later.

'This may be a silly question, since the whole world is in awe, but is Cirque du Soleil well received by the locals?'

'Oh yes, very much so,' Sebastien affirms. 'Everyone has great respect for all they have achieved. And every year Guy shows his gratitude to the province by putting on a show for free.'

'That's fantastic!'

'The headquarters that he built here with the training facility, he deliberately chose a poor part of town and employed local people to bring that area up.'

'Wow,' I say. 'How many people would you say work there today?'

'About eighteen hundred.'

'What?' I exclaim.

'About four hundred of those are in the wardrobe department.'

'My goodness.'

'This is Boulevard Saint-Laurent by the way . . .' He motions beyond the windscreen. 'It bisects the city from north to south. The French-speaking typically live to the east, the Anglophones – that's your people – to the west.'

'How interesting . . .'

'All the way up here you will see different immigrant communities – Jewish, Chinese, Italian, Portuguese, Greek, Arab, Haitian . . .'

'Just like Cirque du Soleil!' I laugh.

'Do you know about the One Drop foundation?' he asks as we turn off into a new neighbourhood, one with more of a trendy, boutique feel.

'One Drop?' I shake my head.

Sebastien explains that Guy Laliberté has partnered with Oxfam to bring water to people in countries where access to this vital resource is lacking – El Salvador, India, Honduras, and so on.

'I went out to Nicaragua last year with one of the touring shows and it's not just the water projects they're working on,' he enthuses, 'they're doing all this great work to promote gender equality and get the young people motivated about building a brighter future.'

'Really?'

He nods intently. 'We ran these workshops with all these kids and teens, got them involved. It was *incredible* . . .'

Watching Sebastien talk about this is like meeting a new person – his grumpy shell falling away as a dynamic, passionate and *com*passionate man emerges.

As we pull up outside Toi, Moi et Café, I turn to him, unable to keep it in any longer.

'Aren't you tired?'

'I'm fine,' he says, unclicking his seat belt. 'I don't need much sleep.'

'I mean of watching over Jacques. Don't you miss having your own *utterly remarkable* life? Being around your fellow performers? Working on such meaningful projects? Doing what you love and what you are obviously brilliant at?'

A cloud crosses back over his eyes. 'Yes, I miss it. Of course I do. But I'd miss Jacques a whole lot more if he were gone.'

'But what if he's not going anywhere?'

'Have you ever thought you had lost someone?' he turns on me, blunt as ever. 'Had someone taken from you before their time?'

I shake my head.

'When I got the phone call, that Jacques had fallen in the frozen lake . . . the line cut out. And while I was stood there, shaking, waiting to reconnect, I thought they were going to tell me he had died.' His lips purse as he fights to steady his voice. 'In that moment, I experienced losing him. I felt it, as if it was real. So when they told me he had survived, it was like I had been given a second chance. That's when I knew I had to be there for him. Because I never wanted to have that phone call or that feeling ever again.'

I sigh. 'But Sebastien, do you really believe he would want to take his own life?'

'Who knows what anyone would do under those circum-stance, until it happens to you. Everyone reacts differently. I have Russian friends at the Cirque who heard that a family member died just minutes before they were going on stage, and they carry on and perform as flawlessly as ever – it doesn't even faze them because for them it's the norm, a part of circus life. The high wire is dangerous, the trapeze is dangerous . . .' He pauses. 'But to feel somehow responsible for another person's death, as Jacques does with Rémy . . .'

'That has to be nigh on unbearable,' I concur.

We sit for a moment in silence. And then I say: 'You know one thing I know for sure?'

He looks warily up at me. 'What's that?'

'Breakfast is on me.'

I don't know that I've seen a more cheerful-looking breakfast platter. My two bright white boiled eggs are sitting in crayon-coloured cups, my toast soldiers are golden crispy strips of ciabatta, the melon (both orange gala and green honeydew) comes in smiley slices, there's a heap of roasted breakfast potatoes, a mini-portion of baked beans, a triangle of cheese and – the pièce de résistance – a baked apple with shiny puckered skin!

My stomach groans with longing.

'I have to take a picture of this.'

'I've never understood why people do that.'

'That's because everything is so beautifully presented here, you're spoiled. You want to spend a bit of time in England, where most things arrive in a hope-for-the-best dollop.'

'You know one of your chefs has a restaurant here.'

'One of *my* chefs?'

'Gordon Ramsay. His restaurant Laurier is just across the street.'

'Have you eaten there?'

'No, but I know he has fish and chips on the menu as well as poutine.'

Oh the dreaded poutine! I can't help but grimace.

'You know you've got to try it. It's the signature dish of Quebec.'

Mercifully our conversation is interrupted by the barista coming out from behind the counter. It seems he's an old friend of Sebastien's and the two chat intensely in French while I sit back with my baklava latte. I kid you not – honeyed latte, flavoured with four syrups (three nut and one lemon), topped with whipped cream and cinnamon.

I'm telling you, I could practically move to Montreal on the basis of this café alone.

It's not just the menu – I love the mix of people in here; all ages appear through the curtains shrouding the front door to take a seat at one of the tarnished copper tables. The floor is wooden, the ceiling dark-beamed, and the coffee has its own silver-scooped filing system behind the bar. I like how the special roasts – from Yemen Mocha Mattari to Jamaican Blue Mountain – are listed on a gold-framed blackboard. I like how the waitress remains smiley and attentive despite the crush and I really like the look of the chocolate gateaux in the glass display case . . .

Maybe I'll come back later for a slice and a slurp of Teaquila Sunset – Darjeeling tea with orange juice, triple sec and golden rum. Wow.

But for now it's time to move on.

We're just heading out through the door, with me using two hands to carry my tummy, when I remember:

'Didn't we have to bring your dad some coffee?'

'He won't drink it from here,' Sebastien replies. 'He's purely an Olimpico guy.'

'Olimpico as in the Olympics?'

'Well, it's really more of a spectator sport place. You'll see. But you do know we held the Olympic Games here in 1976?'

'Mmm-hmm,' I say, though of course I didn't.

'Are you keeping up with the Kardashians?'

'Excuse me?'

'Kim Kardashian's stepdad Bruce Jenner won gold here that year.'

'I didn't even know he was an athlete.'

'Decathlete,' he specifies.

'You're pretty good with all your facts and figures . . .' I smile.

'Well my dad's last girlfriend was a schoolteacher.'

'Busy man.'

'Excuse me?'

'You know, with the women.'

Sebastien stops suddenly. 'Have you slept with more than three men?'

'What?'

'You think because he's been married twice and had one other girlfriend that makes him some kind of player?'

'Oh. No. I'm sorry.' This is awful. Why do I keep upsetting him like this? 'I didn't mean to sound disrespectful.'

'He was with my mother for seventeen years, Jacques' mother for twelve. Can you match that?'

'No,' I say quietly, following him across the road. I'm sticking to neutral subjects from now on. Observations about the city and the range of enticing shops, including this rather unusual furniture store . . .

'Oh look!' I try to jolly things along. 'This sofa cover is made entirely of jeans!'

No response.

He really is ultra-protective of his family members. Ordinarily that would be an admirable trait; he just seems to take the form of barbed wire while doing so.

'I think I'm going to have a quick nose in this bookshop while you're in the café,' I say as he opens the door to Olimpico, all Italian flags and football on TV.

He looks over to Librairie L'Écume des Jours and sighs mournfully, 'I used to go there with Julie . . .'

'I just can't win with him,' I complain to Laurie when I sneakily dial her from the street corner. 'One minute we seem to be getting along fine, and then he'll flare up and take offence at the merest thing.'

'In my experience people who behave like that – all mad at the world – are typically mad at themselves.'

'Hurt people hurt people,' I confirm.

'Right. And I understand that the solution seems so obvious to you – "Move back to Montreal and resume your life!"'

'*Yes!*'

'But he's so blocked, seeing what he's missing might just piss him off more.'

'Oh great.'

'Hang in there. Give him a bit of space. And pick out a cool book for me.'

Laurie and I have this thing that whenever I travel abroad I buy her a book in a foreign language that she will never read but that has a totally intriguing cover or title.

I'm spoilt for choice here:

'LA LIBERTÉ N'EST PAS UNE MARQUE DE YOGOURT.'

'ÊTES-VOUS MARIÉE À UN PSYCHOPATHE?'

I even rather like the look of one of those 'For Dummies' titles in French.

'LE SAXOPHONE POUR LES NULS.'

And then I inadvertently find myself in the maternity section, immediately drawn to a book with a cartoon of a mother holding her little bundle of joy up in the air – as vomit spews out of his mouth in a fountain-like arc towards her face.

Though I may not be able to translate all the captions and speech bubbles, the cartoons are easily understood. On the left page we have *La Rêve*: a slim, pony-tailed woman

power-walking with her babystroller in the park. On the right
we have *La Réalité*: A woman slouched on her couch in front
of the TV, hand in a bag of crisps. And then I discover the
French word for pregnancy – *la grossesse!* How could a country so chic have a word like that for women in their prime?
Or perhaps that's how they feel when they can no longer fit
into their petite Chanel suits.

As I flick through the pages, I am reminded just how much
I idealise being a mum. When you are denied something it's
all too easy to focus on all the picture-perfect moments – all
that dimply glee and squidgy cuddling – and overlook the
daily slog. I don't even have the basics of domesticity down
– my fridge magnet says it all: *I understand the concept of cooking and cleaning. Just not as it applies to me.* And I'm certainly
not the type who could pop a kiddiwink in a backpack and
continue about my business. If I'm really, really honest about
the kind of mother I would have been, the truth is probably
chaotic, exhausted, with finger-paint on my T-shirt and
assorted cereals in my hair.

'Ready?' Sebastien leans his head in.

I fluster a little as I prop the book back on the shelf, hoping
he hasn't seen the title, and hurry to his side.

'What's in the bag?' I ask as we head back to the car.

'Biscotti,' he replies. 'It's my dad's favourite.'

I go to make a comment about him having strong teeth,
but that would probably imply that I'm surprised that a man
his age can still crunch and thus be construed as an insult, so
I say nothing.

What I think, however, is this: *Oh my god, I'm about to meet
the parent!*

21

'I really like this neighbourhood,' I tell Sebastien as I eye the cute terraced houses with their quirky roof adornments, jutting balconies and twiddly ironwork. 'Is this where you grew up?'

'Right here.' Sebastien pulls into a parking spot outside a big redbrick building with angular bay windows, and honks his horn.

Seconds later a handsome, rather robust-looking man appears at the top of the exterior staircase.

'That's your dad?' I peer up at him.

'You sound surprised.'

'He's so young-looking.'

'He's only fifty-six.'

'I suppose it was all the talk of him visiting the physio . . .' Honestly I was expecting someone frail and entirely reliant on his stick. Here he is grinning down at me like some fair-haired Alec Baldwin.

'*Bonjour*, Krista! *Bonjour*!'

He knows my name?

'What do you think of my staircase?'

I look back at Sebastien. 'Is that a traditional Montreal greeting?'

'Tell him you think it's curvaceous.'

'*What?*'

'Do it. He'll love it.'

I take a breath. 'It's wonderfully curvaceous!' I call up to him.

'Yes yes!' he claps his hands together. 'That's right, come on up.'

'Was that the secret password?' I frown.

'It just tickles him because it's irreverent.'

Sebastien explains that, back in the day, the church insisted all buildings had outside staircases so everyone's comings and goings could be witnessed – no covert activity.

'But then the residents got creative with the designs and the sensual curves were considered too *provocative*—'

'You're joking!'

'I am not. So they said all the staircases had to be covered up and boxed in.'

'No!'

'But now, in these more liberated days, they have been exposed again.'

'Gosh. Every city has its story, huh?'

His father reappears on the top step. 'What does a person have to do to get a cup of coffee around here?'

I suppose, after seeing what he did to Jacques' office, I should have guessed that Mr Dufour would not go the minimalist route with his home decor. Every inch of wall and shelf space is housing some award, ribbon, trophy or celebratory photo. There is even a framed ice hockey jersey – red, white and blue.

'Montreal Canadiens,' I read the plaque. 'You used to play?'

'Not me,' Sebastien replies. 'My dad. Still does.'

'Not professionally any more, just with friends,' he explains as he returns from the kitchen with a team mug to pour his Olimpico coffee into. 'That's how I messed up my damn knee.'

'Dad was their star player back in the day,' Sebastien mumbles dutifully. 'Centre forward.'

'I just liked being called "offensive",' he teases. 'Did you bring the biscotti?'

Sebastien slides the paper bag across the table.

'Krista you have to try this!'

'Oh I couldn't take another bite. I totally overdid it at breakfast.'

He snaps me off a piece regardless. 'For later.'

'Thank you!'

'So,' he turns to Sebastien. 'How does it feel to be back in Montreal?'

He shifts in his chair. 'All right I guess.'

'That's it?'

Sebastien shrugs.

'Lucky he's not writing for your website,' Mr Dufour winks at me.

They make some more small talk. Sebastien not really giving anything away, possibly because I am here, and then Mr Dufour says:

'You know, I was helping Mr Tremblay across the street draw up his will and I want you to know that when I die I'm leaving this place to you.'

Sebastien looks uncomfortable. 'Me and Jacques.'

'No, Jacques already has a home. Your home is here.' He sighs. 'When are you coming home, son?'

'Dad we've been through this . . .' Sebastien squirms.

'He worries too much.' Mr Dufour addresses me. 'And I worry about him worrying.' He shakes his head. 'What a fine pair.' He takes a sip of coffee. 'So how is Jacques?'

'He's okay—'

'I was talking to Krista.'

At which point Sebastien decides that he needs to sort a few items in his old room.

I wait until he closes the door behind him before I reply.

'I think he's wonderful. I mean, I only met him four days ago so I can't give you a comprehensive review . . .'

'No, but you can give me the most up-to-date unbiased opinion.'

'Well, then I'd say he's doing very well. All things considered.'

'How is his pain level?'

I hesitate. 'You mean emotional pain?'

He nods.

'It's present,' I say quietly.

'Palpable?'

'Yes.' I can't lie. 'You can see it in his eyes.'

Mr Dufour hangs his head. 'I wish there was something I could do to ease it. But you can't hurry those kind of feelings along.'

'No.'

'Sometimes I think Sebastien is overreacting and other times . . . I just don't know.'

I feel a twinge of concern. Is Jacques more troubled than I know?

He smiles suddenly. 'He has certainly sounded brighter since he met you.'

'Really?' I just know I'm flushing pink now. 'I feel the same way.'

'Sometimes a stranger can do more than family.'

'I hope you don't think I'm intruding.' Now *I'm* worrying!

'Not at all.' He reaches for my hand. 'I don't give pieces of my biscotti away to just anyone.'

I smile back at him. 'Citron-pistachio?'

'Go on, taste it!'

I'm just splintering into it when there is an almighty crash from the other room – an avalanche of books falling? A decade of things shoved onto the top shelf now unleashed?

'Dad!' Sebastien calls out.

Mr Dufour rolls his eyes. 'For someone so graceful in the air he sure can be clumsy on dry land.' He gets to his feet. 'Make yourself at home.'

By which I take him to mean 'Feel free to snoop'. So I do.

Of course I am initially scanning for pictures of Jacques. And there are plenty, all of which leave me with a sloppy look of longing on my face. Except perhaps the group photo where he appears to be partnered with an outdoorsy-looking woman. Still, we all have our exes. Those people we used to orbit around and now avoid. I imagine walking down a long gallery of all my former loves, and I use 'loves' in the broadest sense of the word. As I contemplate each face I respond with a twitch or flinch or sneer or shudder and an endless mantra of '*What was I thinking?*' But the only one it hurts to look at is Andrew. Though, I have to say, the pain feels somewhat dulled today. I heave a sigh. Wouldn't it be nice to leave all these men behind for good? To see one face and feel only positive things. I lean closer to an image of Jacques laughing in the sunshine and feel brimful of admiration and adoration.

All I need now is the reciprocation.

I think I might help myself to a glass of water when an image of a young First Nation girl catches my eye.

Her dark hair is parted in the middle but, rather than being plaited, it is bound with suede laces. Around her neck sits a bone choker, the yoke of her dress is beaded and fringed, her delicate hands hold a collection of feathers. There's a luminous quality to her dark eyes as she looks beyond the camera, the beginning of a smile forming on her lips. Even though she must still be in her teens she looks both poised and purposeful. Just as I take the frame in my hands, I feel Mr Dufour's presence beside me.

'Oh!' I step back. 'I hope you don't mind me looking – she's so beautiful . . .'

'That's Jacques' mother.'

I look up in surprise.

'She's just like him – not a bad bone in her body.'

'Is she . . . ?' I falter. Do I say First Nation?

'Cree,' he replies.

'Wow. Stunning.'

'Of course that's not a recent picture. We were sixteen when that was taken.'

'That's when you met?'

He nods and then smiles wide: 'She would only agree to go out with me if I could learn to spell the longest Cree chief name in history.'

I raise a brow.

'You want to hear it?'

I nod eagerly.

He takes a deep breath and then spells out: 'A-h-c-h-u-c-h-h-w-a-h-a-u-h-h-a-t-o-h-a-p-i-t!'

'What?' I hoot, insisting he writes it down. Ahchuchhwa-hauhhatohapit.

'That's dedication!' I marvel.

'Oh, she was worth it! Best summer of my life. I still think fondly of her.' He sighs. 'But you change a lot from a teen-ager to a man. Especially to a sportsman.'

He looks mildly regretful, like perhaps the game was not worth the sacrifice.

'There were a lot of demands in those days, a lot of adren-alin, a lot of travel . . .'

I nod, not wishing to pry too much. 'Does she still live in Quebec?'

He nods. 'She's away north at the moment. Helping her mother.'

I look back at the other photographs. 'Is Sebastien's mother here?'

He pulls a face. 'We're not on quite such good terms . . .'

'But you were together nearly twenty years!' I can't help but blurt.

'And they were mostly good, but things didn't end well.' He begins opening drawers and rifling through papers. 'She's got to be here somewhere . . .'

I smile. 'I was just curious, there's no need—'

'Here!' He holds out a snap of a blonde woman crouched beside a baby dangling from a doorway in a baby bouncer.

I can't help but chuckle – even as a child Sebastien was catapulting skyward!

'Look at this one!' He shows me another shot of a pre-peroxide Sebastien in double-jointed gymnastics pose.

'So Jacques doesn't have a bad bone in his body and Sebastien doesn't have any at all?' I hoot.

'Looks that way, doesn't it!' Mr Dufour laughs.

'In a way he was preparing for Cirque du Soleil from the age of . . .'

'He started taking classes at five.'

'Wow. And then was it a straight transition through?'

'Well. There was a gap. He stopped for a while.'

My eyes flash towards the door.

'He's gone down to the basement, he can't hear us.'

'Teenage rebellion?' I suggest, tallying up what Sebastien had told me in the car.

'Oh, he took that to a whole new level. There was nothing I could say . . . It got so bad, Rémy had to call Jacques to step in.'

Oh dear, so he was in trouble with the police.

'And Jacques managed to turn things around?'

'At a price.'

I wait for him to continue.

'He had to give up his place in the Iditarod, the year he

was set to break a record. That's months of training and about thirty thousand dollars down the drain.'

My eyes widen.

'Of course Sebastien paid him back the money a few years later. He's been trying to make it up to him ever since.'

'Doesn't he know that he doesn't need to?'

'I think he always felt that if he didn't suffer in some way, if he didn't have to give up something truly precious, then it wouldn't be equal.'

I shake my head.

'Catholic guilt. That's from his mother's side . . .'

I nod. And then I get a little bold. It just seems too good an opportunity to pass up, finding the answer to something that has been bothering me since the first day I met Sebastien.

'It seems like he doesn't want Jacques to get involved with anyone romantically?'

'He just doesn't want him to get hurt. You know, on top of everything else, if he met someone and then that person went away – losing someone else he cares about . . .'

'Right,' I gulp.

And then I realise that when Sebastien said, 'You can't save him!' it may well have been because he felt that it was *his* job – he was the one who needed to return the favour. Especially since he too was connected to Rémy, perhaps even has residual guilt for causing him trouble way back when.

I hear the sound of boots coming up the stairs so switch my attention back to the awards.

'You must be so proud,' I say. 'Of all your sons have accomplished . . .'

Mr Dufour pulls a face. 'They think I'm too proud – I like to display the accolades, solid proof that I did something good with my life.'

'But you've done so much in your own right!' I gasp, surprised he could ever doubt that.

He shrugs. 'It's not where you start, it's where you finish. I didn't expect to be living alone at this age.'

I feel a pang of empathy. That's always been my greatest fear – you give your all but still end up solo. With regrets.

'You know, life can surprise you at any moment,' I tell him in earnest. 'Someone new can take your breath away.' I look back at the photo of Jacques' mother. 'Or someone can come back into your life . . .'

'Speaking of which!' He rouses himself as Sebastien returns. 'Are you going to see Julie while you're here?'

Sebastien groans. 'I've been waiting for you to ask that.'

'I like Julie.'

'I know, Dad.'

Mr Dufour looks at me. 'First time I saw her I said, "That's the girl who's going to give me grandchildren."' He shrugs. 'I'm still waiting, but I haven't given up hope there.'

I feel my nails dig into my palms. Please don't ask me about babies . . .

'I like having them around, children. I like how blunt they are – they sock it to you, right between the eyes!'

'Okay dad, I'm sure Krista wants to be getting on her way . . .'

'And what are your plans for the day, young lady?'

'Well,' I prepare to set myself in motion, 'I'm basically going to try and see as many of Montreal's attractions as possible before sunset.'

'Are you taking her to the Cirque HQ?'

Sebastien gives his father a stern look.

'I bet you'd like to see it . . .' Mr Dufour eggs me on.

'Who wouldn't like to peek behind the scenes of the greatest shows on earth?' My eyes gleam back at him.

'And it is just fifteen minutes' drive from here . . .' He continues his campaigning.

'I thought you needed the car.' Sebastien's eyes narrow.

'Not for a couple of hours. Don't you still have some of your personal items there?'

'Yes.'

'So, it would be a good opportunity to pick them up. And you've got reason to keep it brief if you don't want to get into it with everyone – you're showing a British travel writer around the city and you're on a tight schedule . . .'

Even Sebastien can't argue with that.

'All right,' he concedes. 'But we're in, we're out and we're on our way. Deal?'

'Deal!' I lie.

22

I had expected the building to have an other-wordly design, like Gaudi's free-form fantasies in Barcelona or a multi-storey big top, but it's far more angular and industrial than that – a futuristic version of a Slough office block on the vastest possible scale.

As we make the trek across the car park, I see Sebastien mentally psyching himself up. And me for that matter.

'There's going to be a lot to look at but I need you to keep moving,' he urges.

He's asking a lot. Our first stop is the costume department and my eyes are darting every which way trying to take in all the bolts of fabric, the avant-garde headdresses and row upon row of white moulded heads – casts taken to represent every performer from chubby-cheeked bowling balls to oblongs with imposing Roman noses.

Everyone is busy doing intricate, hand-crafted work – dyeing, stitching, boot-making . . . It's amazing to think how much creativity this one building holds.

'*Sebastien!*' I hear his name called out in every possible accent as we move among the workstations.

Costume, make-up, marketing, canteen, lockers – everywhere we go the reaction is the same: absolute delight to see him again, and then three questions:

'Where've you been?'

'What are you doing here?'

Belinda Jones

'When are you coming back?'

He deftly dodges any definites but with each encounter I see his resolve to keep everyone at a distance slackening. One guy, who I discern to be a Higher Up, tells him that there's a place for him on a European tour leaving next week. And Julie's part of the show.

My heart loops at the possibility. He just nods. The guy then places an arm on Sebastien's shoulder and leads him through to the hangar-like studio where the aerial acts perfect their skills.

It's impossible not to stare at their bodies. Not just because of their highly evolved muscle tone, but also the way they conduct themselves – the grace, posture, flexibility and incredible strength. By comparison I feel like a wobbling blancmange.

And then a petite redhead enters the room, dressed in a shimmering, skin-tight bodysuit that changes colour with the light, her eye make-up a sparkling blaze. It's like the parting of the Red Sea as the performers clear a path for her, a path leading to Sebastien.

I can tell, simply from the way he is looking at her, that this is Julie.

She's deeply engrossed in conversation with another woman and then she registers the hush around her and looks up and sees him. For a microsecond she falters, perhaps not quite believing her eyes, and then she sprints, gazelle-like, towards him. Their bodies collide and then, in a seamless move, he places his hands at her waist and lifts her into the air so that her toes are pointing towards the ceiling and their faces are nose-to-nose. For a second I think he's going to lower her into a kiss, but instead he drops her into his arms, cradling her as he spins around.

Wow. The range of expression in their bodies is incredible.

Around here, if you said 'someone was so excited they did a backflip', you'd meant it.

'Julie!' It's her turn to rehearse.

She signals back to the trainer and then takes Sebastien's hand. 'Will you join me?'

He can't resist for long, everyone is clamouring for him to strip off and step up. I feel a wild flutter of anticipation as he casts aside his coat, fleece, and even his T-shirt. I always thought he was considerably skinnier than Jacques but his form is extraordinary – lean but sharply sculpted, like a true gymnast. He kicks off his boots and walks barefoot to what I know to be silks – those gleaming skeins of suspended fabric that aerialists bind themselves in. I see him apply what looks like resin to his hands, wrap the fabric around and around his hands and wrists until it is taut. He composes himself, starts to run . . .

And then he takes flight.

My heart soars right along with him as he traverses the room on the smoothest arc . . . I can feel the breeze he creates as he swoops past and my eyes tear up as I imagine the sensation of freedom he must be experiencing up there. This is just so right – Sebastien is someone who needs to feel the air all around him, not be tethered to the earth, even via a fast-moving dog-sled.

And then suddenly Julie is up there with him. Her petite form in perfect synchronicity with his as they entwine, climb, twist and then take a freefall drop, ever in motion, working in exquisite harmony with implicit trust. I am in awe. To me, these people are life's true magicians; what they do seems way beyond the realms of human limitation, only here there is no illusion, it's all real. Just way beyond what us mere mortals can even dream of.

*   *   *

I don't want Sebastien to give a moment's thought to babysitting me, or be the presence pulling his mind back to his other life in Quebec, so as soon as he's back on solid ground I tell him I'm going to scoot off and do some sightseeing.

'Did you have a St-Viateur bagel yet?' one chunky bald chap enquires.

'Noooo, it's got to be a Fairmont bagel!' another protests.

'Or you could have afternoon tea at the Queen Elizabeth Hotel,' the one Brit suggests. 'That's where John Lennon and Yoko Ono had their bed-in and recorded "Give Peace A Chance".'

'Really?' I marvel.

'Room 1724.'

'Elizabeth Taylor married Richard Burton at the Ritz-Carlton!' A flamboyantly gay guy elbows in. 'You can have tea there too and you won't find liverwurst on the cake stand.'

'What?' I splutter.

'Better than all that,' Julie reaches out to me. 'The cocktails at the Baldwin Barmacie.'

'That's just across from Toi, Moi et Café,' Sebastien chips in.

'You showed her Saint-Laurent Boulevard?' Julie checks. 'There's a super-cute boutique there called Preloved – everything is one of a kind, made from vintage fabrics . . .'

I'm using my phone to record all their suggestions, unable to keep up with pen and paper.

'This is great!' I cheer as they continue to bombard me. Now I can add such captions as: 'As recommended by Cirque du Soleil's Lithuanian juggler' to my guide.

'Will you be all right getting around on the Métro?' Sebastien checks as he walks me to the door.

I assure him that, as an aficionado of the London Underground, I'll be just fine.

'Just don't confuse the subway with the Underground City.'

'What's that?' I ask, feeling slightly creeped-out as I picture a sinister French-speaking community living amid the sewers.

'It's this insane underground mall – there're two thousand shops down there.'

'Handy in this weather,' I note. 'Wait, did you say two *thousand*?'

He nods. 'It runs for twenty miles.'

'You keep telling me these things about Montreal that are blowing my mind.'

He gives a 'what can I say?' shrug.

'Of course you can go there,' he adds. 'I just don't think it will show you the best of our city. You could be anywhere.'

'Good point.'

And then he asks me a favour – could I possibly drop the car back at his dad's?

'I can show you how to get there in two streets . . .'

I take a deep breath. 'Okay. I can do that.' I may not be able to place my feet behind my ears but I can depress an accelerator pedal and turn a steering wheel.

'And text me later to let me know if you're getting the train back or staying over.'

'Will do.' I go to push open the door and then turn back, 'Do you need to grab anything from the car before I take off?'

'No, I have everything I need here.'

'Ain't that the truth,' I mutter under my breath as I exit.

23

Returning the car to Mr Dufour is as simple as posting the keys through his letterbox – no doubt he's gone out in his perfectly functioning other vehicle. I smile as I descend his curvaceous staircase and even take a picture of it as a keepsake. And then, a few blocks away, I take a second, rather more industrial set of steps – this time down into the Montreal subway.

I need to go three stops on the orange line and then four on the green. Deep breath . . .

I brace myself for the zombie crush, the inevitable knocks and the possibility of boarding the wrong train because I've got caught up in the rush-hour flow and am unable to swim against the tide. But none of it happens. It's busy, yes, but so calm it's actually a pleasure. And, unlike on the London underground, I don't immediately break into a claustrophobic sweat. Back home I have to adopt the demeanour of a Zen master just to get through the experience. Here there are even little arrows where the train doors open indicating the route for those getting off (straight ahead) and those getting on (angled at the side). And people actually follow them. Not in a sheep-like way, but in a courteous, logical fashion. Because why wouldn't you? Why would you obstruct the people getting off, thus creating more problems? Why would you push? Why would you elbow the person next to you just because you can? This civility really is rocking my world. It's just so nice to feel composed instead of hot and bothered.

My personal theory is that there is more trust here – you don't have to try and quell the panic that you won't make it off the train at your stop before the doors close because there won't be any damn fool standing in your way, unthinkingly blocking the exit.

I suppose it comes back to that dad kneeling beside his boy reminding him to be aware of his surroundings and always respectful . . . It's funny the things that hit you when you're abroad. It used to be all the big, flashy wonders that got my attention, but now it's the little things that register – the things that make you feel different *on the inside*.

And then I go and ruin it all by getting off at the stop for Sainte-Catherine Street.

I may be a travel writer but I'm a girl first, and when they told me this was the major shopping centre of the city, I couldn't resist a look. A choice I'm now regretting. This is even more daunting than Oxford Street – the six-mile drag is lined not just with megastores but *behemoths*. Just contemplating all the super-sized commerciality after the darling personalised boutiques of Mile End makes me feel as if I'm contributing to the end of society as we know it. I know I should just walk away, divert down a side street or dip into this cute little church here, but instead I find myself sucked into Canada's oldest department store – The Bay.

The shop's origin is actually English – founded in 1670 as Hudson's Bay Company, back when our ancestors were bartering knives, kettles, blankets, etc., for beaver pelts from the native trappers. The dense wool blankets proved the most coveted item and are still available today in a classic winter-white with a red, green, yellow and indigo stripe. There's something very cool about the design and I consider a purchase until I see the price tag – nearly £250 for the queen-size! There is a fleece throw for about £20 but it's just not the same. Besides, considering that I live in a city shoebox as opposed to a log cabin, I think this probably qualifies as one of those holiday purchases best left in their natural habitat.

Not that there's anything natural about my immediate environment . . . This first time I've seen women in high-heeled boots, until now we've all been united in the desire to be warm and not skid on the snow, but here I'm back in the land of fashion one-upmanship. I don't like it but I continue to wander around until the strip lights drain every bit of joy from me.

'Laurie!' I call out to her from the lingerie department. 'I need you to give me an audio slap! I'm in a shopping trance and self-loathing is paralysing me!'

'Okay.' She immediately rises to the occasion. 'I want you to walk calmly to the nearest escalator and head for the exit . . .'

'All the shoes!' I gasp.

'Krista . . .'

'They even have flip-flops with the Hudson's Bay stripes!'

'Because flip-flops will be the perfect memento of your trip to the Winter Carnival.'

'But they're so cute!'

'Keep moving past them, tunnel vision; all you need is to get back out into the fresh air.'

'There's a massive Guess store across the street,' I say as I emerge.

'You've never bought anything from Guess in your life.'

'H&M!'

'We have that at home,' she tuts. 'You know what you've got to do . . .'

I take a deep breath. She's right. The only way to purge myself of this feeling is to go to a museum.

I choose the Pointe-à-Callière aka The Montreal Museum of Archeology and History, which may seem like I'm over-compensating but in actuality it's the hippest building at the

Old Port. And home to an innovative multimedia experience showcasing Montreal's evolutionary timeline, with red digital numbers counting us up from prehistoric times to the present day. I learn about the natives who came ashore in the fourteenth century to fish, the French who founded Montreal and the British who barged in and took over in 1760. But the coolest thing is when the floor is illuminated, revealing it to be an excavation of the actual foundations of the original colony, established *right here* in 1642!

By the time I emerge it's getting dark and I'm getting hungry. Everything looks profoundly tempting along the cobbled, twinkly-lit streets of Vieux-Montréal, if a little expensive. I peer in the window of Chez L'Épicier where each plate is a delicate artwork – one bronzed scallop dish has a yacht-sail of proscuitto and individual Brussels sprout leaves scattered like fallen petals. I see a dessert of pale caramel cubes and mystery curly peelings topped with what looks like pink cuckoo spit. I also see diners with a larger budget than myself. In my mind I could only really justify such extravagance at the Guy Laliberté restaurant. I know it was around here somewhere . . .

Walking on, gazing in at so many happy, laughing diners while I shuffle through the snow, hungry and alone, I feel vaguely Dickensian. But then I come upon the cosiest-looking eaterie of all – pine tables, low-hanging, red-glowing lampshades and live piano music. It's called the Stash Café, suggesting a more casual vibe, and before I even realise it, I'm seated at a little table near the bar.

It's only when I'm halfway through the menu that I realise the restaurant is Polish.

Golabki, Krokiety, Watrobka z drobiu po Warszawsku.

The English words I spy aren't much more appetising – tripe, herring, cabbage stew . . .

Suddenly poutine is sounding absolutely yummy.

I look towards the doorway – I don't know if I can face stepping back out into the cold. Besides, my glass of wine has just arrived. I take a sip and then another and then decide to go with it. Who knows, perhaps this will be the best pierogi I've ever had. Not that I've actually had one before . . .

The strange thing is that I'm still thinking about that blanket at The Bay. While waiting for my food, I go onto the shop's online store and discover something far better to recommend to our readers – same design but this time a pure cashmere travel blanket with an eye mask and inflatable pillow – currently on sale for about £75. That's more like it. And for the lumberjack in your life – an axe. I kid you not, Canada's equivalent of Harrods has an axe for sale on its website. I have to forward this link to Laurie! Oop! Text.

It's Sebastien.

'*I'm going to stay over and get an early train back. You?*'

Now I feel like I should switch to champagne! This is fantastic news! Fantastic! I have to tell Jacques, he's going to be so thrilled. Our plan is working!

Typically I'd step outside to make a call but it's too cold and I'm too excited. Not that I have Jacques' number, but at least I can call the farm.

'*Bonsoir.*' A female voice answers sounding slightly out of breath and calling off to someone else in French, but too fast for me to comprehend.

'*Bonsoir,*' I reply. 'Is it possible to have a quick word with Jacques?'

'*Pardon?*'

'Er, *est Jacques ici?*' That's not right. *Ici* is here.

She speaks again in French. Only one word stands out – *lopital*. There's something familiar about that . . . Oh no! It can't be! L'hôpital? 'He's in the hospital?' I say out loud.

'*Oui*.'

And then the line cuts out, just like it did when Sebastien got his fateful call. I dial back in a frenzy. No reply – it just rings and rings and rings . . . I feel utterly nauseous, my body instantly quaking. I call again. Still no reply. What now? I look back at the text message from Sebastien. I'd do anything now to leave him happily in the arms of Julie but I can't possibly keep this from him.

My finger hovers over the dial button – of all people for him to receive this most dreaded of calls. It has to be the person who, just a few hours earlier, insisted that no harm would come to his beloved brother. The very same person who engineered this whole trip leaving Jacques unattended in the first place.

Me.

24

Please let him be all right. Please let Jacques live. Please let this just be an awful coincidence – a sudden appendicitis or injection for a dog bite. Not that any of his dogs would bite him, but perhaps he accidentally stood on a tail or got carried away with puppy play – they have very sharp teeth . . . Let it be no worse than that. No falls in frozen lakes. *Please* . . .

The drive back to Quebec is agonising. Sebastien is both anxious and bristling, Julie is trying to soothe him and I am taking the wheel of her Mini Cooper because the two of them had already got into a second bottle of wine over dinner.

Sebastien decided not to worry his father until he knew more, but we're having trouble finding out any details since no hospital seems to have Jacques listed as a patient. And there's still no reply on the main phone at the farm and Sebastien doesn't have any of the staff's personal numbers because, frankly, he never got on personal terms with them.

I feel sick. This was all down to my meddling. In my desire to make things better, it didn't occur to me that I could make things so much worse. If ever Sebastien needed confirmation that Jacques could not be left, I have now sealed the deal. He's going to be at his side until he dies. I get a chill as I think that thought. Please don't let that be tonight.

After three hours of driving in the darkness, we arrive at the car park of the very hospital where Rémy's body was rushed after the accident. Both men, Sebastien tells me, were card-carrying organ donors, so we have to check every department, beginning with the Emergency Room.

My nausea has increased tenfold now.

'And you are certain she said hospital?' Sebastien grills me for the hundreth time as we enter the lift to try our luck on a different floor.

'Yes,' I say. Though I'm actually getting less and less certain as the night progresses.

Until . . . the lift doors open and there, about to step in and join us, is Jacques.

In normal clothes, no bottom-baring gown.

'What are you doing up?' Sebastien demands, clearly thrown by the absence of heart monitors and intravenous tubes.

'Up?' Jacques looks confused. 'I was just going to get some coffees. What are you doing here?'

'They said . . .' He turns accusingly to me. '*You* said he was in the hospital.'

'I am in the hospital,' Jacques confirms.

'But what are you *doing* here?'

A besotted smile forms on his face. 'You're not going to believe this . . .'

'*What?*'

'You have to wait and see.' He turns and presses a button on the lift console.

'*Tell me!*' Sebastien lurches at him.

Jacques looks back at his ashen brother and becomes suddenly serious. 'You thought . . .'

'No, no!' Sebastien protests, turning away.

'Yes, you did.'

'Okay, I did. Jesus.' He hangs his head. 'If I lost you . . .'

'You won't.' Jacques lays a steady hand on Sebastien's trembling shoulder. 'You can't lose me. I am your brother. I am always your brother. Even when you can't see me.' He takes a breath. 'And if you need proof that I would never do what you think I would do, come and look at this . . .'

We exit the lift and follow Jacques down a corridor. About halfway down he gently pushes open a door and reveals a group of people crowding around a young woman with a freshly produced baby in her arms.

For a second I think I might faint. Is Jacques a new father?

'Who is that?' Sebastien asks.

'Look at the baby. Recognise anyone?'

Sebastien looks confused. 'I don't understand, what's going on?'

Jacques gets a wry look now. 'Rémy slept with a girl the night before the accident . . .'

There's a pause while the penny drops.

'That's Rémy's child?!' Sebastien reels.

'Perfect little boy,' he says, looking back at the scrunched face and tufts of inky black hair. 'Seven pounds, seven ounces.'

As we all look back at the baby, I recognise one of the people cooing at the bedside as Johanna Laframboise, a newly inducted grandmother. I dart behind Julie as she turns our way, praying she hasn't seen me.

'I can't believe it,' Sebastien is breathless with shock. 'He lives on. *Rémy lives on!*'

His eyes are glazed with tears now as he throws his arms around his brother – the pair of them clutching at each other, hugging tight as they let go of so much anguish and tension and guilt.

I suddenly feel overwhelmed myself – Rémy has come back to them in a new form: a little being with his whole life ahead of him.

'It's a miracle!' Julie murmurs.

'That's exactly what it is,' I agree.

'And you only just found out?' Sebastien seeks clarification.

'A matter of hours ago. I hadn't had a chance to call you yet—'

'No, no, that's fine. I just . . .' Sebastien's head rocks back.

'I know!' Jacques grins. 'Rémy said he'd met someone but we didn't have a chance to discuss that in any detail. I didn't even know who the girl was. Until now . . .'

Sebastien leans close, 'So who is she?'

Jacques eases the door closed and guides us to the waiting area. When we are all seated, he begins . . .

'Her name is Lily Bechet. She met Rémy at the supermarket when he was running errands for his mother; they went for a coffee which turned into drinks which turned into—'

'Sex,' Sebastien cuts to the chase.

'And the fact is, she didn't even realise she was pregnant until a good six weeks or so after he died.'

'Did she know what happened to him? You know, that it wasn't just that he hadn't called her?' Julie asks.

Jacques nods. 'She saw it on the news.'

'How awful.'

'Apparently she always swore she would never be a single mother and, at the time, she didn't know if she was going to keep it. Then she met a new guy who swept her off her feet and he said he desperately wanted to be a father, but Lily couldn't tell anyone that the baby wasn't his; they would bring it up as theirs and no one would know the truth.' He leans back in the plastic chair. 'But about a month ago, I guess it all got too real for him – the responsibilities, the changes in their lifestyle, and he bailed.'

'Wow.'

'I think it was only a few days ago that Lily told her mother the whole story and then today, on the way to the hospital, she rang Mrs Laframboise and she rang me.' He looks awash with wonder. 'I still can't believe it.'

'Amazing. It's just amazing.'

'You want to come and meet them?' Jacques offers.

'Are we going to be too much en masse?' Sebastien worries.

'Why don't I go and get the coffees?' I quickly excuse myself.

'I'll come with you,' Julie jumps up. 'You guys go visit.'

I'm not sure what drug I need right now to counter the shock of all this, but they must have something for when a worst-case scenario turns out to be the best but still leaves you shaking and disorientated.

'This is incredible,' I hear Julie enthusing. 'I don't mean to be selfish but this one thing could set Sebastien free – there is no way that Jacques would leave little Rémy now. No way.'

'He could still take that European tour!'

'They'd have him in a heartbeat,' she nods. 'In a heartbeat.'

Barely able to contain herself, she reaches out and hugs me tight – all those precision-honed Cirque muscles crushing against my soft flesh.

And then she blinks back her tears. 'I mustn't get ahead of myself but the thought of having him back . . .' She looks near-delirious. 'And I want a baby so bad. I want Sebastien's baby!'

I smile. 'You know Mr Dufour is counting on that!'

And then I have a selfish thought. That all of Jacques' attention will now go to the new baby and grandmother Laframboise. Just as it should be, of course. Besides, I'm going home in a few days and I've got what I said I wanted – Jacques reunited with his second family. And a third one to boot.

As we walk back with the coffees, I now feel very much the outsider. Perhaps I should just leave, not that I know where I am. I could easily get a taxi back to the auberge. If I can just figure out the way to the Reception . . .

'Krista!'

'Uncle Jacques!' I summon a grin as he approaches.

His smile broadens. 'Hey, I like that!' and then he looks directly at me, eyes shining with appreciation.

'We did it!'

'Did what?'

'Got Sebastien moving back to Montreal!'

'He's taking the tour?' I gasp.

'I made it easy on him – I fired him!'

'You did?' I laugh.

'Told him he's got to be out by the weekend.'

'Wow. Tough boss.'

'That's me!' he puffs up his chest. 'And I have you to thank for getting him back to Montreal, hooking him up with Julie . . .'

'Oh no,' I look away. 'Things would have worked out just as well without my interference.'

'Excuse me a moment.'

Sebastien is calling him back. Maybe to ask about severance pay.

That was really nice of Jacques to thank me. But I still feel awkward being here. On the maternity ward of all places. Some cruel part of me says, 'Imagine if you could have been here under different circumstances, having Jacques' baby!' and then even though I'm the one person without a legitimate excuse for tears, they start to trickle down my face faster than I can wipe them.

I'm never going to experience this for myself; never going to have a crowd of hearts zinging with love around me, congratulating me. I'm never going to contribute anything as amazing as a baby to the world. I'm always going to be on the outside looking

in. I'm never going to be able to hold someone and know that
they are truly mine because they are a part of me. I'm always
going to be alone.

Through the blur of my tears I locate the Ladies and then
shut myself in the cubicle and sob as silently as I possibly
can, trying to get it all out and over with. Again. Please just
leave me, I beg all these thoughts; leave me in peace, don't
keep tormenting me like this. I thought we had a deal. Where
are my fir incense sticks when I need them?

As I step back out of the Ladies, I collide with Julie.

'Oh there you are! We wanted to see if you needed a ride
back to your hotel?'

'Um, I . . .' I can't even form a sentence.

'Are you okay?'

'I'll take her,' Jacques cuts in, appearing by her side.

'Oh no, it's fine.' I manage to avoid all eye contact. 'I can
get a taxi. I'll just get my bag out of your car—'

'Put it in mine,' Jacques instructs Sebastien, slinging him
his keys. 'And start her up for me.'

'Are you sure? I don't want to interrupt your time here.'

'You're not. Lily needs to rest now. Let me just say goodbye to Mama Laframboise.'

'Okay,' I say, taking the path of least resistance.

Sebastien, meanwhile, still looks as though he needs a stiff
drink. 'What a day!'

'I'll say!' I almost manage a smile. 'Thanks for the jaunt to
Montreal, it was great.'

'You'll have to come back again and see the show . . .'

'I'd love that,' I say, though my heart sinks a little – that
sounds like one of those things you say when you're never
going to see the person again.

I turn my sore eyes to Julie. 'It was so nice to meet you.
Good luck with everything,' I add, giving her a knowing look.

'And you.' She leans in and gives me another hug, this time of such affection it nearly sets me off again.

And then they're gone and I'm standing in the corridor, and even though I know Jacques is coming for me I just want to run and hide because I don't want to blub all over him and I just can't seem to hold it together right now.

'So, have they decided on a name for the baby yet?' I force myself to ask the appropriate questions as we head outside.

'Yes – René,' he tells me. 'It means to be reborn.'

'Really?' I brighten for a second. 'That's so perfect!'

He stops suddenly. 'Krista, can I ask you a question?'

Uh oh. 'Yes.'

'And you don't have to answer.'

'Okay.' I shiver.

He puts a bear-like arm around me. 'Perhaps we should get in the truck first . . .'

25

Inside his charmingly beat-up vehicle we are blasted with so much heat and airborne dog fluff my mouth gets even drier.

What is he going to ask me? It's obviously a delicate subject because twice he's gone to speak and then appears to have a change of heart.

I am about to cut to the chase and give him the address of my auberge when he blurts, 'My wife left me because I couldn't provide her with a child.'

My mouth falls open.

He looks a little dazed himself. 'You're only the second person I've ever told that to.'

Still I can't seem to find the words but I don't want to leave him hanging. 'I-I only told one person . . .' I begin. 'Until now.' I look back at him. 'Do I have to say it out loud? Like at an AA meeting?'

He smiles fondly. 'Only if you want to.'

I take a deep breath. 'My name is Krista and I can't have children.'

'I had a feeling.' His eyes brim with empathy. 'Your reaction with the puppies, and then today. But I wasn't sure.'

I sigh. 'The day with the puppies was the day I found out that my ex-husband had got a nineteen-year-old sandwich delivery girl pregnant.'

'Oh no!' he groans.

'Yes,' I sigh. 'These young women are so very fertile.' And then I venture: 'What about you – do you know if your wife . . .'

He shakes his head. 'We don't have any contact. She moved to Vancouver for her job. That was our official line – her work took her there and obviously I couldn't leave the dogs . . .'

'Pulled in different directions . . .'

He nods.

I wonder for a moment if he's going to say any more on the subject and I'm glad when he continues:

'We'd been trying for three years before we got everything checked out. We didn't believe the doctors at first, you always hope to prove them wrong. But month after month after month . . .' He tuts. 'There came a point where I actually gave her an out. I didn't want her deprived of being a mother because of me. I mean, you want your wife to have everything to make her happy.'

'And what did she say to that?'

'At first she said we were in this thing together. That she couldn't even think about giving up on us because of this. But now I think she was just trying to make me feel better in that moment.' He picks at the armrest. 'After that I would see this look on her face and I knew she was considering, you know, other options . . .'

'It's a big thing to take away from somebody,' I acknowledge. 'I think Andrew felt I'd somehow negated the contract of our marriage. We'd talked about having kids from the start and I remember him saying, "I didn't know this about you when I married you." Of course neither did I, but I think he felt duped. You know, false bill of goods.' I pull my scarf away from my neck. 'I don't think he even felt that bad about leaving. He never really said he was sorry. In his mind it was as if

I just didn't want it that much any more. But I did . . .' A tear bounces off my cheek.

Jacques reaches across to the glove compartment and hands me a tissue.

'Thank you,' I sniff. 'I keep thinking I've made peace with it but out of nowhere—' I motion to my eyes.

'I know. It hits you hard sometimes.' He twists his torso around to face me. 'I try to think what I would have done, if the situation had been reversed . . .'

'And?'

'I would've been happy to adopt. But then that's what I'm used to with all the dogs; I couldn't love them any more than I do.'

I smile.

'And I have this great friend, Magalie, who was adopted from Haiti by a local family. And she's probably the nicest, sunniest, most accomplished person I know.'

'My best friend at school was adopted,' I tell him. 'Same thing – happiest, most well-rounded, easy-breezy person.'

'Maybe it's because they are so wanted, so loved – their parents had to work so hard to get them.'

'I think you're right. Do you know Tony Robbins – the motivational guy? I heard him telling this story about Steve Jobs of Apple and how he was adopted and he was fixing on the fact that his blood parents had given him up and Tony Robbins said, "But your new parents chose you." And that's what he went with – *he was chosen*. And what a life he had!'

'But your husband didn't want to try that?'

I shake my head. 'He wanted his DNA. His flesh and blood. He didn't think he could have the same attachment to another man's child. Besides, once we knew for sure that I couldn't, he looked at me differently, I could feel the change. I wasn't the future mother of his children any more. I wasn't this magic being who was going to bring more of him into the world. I was just me.' I gulp. 'And it wasn't enough.'

Jacques reaches for my hand.

'It's hard to feel confident and desirable when you know how much you are disappointing someone.' I swallow hard. 'And the words they use . . .'

'Infertile!' He cringes.

'I mean!' I roll my eyes. 'Fertile is a pretty yukky word to start with, and infertile is even worse.'

'Or sterile. That's sexy!'

I laugh out loud. 'I know! It sounds like we've been scrubbing out our reproductive organs with bleach!'

Now he's grinning.

'Barren!' I add in a dramatic baritone.

'Unproductive,' he responds. 'Like we're a pair of slackers!'

We sit with the humour until gradually my smile fades.

'You just wonder,' I begin, 'how you make it up in other ways – I feel I should be doing something remarkable or revolutionary to balance things out.'

'For not contributing to the population?'

'It just seems that people with children *know* they did something meaningful with their life. I don't think there's anything else quite so definitive. Everything seems so blurry to me.'

'I think mums and dads can still search for meaning too. I know my dad is looking for more. Beyond us boys.'

'You're right,' I concede. 'I always seem to torment myself with sweeping generalisations. Every parent has their own experience. Sometimes I just get so frustrated that I didn't even get to try it. Not that it's something you get to try and then decide if you like it.' I roll my eyes.

'Accepting your circumstance is the hardest thing.' Jacques acknowledges. 'That's what I learned when Rémy died. I couldn't accept it. I wouldn't! I was protesting all the way. Willing it to be different.'

'I can't imagine that kind of pain.'

I don't quite have the nerve to take his hand but I do touch his elbow, to show that I care.

'Sometimes you just want your life to have turned out differently. But wishing for something that can't be, that's a wasted wish.'

I blink at him. 'I hadn't thought of it like that.'

And then his phone bleeps a text.

Perhaps it's the fact that we're in a hospital car park but I find myself gasping, 'Is everything all right?'

'It's just the farm, wanting to know if I'll be back in time for the sunrise ride.'

As he taps his reply I take a deep breath in and then try to exhale slowly, happy to have settled down somewhat. So much so, in fact, that I find myself yawning.

'We should get you back to your hotel,' he decides. 'You've had a very long day.'

'I can't believe I was in Montreal this morning!'

And with that, all the heart-to-heart, soul-to-soul, sterile-to-sterile talk is over.

We chat more about his dad and we're just getting onto his Cree mum when we pull up to a snowy bank beside my little *rue*.

Time to part.

'Well,' I say, unbuckling my seat belt. 'Thanks so much for the lift, and congratulations again on the new addition to your family!'

'Isn't it wonderful?' He beams. 'I can't wait to see if he has any of Rémy's traits.'

'What did you like most about him?' I'm suddenly curious. And not quite ready to say goodnight.

Jacques thinks for a moment and then says, 'His energy – he was always game for anything, always ready to go. And he really stood up for what he believed in.' He smiles. 'He was a good friend to me.'

I don't quite know what to say now, so I go to open the door, without much success.

'Here, let me get that, it sticks sometimes.'

I think he might lean over me again, but instead he gets out of the car and walks around to my side.

'Thank you,' I say as he helps me out.

'And don't forget your bag . . .' He reaches into the back seat, grabbing it with one hand and then offering me his free arm. 'I'll see you to the door.'

'All right,' I say as I contemplate the slippery path. 'But I apologise in advance if I take you down with me!'

'Don't worry.' He pulls me closer. 'I've got you.'

My heart heaves happily. I really don't want to say good-night. I don't want him to go. But he has a sunrise ride and it's not so very far off daylight now.

'Do you have your key?'

He unlocks the door at the top of the steep front steps and then switches places with me. I love how gallant he's being, the only snag is that now I'm towering above him – for me to lean down for a hug would surely unbalance us both and I don't want him falling back and cracking his head and ending up at the hospital for real.

'Goodnight then,' I say.

He reaches for my hand and kisses it softly, then rests it for a moment upon his cheek. 'Goodnight Krista.'

As the door closes between us, I merely step to the side and lean against the wall, not wanting to disturb the feeling I just experienced. I can hear a voice in my head say, 'I love him! I love that guy!'

And I don't necessarily mean 'in love' because of course it's too soon for anything except infatuation, but there's something about him that just slays me. And comforts me. And warms me. And intrigues me. And makes me yearn for the next time we will meet . . .

26

I don't hear from Jacques at all the next day.

It's actually the first day since we met that we haven't had some contact and I'm all too aware of his absence. Especially after feeling so close last night . . .

I awoke late this morning, still a little shaken from all the emotion of the day before. Breakfast was already over so I headed to a diner called Buffet de L'Antiquaire, on account of it being in the antique district of Lower Town. It's one of those places where you can see your eggs and bacon sizzling on the giant oven plate in front of you. I like that. And I liked that it wasn't too fancy because I wasn't feeling too fancy myself. I can't quite stave off the notion that I'm back to being just me again. Is it done? I wonder. Is the cycle of Jacques complete? Or is he simply regretting revealing something so personal last night?

I drain the chunky white coffee mug and prepare to pay the bill. I really have no business feeling so sad. Maybe I'm just lonesome after yesterday's social whirl – adding Mr Dufour, Julie and all those Cirque du Soleilers to my list of encounters – and having no one to meet up with today. Annique and Gilles think I'm still in Montreal and I didn't want to encroach on their free day. Besides. I have plenty to do. This is my ideal chance to mooch around the shopping area of Petit Champlain entirely at my own pace.

This really is Christmas Card perfect – as designed by

Beatrix Potter after a field trip to Europe. There's even a bunny-motif bistro. (Albeit named Le Lapin Sauté, translating as 'the sautéed rabbit'.) I opt instead for Le Cochon Dingue (the foolish pig!) and a bowl of hot chocolate to revive me after several hours 'window-licking' at the upmarket galleries, jewellers and, most significantly, La Fudgerie-Boutique.

While sitting and sipping I read more about the One Drop Foundation that Sebastien told me about. This is the first I've heard of World Water Day (held every March) and the concept of 'eating less water' – apparently it takes between 2,000–5,000 gallons of water to produce the food one person eats in one day! And ten gallons to produce one sheet of paper. Must start writing smaller in my notebooks.

And then I find myself gazing out of the window, looking over at the ferry port, which only serves to twang me again. It's amazing how, in such a short space of time, everywhere here is loaded with memories. The Auberge Saint-Antoine is just around the corner. How different things were then. How lucky I am to have been able to get to know Jacques in the interim. And yet it's always a mixed blessing liking someone that much. Thinking about him makes me feel a little nervous. Something happened in the car between us last night, and on the auberge doorstep, and I feel like I can't do without that connection now. And that's when I always mess things up – when I realise I have a need for someone. I'm surprised I even want to put myself out there again after Andrew. But I do. I don't think Jacques would ever hurt me, not intentionally. But things are still ambiguous between us. It certainly meant a lot to hear from his father that I have brightened his spirits. But in a way beyond friendship and empathy? I still can't tell.

*   *   *

I try to distract myself with a visit to the Museum of Civilisation, aka the Museum of Human Adventure! It's a modern, multi-storey experience, and I get a little boost when I discover the First Nation exhibit, giving me the opportunity to learn more about Jacques' heritage. (Now if they just had a floor dedicated to ice hockey, I'd be sorted.)

The resourcefulness of these people is amazing – they used every element of a tree or animal or bird to turn into clothing, snowshoes, drums, headdresses, basketware, hunting and fishing equipment, baby papooses, artworks, etc., etc. Their craftsmanship is an inspiration.

I'm just leaning in for a closer look at the stitching on the birch-bark canoe when my phone bleeps a text. In my urgency to read it I send the phone flying into the display. There is no guard to hand but I know I'm being filmed so I try and mime to the camera what just happened to explain why I am now stepping into the scene. Oh no! A school group has just entered the room! Instead of grabbing my phone and hopping back over the barrier I choose instead to duck into the tepee.

My heart is pounding as I back to the furthest corner. Why did I do that? This wasn't supposed to be a game of Hide & Seek. I'm stuck in here now! What if it was a message from Jacques? What if I've got a five-minute window to accept the invitation of a lifetime?

For what seems like an eternity I listen to the teacher lecturing at the children. And I can't even learn anything because it's all in French.

And then my phone starts to ring.

Which is when I recall waking up in the middle of the night and deciding to change my ringtone to 'Ice Ice Baby'.

On the upside, it makes it easier to locate.

'Sorry, sorry!' I say as I crawl towards it on all fours,

catching my foot on the barrier in my haste to leave the exhibit and then hobbling to the door. Now I'm *really* glad I can't understand what the teachers are saying.

When I do finally get to look at the screen I discover the text is from Gilles.

I slump with disappointment.

He wants to check that I will be free to go to the studio tomorrow to review all the photographs from the trip. Six p.m.

I have no reason to say no. 'I'll be there.'

The call, however, was from Laurie. Always a pleasure to hear from her.

'How's it going there in snowglobe world?' she trills when I call back.

I have so much to update her on, but something tells me to let her go first.

'As I matter of fact I do have some news . . .' Her voice is charged with excitement.

'Yes?'

She puffs out a breath then squeals. '*I'm moving to New York!*'

My stomach flops to the floor.

'Krista?'

'I'm here! I'm just in shock!' I say as I move to the nearest bench. 'Tell me everything!'

'Well, you remember that personal shopper girl I met on my last trip? The one who is just as obsessed with London as I am with New York?'

'Brianna?'

'That's right. Well. She lost her job but she has some savings, so she wants to come to London for as long as possible but she can't get out of her apartment lease—'

'So you're going to take it over?'

'We're going to do a straight swap. I stay at her place, she stays at mine. Just for three months to see how it goes, but maybe by then I will have figured out how to get a visa . . .'

'Wow!'

'And I can carry on doing my work for Va-Va-Vacation! – no real need for me to be there in person.'

Oh but there is, I think to myself.

'And how cool will it be to say that we've got a New York office?'

'Very cool,' I reply. 'But what are we going to do about Teatime?'

'Well four p.m. in London is elevenses in New York . . .' She giggles. 'I'm sure we can work something out.'

'Right.' And then I snap myself into yay-for-you mode. 'This is amazing, Laurie, just what you wanted!'

'Well, it's a step in the right direction. Maybe I'll actually meet someone this time and he'll propose and all my problems will be solved!'

'How soon are you going?'

'Next week!'

'Oh my god!' I close my eyes.

'I was thinking – I'm going to my folks for a couple of nights, but after that why don't you come and stay with me until I go, so we can have max chat time.'

I smile in gratitude. 'That would be wonderful.'

'And of course you can visit me in New York any time you like.'

It hits me again – she's really going.

'W-whereabouts does she live?' I try to ask the appropriate questions.

'Little Italy!' She whoops. 'My favourite part of town, I'll be able to walk to Bread!'

As much as I was longing for some company, I now feel I need to get off the phone so I can process this information, come to terms with it, and then go back to Laurie with some genuine well-wishing, rather than trying to drown out this voice in me that's whimpering, '*Please don't go!*'

'Oh!' Laurie exclaims. 'That's her on the other line now, gotta go!'

I stand there motionless for a good few minutes. I can't even fathom Laurie not being there in the office. She is my rock and source of all hysterical laughter. It's just going to be so drab without her. As wonderful as it is to go on all these trips, it's so nice to have someone to come home to. Someone who, when you are with them, there is no other place you would rather be.

I force myself to walk over to the door but feel so daunted by the hike back to upper town I can't quite bring myself to open it. Suddenly I have no energy.

But then I remember the funicular, just a few minutes from here . . .

As the metal cubicle grinds me up the hill, with all the strain on its mechanics and none on my knees, I wonder how it can be that one day your life can be filled with such purpose and the next you feel utterly adrift . . . How *do* you get back on track?

'Oop!' I am jolted, quite literally, by our arrival at the Château Frontenac.

Crazy that I have yet to go in when it really is the iconic centrepiece of the city.

We were actually due to dine here the evening I diverted Annique to Wendake, doing us out of lobster night at the buffet. Right now I'd settle for a chai latte – apparently there's a Starbucks within these walls; it's just a matter of locating it.

'Hello you!'

A large, long-haired, pink-tongued dog greets me as I push through the polished brass doors from the main courtyard. He has no lead and seems to consider himself to be in charge of the lobby area – a grand affair with dark wood panelling warmed by glowing candelabra and gold-patterned rugs. I look around for his owner and find hotel employee Genevieve smiling at me.

'This is Santol. He's our dog concierge.'

'Ohh!' I smile back at her. 'Is it okay to . . .' I go to kneel beside him.

'Oh yes, he loves the attention!'

It feels so good to rummage around his wavy black fur and flip his floppy ears. Even more of a tonic than a chai!

'What is he?'

'Bernese Mountain Dog crossed with Labrador Retriever – so Labernese.'

'Really? I haven't heard that one before!'

'He's also a former guide dog.'

'That's so lovely!' I run my hands over his pure white toes. 'What a nice welcome to the hotel!'

'He's certainly a disarming presence,' she agrees. 'We've had businessmen in suits lying on the floor with him before now!'

At which point Santol rolls over, offering up his vast expanse of tummy. He makes me feel so good I nearly buy the soft toy version of him in the gift shop. Instead I purchase some healing paw balm – my thinking being that, if I ever do get to see Jacques again, I could make it a present to Sibérie, since she was my first dog encounter here in Quebec. Maybe that could be excuse enough to go there tomorrow – I just wanted to come and see the dogs one last time, have one last mush!

At least I still have the dog-sledding race to look forward to. Although it would be more fun if Jacques was racing. I wonder if there's any possibility he is considering doing it now? Not that everything is suddenly fixed after last night but maybe his attitude has changed? He could race in Rémy's honour now. And any prize money could go into a little fund for René.

There I go, meddling again. Planning out someone else's life when I should be focusing on my own. Ordinarily I'm pulled forward with thoughts of my next trip. But now I think, 'How can anywhere compare to how I feel here?'

I pause for a moment and watch an elderly woman making handmade Carnival sashes – the craftwork is authentic and the price reflects the hours of painstaking finger labour. I see a father purchasing a set for his entire family. There's certainly some old money in this place – gotta love these grand dame hotels, they will endure.

Dropping down to the lower level, I nose around a shop with furs dyed in regal hues from scarlet to pansy purple to midnight blue, and then I locate Starbucks.

I'm perusing the hotel leaflet I picked up in Reception while waiting to place my order when it occurs to me, 'Why have the very same chai latte that I can have in fifty-eight countries in the world, when I could be having a unique Winston Churchill martini in the Saint-Laurent Bar while sitting beside the fire?'

As the man himself once said: 'I am easily satisfied with the very best.'

I sit there for nearly an hour, staring into the yellow flames, watching the logs crack and ashes crumble. It's a comforting place to be and I focus on being pleased for Laurie. We can still Skype. She can carry me on her iPhone when she goes to her local café and we can chat away. I mustn't be sad about this. I don't want to spoil it for her.

'Oh Laurie! This is so fabulous!' I text her. 'I'm so happy for you!'

With my second martini the distinction between fantasy and reality blurs further. I am no longer just a girl with an uncertain future, visiting this city for a few days – this is my world. It's luxurious and cosy and steeped in history. When I'm done the barman directs me to the terrace restaurant to take a look at the collection of Fifties ski posters and a photograph of Grace Kelly when she was guest of honour at the Carnival in 1969. Her ballgown is a frillier, flouncier version of the gold extravaganza she wore in *To Catch A Thief* and, as I ascend the (highly curvaceous) marble staircase, I imagine myself to be skimming the steps with shimmering fabric.

Pausing halfway I wonder if I might do a little twirl while no one is looking, and that's when a man in a long camel coat and dandy moustache comes clattering down the stairs like something from an old movie himself.

That aftershave . . . I inhale as he passes.

He's already on the last step when I hear him say, 'Not going to set the dogs on me this time?'

I spin around. The sly tone of voice is unmistakable, but everything else is unrecognisable – the cut and tint of his hair, the addition of a moustache, his now dark brown eyes.

'H-how do you do that?' I step towards him.

'You think your Wolfman is the only person who can have different-coloured irises?'

'But your chin, the dimple is gone . . .'

'It was never there in the first place.' He grins. 'I shaded it in – people focus on a detail, so that day they remember me as the light-haired man with the cleft chin. Today I am the dark-haired man with the moustache! I can go wherever I please.'

'But why reveal yourself to me?' I falter. Especially after the last scenario, I think to myself, with more than a twinge of guilt.

'By the time you report me I'll change again. I am not a man of limited resource.'

I find myself reaching for the handrail to steady myself. This is all a bit much.

And then I look back at him. 'That day at the ferry, where did you go?'

'Into the water.'

Before I can say, 'I knew it! I knew I saw a flipper!'

He says, 'No. I'm joking. I have a place down there at the port. I just went home.'

I can't help but snort. 'You really are audacious!'

He shrugs. 'So where to now?'

My stomach growls in response.

'Dinner.' He nods with a smile. 'Where?'

'Well,' I begin, already forgetting that I should be calling the police. 'I wanted to check out the Voodoo Grill—'

'Oh to be young and fashionable.'

'I think my readers would like it.'

'Ah yes, your Va-Va-Vacationers.'

Of course he knows already. Probably Googled me when he worked out my name from the hotel registration.

'It's a good choice, the food is surprisingly high quality for a place that plays music so loud. And there's an Anglophile waitress with a regal demeanour that will take special care of you once she hears your accent.'

He really does know this city inside out.

'Where I really want to go is Aux Anciens Canadiens,' I venture. 'But I suppose you'll say it's really touristy . . .'

'Do tourists go there? Yes. But I hear the Quebec meat pie is unmatched.' And then he gives me a sideways look. 'Of course, I'd recommend Restaurant L'Initiale, but now you can't get a table for all the policeman eating the stuffed quail.'

I don't mean to laugh out loud but I do. He does have a certain charm.

Then, in a surprisingly humanising move, his stomach growls.

We look at each other.

And before I know it, I hear myself inviting the closest thing Quebec has to an outlaw to join me for dinner . . .

27

Aux Anciens Canadiens wins on proximity, just a scurry and a sneeze from the Château.

There's a storybook quality to the dinky whitewashed stone building with its pointy scarlet roof. And I consider it rather daring that they have both an ice sculpture *and* a firepit, one either side of the front door.

Inside has a country feel, with blue check tablecloths and waitresses in peasant outfits with black bodices and white puff sleeves.

We're barely situated in our wooden booth and our order is in.

'She will have the pea soup grand-mère, Quebec meat pie and, for dessert, the maple syrup pie. And I will have the onion soup au gratin, the Lac Saint-Jean pie with wild meats and the fudge dessert.'

I'm about to protest at the presumption of his ordering for me when he says, 'That way we get to try all the classic dishes on the menu.' Which actually seems like a really good plan.

'So.' He leans across the table to me. 'Go ahead.'

'Go ahead what?'

'I know there's a question you are burning to ask.'

'One question?' I scoff.

'Well, which of the many is most pressing?'

'Hmmm,' I muse. 'I'm torn between asking you why you

do what you do and what you look like when you're being yourself.'

He shrugs. 'Not so very different – it's not like I'm wearing a prosthetic nose or anything.'

'So you say . . .' I narrow my eyes at him.

He laughs. 'Of course the moustache is stick-on.' His hand goes to his upper lip. 'Do you want me to peel it off?'

'Only if you think it's going to end up floating in your soup.'

He laughs again.

'Tell me.' I'm leaning in now. 'What did you look like when you were a little boy?'

He thinks for a minute and then says, 'Basically a little surfer dude in a Harry Potter blazer.'

'You were blond?'

'White blond,' he confirms. 'And I never wanted it cut.'

'Posh school?'

'The poshest.'

'Rich parents?'

'The richest.'

I study him for a moment. 'And you've been acting up since you were a child?'

'I suppose you could call it that. I just didn't like to be cooped up in the classroom, going over and over the same stuff – I got it the first time! I wanted to be outside. Pretty much doing anything I could to piss my father off.'

'And why would you want to do that?'

There's a flare of annoyance in his eyes now. 'If you met him, you'd know.'

'I'm sure your therapist has told you that you were just trying to get his attention.'

'What makes you think I've got a therapist?'

'Well,' I take a sip of the wine he has selected. 'You seem to like mystery and intrigue and I would imagine you are your own biggest puzzle.'

'*Merci*,' he says as the soup is set before us. 'Eat it while it's hot.' In other words, I'm not responding to that.

Both the pea and the onion soup have that lovely home-made quality that makes it feel like a tonic. Though apparently for me it is acting as a truth serum.

'You know if you're still waiting for your dad's approval, I think you're wasting your time.'

The soup catches in the back of his throat.

I quickly hand him his glass of water. 'I don't mean to sound harsh but I've seen it before on these rehab shows, rich kids of all ages turning to drugs because their dad was too busy making millions to take the time to validate them. If it hasn't happened yet, it's never going to happen.'

'Why would you say that?' He looks genuinely shocked.

'Aside from the fact that my tongue has been loosened by alcohol?'

'Yes.'

'Well, firstly I don't want to see you self-destruct.'

'And why would you care if I did?'

'It's my weakness,' I reply. 'I'm just made that way.'

'And secondly?'

'Because if you can accept that it's never going to happen, that he's never going to tell you what you want to hear, it will set you free. Why waste your life wanting something you can't have?' I mop up the last of my pea soup with a ragged corner of bread. 'Besides, there's someone whose opinion is way more important.'

'Please don't say God.'

'Yours. It matters the most what you think of yourself.'

'And what do you think of *yourself*?' He turns the tables on me.

I think for a moment and then say, 'Let me put it this way.

My mother thinks I'm a gadabout. That I'm on a fruitless quest. That wherever you go, there you are – so what's the point in leaving the house? She thinks I've got nothing to show for my travels. Nothing external or material anyway. Meanwhile, I think I'm an adventurer. I believe travel broadens the mind. It inspires me and makes me fall in love with the world all over again. So who is right?'

'Doesn't it bother you that she's got you all wrong?'

'It doesn't matter because that's not the point – my lesson is to let go of wanting her approval and her lesson is to accept my choices.'

He blinks back at me.

'And yes, I've watched a lot of Oprah Winfrey.'

'Is it partly true though,' he ventures, 'that you travel to escape?'

'I travel to discover,' I tell him. 'And to stop me becoming jaded or stuck in a rut.'

'And bored?' he asks. 'That's my major affliction.'

'Have you been to India?'

'Yes.'

'Africa?'

'Yes.'

'I think you must be doing it wrong,' I decide.

Finally a smile from him. 'I've bungee-d and abseiled and free-dived on virtually every continent but I've been doing the adrenalin junkie thing so long it's getting harder and harder for me to get a high.'

'Have you tried drugs?'

'Is that your suggestion?' he splutters.

'Noooo!' I exclaim, horrified. 'I just thought you might have a predisposition for them.'

'I do. Which is why I don't take them.'

'Thank goodness for that. Oooh red cabbage! I love red cabbage!'

'It doesn't take much to make you happy, does it?'

My first forkful of pie makes me a whole lot happier. You can keep your fancily presented fare drizzled with this and wafted with that: give me flavour! And melt-in-your-mouth flaky pastry.

'It's actually kind of like a Cornish pasty, only more refined. Have you ever had one of those?'

He nods. 'I spent a week surfing in Newquay.'

'What did you think of England?'

'You guys are funny.' He gets a gleam in his eye. 'And not as polite as people say.'

'Oh, our days of being the epitome of good manners are long gone.' I tut. 'I think that's one of the reasons I like it here so much. It feels so much more genteel.'

'What a sensitive soul you are,' he teases. 'It's too genteel for me. I need more passion.'

'And challenge?' I say, as an idea starts to form. 'Have you ever been fully absorbed in a project?'

'Well,' he pauses. 'If you can call my current activities a project, I do get a kick out of planning the details and logistics. Taste this . . .'

He pushes his plate towards me.

'But how long does that last?' I persist. 'A few months?'

'More like weeks. I work fast. ADD fast.'

'You know there's a medication for that?'

'Yes, but I keep thinking there must be something out there that could captivate me . . .'

I sit forward, my heart palpitating with excitement. 'I think I might have that something. Real life-or-death stuff.'

He looks curious but not convinced. 'And what would that be?'

'I don't want to say.'

'Why not?' He looks bewildered.

'Because I think it's perfect and you'll only pick holes in it.'

'And why would I do that?'

'Because I can't explain it properly right now. I don't have all the facts and figures in my head. You'd have to read about it for yourself. There's a website . . .' I take out a pen and carefully write out the address for him.

He reaches to take the scrap of paper from me but I hold back.

'Not yet.'

'Not yet?'

'I'll give it to you when we part. So you can contemplate it when you are by yourself, no distractions.'

His eyes narrow at me. 'Are you going to try this pie?'

I smile and take a forkful. 'Mmm, that's good too,' I enthuse. 'Just don't tell me what the wild meats are.'

Another glass of wine and the talk turns to romance. It seems apparent that the only woman who could truly hold his attention is Angelina Jolie. And she's already taken. Although, I have to say, I think the exotic creatures speaking in tongues at the Cirque du Soleil training facility could give him a run for his money. But I don't mention them at this juncture because they are all part of my masterplan.

Meanwhile he neatly pegs me as a woman who goes for 'fixer-upper' men. I am slightly on edge, wondering if he's going to reference Jacques again after his earlier 'your Wolf-man' comment. But he leaves well alone. And it actually occurs to me that Jacques is not so much of a troubled soul as someone who is suffering circumstantial pain. Which is different. He's obviously quite together in every other way. And he's found his passion, unlike the man sitting before me, constantly questing for a new high.

We find one rather sooner than we might think – albeit of the sugar variety – with the arrival of dessert . . .

After the first bite of maple syrup pie I am loathe to trade with his fudge pie, although they are actually quite similar – like treacle tart or pecan pie without the pecans.

If I had a dollop of Devon clotted cream on top I could die happy. And I say as much.

'Nothing left to do?' He asks me. 'Before you ingest that fatal blob of cream?'

I titter. 'Of course. I still have dreams.'

'Such as . . .'

I think of the one nearest to my heart – the fantasy of husky-sledding, maple-syrup tapping, summer picnics and autumn travels with Jacques.

'That seems like a good one,' he comments. 'Judging by the look on your face.'

I heave a wistful sigh. 'I'm trying to stop wishing for things that I can't have because then it's a wasted wish.'

'All right, then tell me what you think *might* be possible.'

'Well . . .' I tap my nails on my coffee cup. 'I'd like to see the aurora borealis. And be part of a dog-sled race. And eat a whole maple syrup pie.'

'One of those I can make come true right now.'

He summons the waitress but then surprises me by requesting the bill.

'So I take it we're not going with the maple syrup pie option?' My heart slumps a little.

'Come on,' he says, throwing down a flutter of notes as he gets to his feet.

'Th-thank you for dinner!' I stammer after him. It really was perfect. 'Where are we going exactly?'

'Give me five minutes and all will be revealed.'

'All?' I repeat, slightly concerned.

But this time he doesn't reply.

28

No sooner are we out on the street, he turns to the left and strides confidently down the hill. Meanwhile I am still inching along, making sure I have something to grab at should I skid on the ice.

'You're like a little old lady,' he laughs as he turns to check on me.

'Oh don't!' I call back. 'The other day I had an OAP help me across the street!'

'I think we need to set up a zipline between the buildings so you can get around a bit faster.'

'Sounds more like your style.'

He smiles as he returns to my side. 'You know, a guy actually walked on a tightrope between the top floor of Château Frontenac and the Price Building over here . . .' He points to a stunning Metropolis-style skyscraper with a Kryptonite green glow at its peak.

'You're kidding!' I gawp up at where he would have tiptoed across.

'Took him fifteen minutes. No safety net.'

'It wasn't you, was it?'

'No!' he chuckles. 'It was a Frenchman, on official business – part of the four hundredth anniversary celebrations for the city.'

'Ohh.'

'But I think I might have a quicker way to transport you.'

Before I can speculate on what that might be, he bends

down, throws me over his shoulder and jogs down the street with me squealing all the way.

We're practically back at my hotel when he sets me down.

'Oh my god!' I grip at my heart. 'That was crazy!'

I'm still experiencing the sensation of being jiggled upside down and grabbing at the cashmere of his coat when he takes my hand and leads me away from my auberge, towards the art deco doors of the Hotel Clarendon.

At which point I dig in my heels.

'What are we doing here?'

'They have a room with a particular view . . .'

I know I probably should walk away but curiosity gets the better of me, and we are so close to my auberge I feel as if I have my own safety net of sorts.

'Coming in?'

'Yes,' I reply. With only the faintest echo of Laurie's caution to misbehave with the right person . . .

The lobby is creaky with historic charm – vintage luggage trunks, potted palms, even one of those wrought-iron reception cages. I half expect Hercule Poirot to be studying us from behind a newspaper.

'*Bonsoir*,' he greets the receptionist. 'Do you have room 409 available?'

She checks and tells him yes.

He takes out a bundle of notes. 'How much?'

'How many nights?'

'Just one.'

'Er,' I tug at his sleeve.

'Don't worry, we'll only be there an hour.'

'Oh great!' I roll my eyes – way to make me feel like a prostitute.

'Do you need any help with the baggage?' the receptionist asks.

'No I can manage her.' He winks at me.

I go to reprimand him but realise I don't even know his name – not that he'd even tell me his real one. Besides, he's already at the lift.

Again I hesitate.

'Trust me,' he says, holding the door for me.

'Well that's just the problem,' I sigh. 'I don't.'

Room 409 is warm, spacious, and dressed head to toe in a soothing sage. Deliberately avoiding the bed, I make a beeline for the old-fashioned desk and peer out of the window to its right – there's my darling Auberge Place D'Armes! I can almost see myself over there, sitting alone with my laptop in my fleur-de-lys attic, had the evening taken a different turn.

I hope I'm not crossing into dangerous territory here. I suppose I could always grab an icicle off the eaves and wield that in lieu of a knife.

'Come join me in the bathroom!' I hear him call to me.

'What kind of an offer is that?' I frown, peering tentatively around the door frame.

He's patting the closed toilet seat. 'Come sit!'

'You know there's a sofa out here?'

'But this is the best view.'

I must be in his thrall because I do as he says, albeit perching on the very edge.

'Now what?'

'Open the curtains.'

I lean forward and swish them apart. Down the street I see Simons department store and Le Sachem – the First Nations shop where I stocked up on incense sticks and pondered the appeal of earrings with mink baubles. I see the black night sky and then what I think are streaks of city colour reflected on the water . . . Only instead of your typical street lamp yellow a luminous purple seeps into emerald green then merges with vivid orange, now electric blue . . .

'You're looking at the aurora borealis.'

I twist back to face him. 'I thought we had to be out in the wilds to see that?'

'Not this one – that is the name of the city's light installation. The colours are playing on the grain silos at the Old Port.'

I lean closer. I can just about discern the towers now. The merging and changing of the colours is hypnotic.

'I like the purple best,' I tell him.

And then his thigh starts vibrating.

'Excuse me a moment,' he says, consulting his phone and stepping into the other room.

I kneel closer to the window, arms resting on the ledge, looking like a little kid saying her goodnight prayers to the stars. In my mind my black coat becomes a white nightie and my hair coils into ringlets. If I squint a little I can see Peter Pan swooping and prancing around the snow-spangled rooftops.

'What's that other building down there, the one that's all lit up with pink?'

I wait for a response but none is forthcoming.

'The one on the corner.'

Again, nothing.

I go to call his name but realise I still don't know it.

'Oh Master of Disguise!' I get to my feet. 'Did you fall asleep in there?'

I peer into the shadowy room. 'Hello?' I turn on the lights just to be sure he's not hiding. And then check the wardrobe and under the bed.

Nope, he's definitely gone.

I sigh. What did I expect? This is entirely in keeping with his behaviour to date.

I look at my watch. It's pretty late. I wonder if I should wait here – he might have needed to step outside the building to take the call; lord knows his conversations would need to be private.

I wander back to the desk and pick up a be-ribboned package of chocolate-covered cherries, or '*cerises enrobées de chocolat noir*' as the French far more seductively describe them. I'm thinking these will make a very nice going-home present when my phone rings.

'Talk about leaving a girl hanging—'

'I'm sorry, I've had such a busy day.'

'Jacques!' I gasp.

'We had a big group in for a night ride, I'm only just getting back now.'

'Oh-h,' I croak, still too surprised to form a whole word.

'Sorry, it was a bit noisy out there, I'm inside now.'

Just as well he couldn't hear me. Or see me for that matter – just how would I explain my current situation?

'I missed seeing you today.'

My heart dips and swoops. I can't believe he said that!

'Me too,' I smile into the phone.

'I was wondering if you might be free for dinner tomorrow night?'

A huge grin takes over my face. 'Yes!' Oh my goodness! 'I'd love that!

'I have a six p.m. meeting in town so I could pick you up after that?'

'Fantastic! In fact, let me give you the address of Gilles' studio. We'll be going through the photos and I'm not sure how long it's going to take but you could come along and help us put names to the dogs' faces . . .'

'Sounds like fun!'

'Marvellous!'

'So,' he sighs. 'Sleep well!'

I will now! I think to myself.

There's just the matter of transferring back to my own hotel room.

As I descend in the lift I wonder if I need to officially check out? But what if he does come back? I don't want to do him out of a room he's already paid for.

'*Oui*, madame?' the receptionist responds to my hovering.

'Did that man I was with say anything before he left?'

'I didn't see him leave, madame.'

I nod. Of course not. 'So no message for room 409?'

'No.'

'Okay. Well, here's the key.'

'*Merci*.'

'He was just showing me the lights on the grain silos.'

She nods. I'm sure she's heard it all before.

I step out of the heavy doors and into the frisky chill of the night. It actually feels good. Cleansing. I edge back to my hotel with a very different mindset to how I began the day. Earlier I was verging on melancholy but now I have so much to look forward to, I feel so very lucky. A real dinner date with Jacques! I wonder where we'll go? Not that it matters, I just love to be in his company . . .

I'm settling into my bed when I hear the jangle of an alarm followed by wailing sirens. But I don't even bother putting in my earplugs – the mood I'm in, it sounds like the sweetest lullaby . . .

29

I breakfast on pious oatmeal and purifying green tea and then, with half an hour to spare before Annique picks me up, decide to take a closer look at the pink-lit building from last night. (From my guidebook I've deduced that it is the Musée de L'Amérique Français, the oldest museum in all of Canada, set on the site of an old seminary or theology college.)

I step out with enthusiasm but can't help but feel a twinge of guilt when I see the Hotel Clarendon squaring off at me on the street corner. I have to say I hope that's the last I see of Mal, as Laurie nicknamed him during our early morning exchange.

'Don't be surprised if he's flying your plane home tomorrow!' she teased.

'Oh don't!' I wailed. 'I wouldn't put it past him turning up as a stewardess.'

'I still can't believe you fell for his, "Come up and see my aurora borealis" line! It's even worse than etchings!'

'I know.'

I'm starting to feel a bit sordid about our fraternising last night. If only I'd known Jacques was going to ask me to dinner, I would've been more than happy with a slice of quiche and an early night.

I turn the corner and then immediately stop in my tracks. The building has been cordoned off and there are police and TV crews bustling outside.

I actually recognise one of the policemen and quickly backtrack, not wanting to get myself a reputation as a crime scene regular. That's when I find myself looking up at the Hotel Clarendon, and the window looking down on this very spot. The window I was standing in last night. Slightly regret chatting to the receptionist now, drawing extra attention to the fact that Mal had gone scuttling out into the night. And then I realise he could be up there right now and I give a little shudder.

Not sure quite what else to do, I scuttle back into my auberge Reception.

'Gosh, there's a lot of commotion outside,' I breeze innocently. 'Do you know what happened?'

'There was a *cambriolage* . . .' The receptionist clicks her fingers trying to think of the word.

'A burglary?' I voice my worst thought.

'*Oui.*'

'What did they take?'

'There was a collection of bishops' rings in the museum. Very rare. Very valuable.'

So now he's a jewel thief.

She goes on to tell me that a fake Bonhomme was arrested down by the ferry – a decoy paid to send the police in the wrong direction . . .

I think I need to lie down. I go to turn away but then she says, 'We have another package for you.'

Oh no. I gulp. I don't even want to take it. I get the feeling it will only draw me in deeper.

As I stand paralysed I have a fleeting thought about packing up and leaving a day early, just to escape all the complications, but how could I possibly miss out on my dinner date with Jacques? Just thinking of him now makes my insides melt like brie.

Besides, I'm sure I'm worrying unnecessarily. Mal wouldn't want to get me in trouble. We got along. We had a good time. Oh god, am I his alibi?

'No officer, I was in Room 409 at the Hotel Clarendon with Krista Carter, just ask her.'

That would go down a storm with Jacques, I'm sure.

'Here it is.' The receptionist presents me with a bubble-wrapped box.

'Thank you,' I wince, and take the ticking time bomb up the stairs with me.

For the longest time I can't bring myself to open it.

'You have to!' Laurie insists.

'Do I though? What if I took it back downstairs and told them to say I never picked it up. I could change hotels—'

'Again?'

'What if I went back to the Hôtel de Glace?'

'Yes, because you really want him to track you there in the middle of the night.'

'Good point,' I shiver, imagining trying to get away from him while still wearing my sleeping bag, hopping along like I'm in a sack race.

'The snow sweeping over your footprints, leaving no trace.'

'All right, all right . . .' I begin pacing the floor.

'Listen, if you play your cards right tonight, you could end up back at chez Jacques and what could feel safer than that?'

'Nothing,' I concur. Even someone as off-the-wall as Mal is no match for ninety-eight huskies, a Samoyed and a German shepherd that already knows his scent.

'Do you think I should tell him?'

'What – that you were dining with the enemy? Or that you checked into a hotel room with him?'

Oh cripes. That doesn't sound good. 'Could I pretend that I was investigating him, trying to get a handle on his identity?'

'Have you opened that package yet?'

'No.'

'Well if you want to do it with me here, you have to do it now. I've got a conference call with Miami tourism in five minutes.'

'Florida,' I murmur. 'Don't they have a lot of witness protection relocations there?'

'Krista!'

'Okay.' I sit down on the bed. 'I'm doing it.'

I tear off the bubble wrap and then slowly slide up the lid of the dark blue box.

'Oh my god.'

'What is it?'

'Oh my god.'

Laurie squeals with impatience. 'Severed elk toe, what?'

'It's one of the rings from the collection.'

She gives a breathy inhale. 'What's it like?'

'Beautiful – pale amethyst in an old gold setting. Kind of like a big cocktail ring.'

'Is it a gift?'

'Wait, there's a note.' I open the piece of paper. 'I'll trade you the rest of the rings for that email address.'

'What email address?'

I lean back on the headboard. 'I made this big deal about having the perfect solution to his hyperactive brain and compulsion to live on the edge.'

'What was it?'

'It's actually to do with Cirque du Soleil. They've got this charity programme called One Drop . . .'

I give her the lowdown.

'So, you're hoping he'll switch over to the good side?'

'Well that was before I started thinking he was really crazy. I don't want to inflict a psychopath on them.'

'But what if he's not? What if he does have all this money and he's just been looking for the right place to spend it?'

'That's what I was thinking!' I sigh. 'So what do I do now?'

'You make the trade.'

'Seriously?'

'Somewhere public, of course.'

'The note says to meet him at the ski joring event at the Carnival.'

'And what, pray tell, is ski joring?'

'I don't know, but I've been meaning to find out.' For a second I'm in a daze, and then I gulp. 'You don't think I'm in any real danger, do you?'

'Take Annique with you,' Laurie advises.

'You really think she's the best bodyguard?'

'At least you know everyone will be looking your way with her around, so there'll be lots of witnesses.'

'Oh that's comforting.'

'Listen. I really think he's all about the thrill. I don't think there's malevolence there, do you?'

'I don't know any more.'

'I think he just did this to impress you.'

'Why would he want to impress me? I'm nobody.'

'These flamboyant types have to have an audience.'

'But why me, Laurie?'

'You say yourself you are one of life's observers. And you're curious. He knew you'd pay close attention to him.'

I sit forward, head in my hands.

'I've got to go.'

'I know,' I tell her. 'Have a good meeting.'

'And you.'

❄   ❄   ❄

This is utterly surreal. And more than a little scary. Is this what happens when you say you want more life in your life?

Without being conscious of what I am doing, I try the ring on. These bishops must have had small hands back in the day because the fit is exact.

I walk into the bathroom to admire the most expensive piece of jewellery I've ever worn.

Shame it's stolen property.

That now has my fingerprints all over it.

Oh no! Now I can't get it off! Immediately I start to panic. Annique will be here any second—

There's a rap at the door.

What if it's the police?

''*Allo?*' for some reason I choose to speak with a French accent.

'*C'est moi!*' Annique sings. 'Ready for our final fling?'

'Just a minute!'

All I can think to do is cover the ring with my bulkiest glove and then hope that my hand shrinks in the cold. Which I'm sure it will.

I just wish I hadn't tried it on my ring finger . . .

'Everything okay?' Annique picks up on my anxious energy.

'Yes, yes. Um. Do you know what time the ski joring is?'

She consults her list. 'It's just starting now.'

'Can we go straight there?'

'No problem.'

We're halfway up the hill before I think to ask, 'What exactly is ski joring?'

Naturally it is one of the most daredevil activities of the Carnival – a charging horse drags a skier around a track while he performs jumps and slalom zigzags at maximum speed – because skiing and horse riding simply aren't sufficient bone-breakers in their own right.

As soon as I hear this, I know Mal won't be a mere spectator. I just wonder if I'll be able to single him out in his ski goggles. But, really, why am I even worrying about that? He always finds me.

Here we are at the Plains of Abraham and the ring is still stuck. I'm sure my hand would indeed shrink if I could remove the all-too-insulated glove and let the icy air get to it, but there are police everywhere and every time I pass one I only feel myself getting *hotter*. What the hell am I going to do? Have Mal tie a piece of string to it and then take a downward slope at 70 mph? I just know I'd either get dragged down behind him or lose a finger. What I need is a tub of butter.

It's then I see the Queues de Castor pâtisserie stand.

'Beaver tails!' I exclaim.

'Have you tried one yet? They are delicious!'

'I had a little bite the other day but I could really do with one of the maple butter toppings . . .'

'We'll come right back after the ski joring.'

'Actually I need it now.'

Annique's nose wrinkles at my desperation. 'Okay . . . Just make sure you don't get it all over you like the maple taffy . . .'

'Good point,' I say, accepting the pastry from the lady in the kiosk. Turning away from the masses, I stuff my gloves in my pockets and then, as gross as this is, rub my whole left hand in the sugary-buttery topping.

'Come on, come on!' I urge.

I give one almighty yank, and with that the ring shoots off into the snow.

'Noooo!' I fall to my knees, desperately trying to find it before it gets trampled by Carnival-goers or swamped in slush.

Come on, come on – show yourself!

Belinda Jones

'Is this what you are looking for?' Annique holds the ring up in front of my nose.

'Yes!' I puff, snatching it back. 'Gosh, thank you! Family heirloom, would've been in so much trouble had I lost that.'

'Really? Because it looks a lot like the rings on the front of all the newspapers this morning.'

I look back at her, unable to speak.

She eyes my sticky hands. 'If I give you a Wet Wipe, will you tell me what's going on?'

I decide to come clean. Mostly because I can't think of a convincing enough lie at such short notice. But also because I am asking Annique to walk into the dragon's lair with me.

She is surprisingly unfazed. 'Is that him? Is that him?' she asks when we reach the event track. 'If I could just see that chin!'

'Oh, that's long gone,' I tell her.

We watch one skier (dressed in yellow and grey) complete the course and another (in red) begin, but I don't get a gut reaction until the next competitor sets in motion. There's a very particular amethyst flash to his otherwise black ensemble . . .

I can't even bring myself to say, 'That's him!' I just watch with my heart in my mouth as he swishes and leaps, knees to his chest, with a mixture of finesse and abandon, causing gasps and cheers from the crowd. I swear he even gives us a little salute as he curves past. Impressive. With that athleticism he's going to fit right in at Cirque du Soleil. That's if he doesn't get incarcerated first.

'Now what?' Annique asks.

'I think I should stand a little way off to the side, it's too crowded here.'

'Okay,' she nods. 'I'll wait right here.'

I have never felt more self-conscious as I head towards the horse trailers. My eyes are working overtime, checking for

Mal, the police and even Jacques, who typically appears at just the right moment but today . . . Let's just say I'm looking forward to seeing him tonight and not a moment before . . .

And then I see the skier with the amethyst flare heading towards me. My stomach pogos upward but then hesitates mid-air – there's something unfamiliar about his gait. His outfit has a looser fit . . . And then he raises his goggles and I see a very different pair of eyes. Whatever Mal's disguise trickery, switching race would require some special CGI skills. I go to speak but he walks right past, ignoring me. Now I'm foxed. I'm about to turn back to signal to Annique that it's not him when I hear a naying and braying in my ear.

'You switched!' I gasp as I turn and find Mal now astride the horse.

'Well, I thought I'd better have a built-in getaway vehicle this time,' he says, scanning the horizon. 'Do you have the piece of paper for me?'

I nod. 'Do you have the jewels?'

I can't believe I just said that. How is this my life?

'I do. Ready to trade?' And then he hesitates, leaning back in the saddle and placing a hand on his hip like some kind of dandy. 'Did you know that amethyst was thought to ward off drunkenness?'

'What?'

'It's true, there's nothing worse than a drunken bishop—'

'Stop!' I complain. 'You're making my head hurt.'

He laughs and then throws the velvet bag over to me. It doesn't feel as heavy as I was expecting. Mostly because it contains nothing but a dozen or so boiled sweets.

I look up in confusion. 'What's going on?'

'Oh Miss Carter . . . Did you really think that was me?'

'It wasn't?!' I don't know which is harder to believe.

He raises his nose in the air. 'I rather feel someone might

be taking my bad name in vain, trying to get me to take the fall for their far larger crime.'

'How would that even work?'

'It didn't take much to convince you I was guilty.'

'Well, you did send me this!' I protest, holding up the ring.

'It's a fake. I was just messing with you.'

I roll my eyes, utterly exasperated. 'Haven't you got anything better to do with your time?'

'Obviously not.' And then he smiles. 'I think you might be my favourite foil.'

I heave an almighty sigh, eager to expel the built-up tension from my body. And then I look back up at him. 'All these pranks, really, it's got to be more than boredom.'

He narrows his eyes. 'I feel another of your theories coming on.'

'I was just thinking that maybe, because your dad didn't set any boundaries, you have to test the ultimate authority – the law.'

He smiles. 'If I had my shrink here, I'd trade her. You're much better.'

I can't help but snigger. But then I get serious as I extend the folded slip of paper towards him.

'I want you to have this anyway. So you can start using your powers for good.'

'As opposed to evil?' he taunts.

'You're not evil; you're just lacking a purpose in life. I really think this could be the answer. Promise me you'll read every word on the website before you judge.'

He tries to take it from me but I hold fast.

'Promise me.'

He waits just long enough to let me know that he's thought this through and then says, 'I promise.'

'You could really make a difference.'

'I could?' He looks unconvinced. 'Why?'

'Because you've got imagination and flair and you know how to get around tricky obstacles and you're smart and you could be whoever they needed you to be to get the job done. And you're not afraid of anything. And you know what else?'

'What?' he says, serious himself now.

'You could become someone you really admire.'

Now he is still.

'And!' I continue. 'You could fall in love with a contortionist from Belarus.'

He cracks a smile. 'Really?' Then, holding my gaze, he leans forward so that his face is level with the horse's mane.

'Why Krista, I'd almost think you believed in me.'

There's something so vulnerable in his voice that my eyes immediately start to prickle.

'I do,' I say softly. And then a single tear splashes onto my cheek.

He reaches down and gently transfers it to his fingertip. 'One drop.'

I blink, amazed. Does he already know?

But then the mood suddenly changes – the horse begins pacing and jerking its head.

'They're coming for me.'

And then with a rousing, 'Hah!' he's gone.

30

When I return to Annique I'm a little shell-shocked.

'So he's innocent?'

'Well, I wouldn't go that far. But he didn't steal the jewels.'

'Hmmm,' she muses. 'That's a lot of drama for nothing.'

'Not entirely nothing,' I counter. 'At least this way I get to keep the ring!'

'Oh yes!' She laughs. 'Though you might want to wait until you're back in London to wear it!'

And then her phone jingles. It's her daughter Coco.

'She forgot her school project.'

'Do you want to go and get it?'

'Well, we still have more of the Carnival to see . . .' She looks conflicted.

'I can do that, honestly, go! We can meet up later at Gilles' studio.'

'If you're sure?'

'Yes, and take this bag of sweets for her class.'

'*Merci, merci!*'

'One quick thing,' I reach for her arm. 'Do you still have the pass for the Hilton Executive Club?'

'I don't. But if you're looking for a room with a view you can see everything from the top of the Observatory. Or Loews if you could do with a rigid drink.'

I smile. 'Is that the one with the revolving restaurant?'

She nods.

'Then I'm sold.'

I like the idea that the revolutions might somehow counter my own spinning head.

I feel rather self-conscious as I enter L'Astral – the circular dining room is considerably more sophisticated than I was expecting. I appear to be the only pink-nosed, wind-whipped tourist, while everyone else looks polished and affluent.

Still, I'm too entranced by the view to leave. It is just as magnificent as my first day here. Only this time I can see the Plains of Abraham, and thus the Carnival, in its entirety.

Methodically I scan from the entrance to the big wheel to the bistro tent to the sleigh rides, up to where the ski joring took place, and beyond to the huge ice circuit where Annique and Gilles taught me to skate. I just want a glimpse, to know he's all right. *Could that be him?* No. False alarm. I take out my phone and check on the local news to see if anyone has been caught or charged.

Nothing yet.

Which is good. I think. I hope.

A minute passes. I check again. Still nothing. Then I type in 'amethyst' and 'drunkeness' and to my utter amazement I find a link that confirms Mal's claim – that the sheer purple quartz was named from the Greek word '*amethystos*' meaning 'not drunken'.

And so I settle in – cocktail in one hand, cocktail ring embedded in the palm of the other – and gaze out at the subtly changing scenery, gradually making peace with the fact that I may never see him again.

Finally, the sun sets.

Now the day is gone and the night belongs to me and

Jacques. There's just the matter of reviewing the photographs at Gilles' studio . . .

I wasn't expecting much more than an outsized computer screen to click through the digital images, but it turns out Gilles has a passion for old school photography and has been mixing it up all week. He's even strung up a few prints on a line with wooden clothes pegs.

'Are you for real?' I laugh as I enter.

'Well, it beats hunching over a light box!' He grins. 'Though we'll be doing that too!'

'I daren't even ask how many you've taken . . .'

There are piles on every surface.

'Well, I have edited them a little – the ones I know you'll hate: the double chins, the eye wrinkles—'

'All right, all right!' I hush him. 'It's a good thing you let your pictures speak for you most of the time.'

He grimaces an apology and then asks, 'Where would you like to begin?'

'At the beginning, of course!'

And so Gilles takes me on a technicolour retrospective of my trip. From the Hôtel de Glace to the snow sculptures, the hair-raising Tornado ride, the sticky Cabane à Sucre, me in a post-Caribou fondue rapture (didn't know he was photographing that!), the exhilarating dog-sledding, the gorgeous, playful fluffy puppies, our shopping trip and bistro lunch, posing in my sash bikini with Bonhomme, the insanity of the Snow Bath . . . So many memories I have been holding in my mind, now here in the form of tangible images.

'Wait! Go back!'

'To the fusball game?'

'Yes, yes,' I urge, scooching forward. 'Can you zoom in on this man?'

It's Mal. In disguise, of course, but it's him nonetheless. I can't believe Gilles captured him on film, without even realising. It pleases me to know that I have a little reminder of him. Even if it is the moment just before I set Niko on him.

'Ready for the next?'

There are some wonderfully chilling photos from the ferry and then a familiar-looking wolf-pelt and fire pit . . .

'When did you go to Wendake?' I ask, amazed that he has so many beautiful shots of the First Nations hotel, even the artsy restaurant platters.

'When you were in Montreal,' he replies. 'Annique said it was worth photographing.'

'And it is,' I confirm. And then I give him a sideways glance. 'So how's it going with her?'

He looks a little awkward. 'Annique?'

'You can tell me. I want her to be happy.'

'It's not that.' He heaves a sigh. 'It's just . . .'

'Yes?'

'She is perfect in every way.'

'How awful for you,' I roll my eyes.

'Except . . .'

Oh dear. Here we go. '*Except?*'

'I don't know if I'm ready to be a father. It's a big step. She has asked if I want to meet Coco this weekend and I don't know if it's a good idea.' He sighs and rubs his brow with both hands. 'I mean, I'm only twenty-three, my career is still developing—'

'Wait,' I place my hand on his arm. I can't have heard right. 'You're twenty-three? How is that even possible?'

'How is it possible?'

'I thought you were in your thirties!'

'Well, I haven't been getting so much sleep lately . . .'

'Not because you look haggard!' I tut. 'You said you'd been

modelling for ten years and then working as a photographer for six . . .'

'It's true. I was a child model. I started when I was about seven and went through to my teens, then I started assisting . . .'

I sit back in my chair. This is quite a shock to me. Puts a whole new spin on things. 'Does Annique know?'

'She knows I'm younger, just not how much.'

'Well,' I puff. 'That could be your solution right there. If you tell her the truth, then she'll automatically look at your relationship in a different light.'

'You think?'

'It doesn't mean she'll like you any less, she'll probably just give the future a little more consideration.'

'So you think I *should* tell her?'

'Honesty is the best policy,' I say, though not the most thorough practiser of what I preach. 'She'll probably ease up a little regarding Coco and then you guys can just take your time and see where things go.'

His shoulders lower. 'That sounds good.' And then he places his hand on mine. 'Thank you.'

'Knock-knock!'

'Jacques!' I brighten at the sight of him.

He looks suspiciously happy too.

We walk up to each other, shimmering with good cheer, yet still unsure of an appropriate greeting. And then he notices the photos of his dogs on the 'washing line'.

I'm not sure if he says '*Mes chiens*' or 'My children', but I suppose in this case the words are interchangeable.

'Big day for them tomorrow.'

'You're racing?' I gasp.

He nods. 'That's what my meeting was about. I was just getting my registration approved.'

'Oh Jacques!' Now I hug him. 'I'm so excited. Right through town?'

'If you get a spot by the Château you can see us take off and finish.'

Gilles gives me the thumbs-up.

And then I rein in my enthusiasm. 'Do you still have time for dinner?'

He looks a little shy. 'If you like, I could cook for you. I'm sure you must be a little bit tired of restaurant food.'

'Oh I would love that! We just have to look at the general scenery pics and we're done.'

'Great. Is it okay if I look around?'

'*Bien sûr*,' Gilles gives him the go-ahead.

I have to say, these cityscapes and Carnival overviews are nothing short of stunning. I love how he chooses one aspect as a focal point and then uses the background as a chorusline to the star feature. And this curved lens effect is amazing. In fact, all the images, I think as I scan back through the collection, have so much life and personality to them. This may be Va-Va-Vacation!'s best collection yet.

'You've done a really good job, Gilles,' I concede. 'You should consider doing this for a living.'

For a second he looks confused, as if I mean it.

After all the tension of the day, this is all I need to crack me up. Which sets Gilles off. Which makes me worse.

Suddenly we hear the sound of a door slamming.

I turn around and find Jacques gone. 'Where'd he go?'

'You think we made him jealous?'

I stoop to pick up the pictures he knocked to the floor in his haste to leave. And then I freeze.

Oh no.

I turn on Gilles. 'The double chins you remove and these you leave lying around?'

It's the pictures of us kissing at the ice hotel. Pillows drooping by our side, feathers fluttering in the air.

His hand flies to his mouth. 'I was going to show you and then put them away, I-I'm sorry—'

'You're crazy!' I blurt. 'What if Annique saw them? Can you imagine how she'd react?'

'How I'd react if I saw what?'

She's standing right behind me.

Before I can even speak she's taken the pictures from my hands.

It would be bad enough if she'd slapped Gilles or raged her fists against his chest, but she doesn't. Instead she turns to me and says, 'This has been going on since the Hôtel de Glace?'

'No!' I gasp. 'It was just one weird moment—'

'I thought we were friends.'

And then she leaves.

For a moment Gilles and I stand there in shock. This is worse than the decapitation of the snow sculpture.

'I'm going after her.'

'Hurry!' I implore.

'Can you lock up for me?'

'Yes! Just go!'

I sit down, a little weak-kneed from obliterating so many relationships in a matter of minutes.

I take out my phone to call Jacques, not that he'll answer. Perhaps a text would be better. But what should I say?

'*It's not what you think!*'

'*It didn't mean anything!*'

'*It was just one time!*'

Only clichés come to mind. Though, 'It happened before we met!' may be a good way to start.

It's just unfortunate that I lied to his face the other day when he said he thought Gilles had some kind of attraction

for me. I didn't mean to be deceiving, it just seemed unneces-
sary to go there. Of course, if I had confessed then, perhaps
he wouldn't have run out on me tonight.

I start and then delete half a dozen more text messages,
ultimately sending:

'*I'm so sorry Jacques. Those pictures give completely the wrong
impression. I hope you will give me the chance to explain.*'

It's still not right. But I don't know what else to say. Half of
me feels it's a thankless task trying to win him back – for
what? I'm leaving tomorrow. Why would he bother with the
emotional upheaval? After all, as brief as that moment was
with Gilles, it still means I was kissing another man a week
ago and that doesn't paint me in the best possible light . . .

I slope back over to the laptop and focus on reviewing the
final images, trying to keep the hysteria at bay. I can't believe
that just happened. I can't believe I got so close to having a
cosy night with Jacques, only for some stupid pictures to ruin
everything!

I linger as long as I can, hoping he will return – either my
text or to the studio, but he does neither. And then it dawns on
me that I don't want to be here if Gilles and Annique come
back so I hurriedly gather my things and leave Gilles a note to
say I'll see him tomorrow at the starting point for the dog-
sledding race. But then I change my mind – the last thing
Jacques would want to see before he took off would be me
squished alongside Gilles. So I scrap that and write a new note
saying, 'Meet me at Château Frontenac Starbucks at 11 a.m.'

So what now?

With my dinner plans gone awry, I decide to eat at my
auberge restaurant *Le Pain Beni* – blessed bread for a cursed
girl.

The waitress seats me beside a lively mural featuring two
nuns.

'You've got the right idea, sister,' I mutter under my breath.

With not much of an appetite, I go straight for dessert and order the banana cognac flambée Annique's friend had raved about – but I can't eat it. It seems too much of a treat. I'm in a suffering mode. I need poutine.

After checking back at Reception – 'No messages? No packages?' – and then checking my phone a dozen times more, I head down the road, once again passing the Hôtel Clarendon, the Musée de l'Amérique Française, Simons department store and so many of the shops we dipped into on our 'window-licking' excursion. My brow rumples further at the sight of Les Frères de la Côte – the bistro where we had lunch, back when Annique liked me.

I hurry past, turn right on Côte du Palais and there it is: Chez Ashton, which sounds terribly chic and exclusive but is in fact Quebec's answer to McDonald's.

The menu offers fast food burgers, hot dogs, 'rosbif' and trough-loads of their signature dish of poutine.

It comes in three sizes – regular, mini and – clearly for those people who feel compelled to say they've eaten it but are frankly terrified – *bébé*.

To think that I could be sipping wine while Jacques conjures up his 'spécialité de la maison' but instead I'm sitting alone at a fluro-lit table surrounded by a coach-load of teenagers preparing to eat what looks like prison slops out of a foil carton with a plastic fork.

I heave an almighty sigh.

Bon appetit!

31

Laurie is positively reeling from all the drama.

Stolen religious jewels! Skiing with horses! Secret tryst photo-scandals!

But the thing that really sends her ergonomic chair spinning is this:

'You actually liked the poutine?!'

'I don't know what to say,' I sigh down the phone. 'It was sooo delicious. I think it's like Marmite in that you love it or you hate it but if it hooks you then it sets up a craving that no another food on earth can satisfy. I actually fancy another portion right now.'

'*For breakfast?*' Laurie wretches.

'Don't knock it till you've tried it.'

'I'd say bring me some back, but the thought of those cheese curds after an overnight flight . . .'

'Do you know they actually squeak when they're fresh?'

'Krista,' Laurie adopts a serious tone. 'Do you think perhaps that you're fixating on the poutine as a way of not dealing with what happened with Jacques? Not to mention the fact that this is your last day in Quebec?'

I slink lower beneath the covers. If I don't get up then the day can't start.

'What are you going to do about him?'

'What can I do, realistically, when I only have a matter of hours left and he'll be tied up with the race for most of those?'

I puff. 'Even if I could make it right with him, what would that mean beyond today?'

'Being a bit defeatist, aren't you?'

'I just realised my infatuation with him is a fantasy – I'm all caught up with my feelings for him and not really looking at the practicalities.'

'I thought you said that you could see yourself living on the Île D'Orléans mushing huskies, tapping maple syrup and speaking French with a Bromley accent.'

'I could.'

'And what about that little puppy-child that needs a mummy?'

'Teddy,' I sigh, panging as I remember the moment at which he emerged from Jacques' jacket. 'But what are the odds of him inviting me to stay? I mean, as holiday romances go, we didn't even get to the romance part.'

'That's because he's had a lot going on emotionally. It's not like some drunken Ibiza bar hookup.'

'Hold on – there's another call coming through.' I look at my phone.

'Who is it?' Laurie demands.

'I don't know, I don't recognise the number but it is a 514 area code . . .'

'Answer it!'

'Hello?' I fail to disguise the caution in my voice.

'Krista?'

'Yes?'

'It's Sebastien.'

'Is everything all right?' My thoughts immediately go to Jacques.

'Yes, I just need to ask a favour.'

'Go ahead . . .'

'There's a church opposite your hotel, can you meet me there an hour from now?'

'Yes . . .'

'I'll explain when you get here.'

And then the line clicks off.

'What do you think he wants?' Laurie asks when I bring her up to speed. 'And why a church?'

'I have no idea. I just hope he doesn't know about the pictures with Gilles; he's extremely protective of his brother.'

'You'd better get ready,' Laurie urges. 'And dress for all eventualities.'

'Laurie?'

'Yes.'

'You're such a good friend, always there for me.'

'Oh don't start!'

'I mean it.'

'Just bring me back a bottle of Caribou and we'll call it quits.'

As I layer on my clothes I feel nervous, curious and sad all in one. Is there any way for this situation to turn around? The thought of going back to my life in London seems nigh-on unbearable.

Time to go. I'm halfway down the stairs when I collide with Annique.

'Oh!' She takes a step back. 'I was just coming up to see you but obviously you're headed out.'

I look at my watch. 'I've got five minutes.' And then I think that sounds callous so I explain, 'I have to meet Sebastien – he needs some kind of favour.'

'Sebastien? Did you resolve things with Jacques?'

I shake my head. 'I sent him a text but he didn't respond.'

'Perhaps his phone doesn't accept texts?' she offers.

'Perhaps. What about you and Gilles? Is everything all right now?'

She sighs. 'No. But it's okay. It's for the best.'

My shoulders slump. 'Annique, you have to understand I hadn't even met you when it happened and I had no idea that the two of you were—'

'No,' she cuts in. 'But he did. He knew.'

'I know he thinks the world of you . . .'

'Do you know how old he is?' Her chin juts the question. 'Or rather I should say, how young?'

'I just found out yesterday,' I say in a small voice.

'You consider his age, the fact that he's not ready to be a father, the fact he was kissing another woman two days after we met . . .'

I grimace. 'Well, when you put it like that . . .'

She checks her watch. 'You need to get to your appointment.' She leads me back down the stairs and pushes the bar on the door. 'If I've learned one thing, it's that I need a man who has all the time in the world for me and for Coco.'

It is precisely at this point that I look across to the church and see Mr Dufour waiting in the car park. Retired, mad about kids . . . I turn back to Annique.

'How do you feel about older men?'

She shrugs. 'It might be time.'

'I want you to come and meet someone.'

'Ohh, not now, I have Coco with me – she's just waiting in the souvenir shop.'

'Actually, she would be a bonus as far as this guy is concerned.'

'Really?'

'Absolutely.'

So now there are three of us heading for the church.

I understand the choice of venue now – this is where all the sled-dog vans are parked, bringing with them the distinctive smell of hay and revved-up dogs.

'Krista!' Jacques' father does his classic welcome cheer.

'Hello, Mr Dufour!'

'Call me Philippe.'

'Philippe, I'd like you to meet Mademoiselle Coco.'

She is a darling little girl, eyes like chocolate buttons, hair braided with bright pink bows, sticking out from her jaunty cerise beret.

He doffs his cap with a swooping bow, causing her to giggle and respond with a curtsy.

'And this,' I pause for effect, 'is Annique.'

His eyes widen to take in her beauty. '*Enchanté . . .*'

'She's even prettier on the inside.'

He looks back at me to check my sincerity and I give him a nod of confirmation – she's the real deal.

'Would you like to meet the dogs?' He turns his attention back to Coco. 'Give them a lucky paw-shake before they race?'

She looks excitedly up at her mum for approval.

'That would be lovely,' Annique confirms.

'After you . . .' Mr Dufour motions towards the truck. But before he follows them, he turns back to me and husks, 'I think I just met my new wife . . .'

I'm just thinking that I should probably have asked where Sebastien is when he appears beside me.

'Thanks for coming,' he puffs, a little out of breath.

'Everything all right?'

'Just running around setting up for the race. Jacques is already at the start with the first group. I don't know if you know but we run a couple of teams each year?'

'No . . .'

'And I was due to race second but,' he gives an exaggerated grimace, 'I've got this twinge in my arm and I can't risk messing up my body before the Cirque du Soleil tour. You understand?'

'Of course.'

'So you'll do it?'

'Do what?'

'Race in my place?'

I stare at him in disbelief. 'You can't be serious.'

'Why not?'

I give an involuntary snort. 'You've seen what happens when I mush under pressure – I land flat on my face!'

'You'll be fine.'

'Sebastien!' I despair. 'I can't believe you're being so blasé about the Dufour reputation. What if I completely mess up? Which is really likely considering I have done this precisely twice before and only out in the snowy wilds – I don't know anything about careering through a town centre with hundreds of whooping people lining the trail.'

'Oh you'll love it, it's a total trip.'

I blink at him. This must be a wind-up. It has to be.

And then it strikes me . . .

'If you knew an hour ago that you weren't going to race, why didn't you ask one of the other guys or Lucy . . .'

'Because it has to be you.'

Before I can probe him further he adds, 'And it has to be now.'

At which point Mr Dufour comes around the corner with six super-charged dogs, rearing up on their hind legs with excitement.

'You're not going to deny them their race now, are you, Krista?'

Oh cripes, he's in on it too!

'You can do it!' Annique encourages.

I want to point out that she's in no position to be allowed an opinion since she was curled up in a hungover ball when we were last at the farm.

'I asked them to run faster than they ever have done in their life,' Coco adds.

'Thanks for that,' I mutter, feeling faint with anxiety.

As we progress up the hill to the starting point, Sebastien continues with his pep talk.

'You can't mess this up.'

I give him a 'Be real!' glare.

'What I mean is, this is a fun race, a Carnival attraction. You're not going to make or break us.'

'Then why is it so important?'

'Because I don't want the last image Jacques has of you to be the one he saw in the photo studio.'

My stomach drops like a stone. He knows.

'I feel awful about that,' my brow crumples. 'It was just a fleeting moment—'

He holds up his hand. 'I know. I saw Gilles on the way in. Jacques wouldn't speak to him but I did.'

I heave a sigh. And then I startle: 'I'm supposed to be meeting Gilles at Starbucks—'

'I already told him you had other plans.'

I give Sebastien a steady look. 'Do you really think me doing this is going to make a difference? It won't just annoy Jacques more?'

'Listen, you're not the only one around here with devious ways of fixing situations.'

I raise an eyebrow.

'And don't act all innocent with me. I know Montreal was your idea.'

I bite my lip.

'So you see, I owe you.'

An announcement is made over the tannoy. Sebastien translates for me:

'It's your turn.'

I take a breath, the mere influx of oxygen making me giddy. I can hardly hear the dogs barking for the rushing in my ears, but I can feel them straining, yanking at the sled.

'*Set us free! Set us free!*'

Sebastien places his hands over my trembling mittens.

'Trust the dogs, trust yourself. Lean to the left, lean to the right. And enjoy it – in approximately three seconds you will be the star attraction at the Quebec Winter Carnival!'

Oh my god!

And with that, we're off!

It's an interesting thing being a writer. Nobody cheers and whoops as you sit at the laptop. There are no crowds of people peering over your shoulder, elbowing at each other to get a better look at your adjectives or gasp at your innovative use of punctuation. You might get a compliment after the fact, but the actual act of writing is about the least likely 'spectator sport' you could get.

So this rush, this frenzy, this sky-rocketing adrenalin is all very new to me.

Not that I can really take any of it in. Other than passing through the archway as we exit the Old Town, I don't think I could even describe the route that I am currently pounding down. I am soley focused on the dogs. I try so hard not to panic-brake as we plunge downhill but a few times I get a 'runaway train' sensation and have to slow them just enough to keep my hysteria at bay.

Out of some mysterious instinct I feel my knees bending and flexing in response to the motion, and when we take a steep slope I hop off the sled and run myself. For a few seconds after I jump back I enter the zone. I have just enough time to think, 'This is the best!' before we take a sharp right and the Château Frontenac comes into view.

The cheering intensifies.

'*Allez, allez!*' I request one last burst of energy from the dogs and they oblige.

Suddenly it's all over.

And then it's all hands on deck – Sebastien and his father running towards me to take over and handle the dogs. My legs almost buckling as I step off the sled.

I did it! I can't believe it but I did!

And then I see a surprising pair of arms advancing to embrace me.

'Madame Laframboise!'

'Bien fait, vous êtes tellement brave!'

'Th-thank you!' I say, though I have no idea of the exact translation, it seems positive. She's still hugging me when, over her shoulder, I see a man approaching.

And that man is Jacques.

'I didn't realise you two knew each other.'

'She's a good girl,' Madame Laframboise places her hand on my cheek. 'She cares about you very much.'

I blush and look at the ground.

'It was you?' Jacques steps closer. 'You're the reason she called me?'

'I'm sure she would have any way, with the baby coming . . .'

And then I look up at him. This is my chance to speak. I have to at least try to make him understand.

'Jacques, I'm so sorry about the picture, I—'

'No,' he stops me. 'I'm embarrassed about how I behaved. I don't normally get that jealous. There was just something so . . . I don't know, *pure* about how I felt about you and when I saw that, just the thought of another man . . .' He shudders.

'It was the briefest moment—'

'I know,' he soothes me. 'Sebastien told me. And he showed me just how brave you were willing to be for me.' He rubs his hands over his face. 'I can't believe you just competed in the *La Grande Virée*!'

'I'm still in shock myself!' I laugh.

He takes a step closer. 'You were wonderful! On fire!'

'Really?'

'Jacques! Krista!' Sebastien interrupts, beckoning us over. 'They have the results.'

Thanks to me, this is the first year in ten that Jacques does not come out as overall winner. And he says he couldn't be happier.

'It's time for a change, time for something new.'

And then he pulls me into a big squishy Puffa hug and kisses the top of my head.

'Tell me, it's not true that you're leaving today, is it?' he says, looking down into my eyes.

I give the slightest nod.

'Can't you stay just one more day? I owe you a dinner. I'll get your flight changed. We can have the whole evening to ourselves – just you, me and a hundred or so dogs.'

My smile becomes a mile wide. 'Sounds like a dream!'

'Then you'll stay?'

'I'll stay. With you.'

He looks as if he might burst with delight. I feel the same way.

'So you'll check out of the auberge and check in with me?'

I nod, desperate to squeak or squeal or roll in the snow like Jupiter is doing right now. This is beyond wonderful! I'm all but soaring with joy!

'Okay, well, we'll get finished up here and then let me know when you're ready and I'll come get your bag. And you.'

I so desperately want to run all the way, but I don't want any broken bones or concussions before what could be the best night of my life, so I inch across the road in my usual eighty-year-old-with-an-invisible-walker mode.

As I come through the front door the woman on Reception jokes, 'No messages, no packages!'

'That's okay,' I chirrup.

'But there is a man waiting for you in the restaurant . . .'

32

My face falls. This can't be good. I almost daren't look in. I just couldn't bear it if anything got in the way now . . .

As I walk past the beige-clothed tables, I study every male I see, just to be sure that the complexion and eye colour isn't a variation on you-know-who.

But then I see one face that has remained the same from the first day I arrived – Gilles.

'I got a booth away from the window so no one would see us.'

I slide onto the opposite banquette.

'Jacques is coming to get me here so I haven't got long.'

'That's okay. I just wanted to tell you . . .' He looks a little lost for words.

I want to reach across and touch his hand but think better of it. Instead I simply say, 'I'm sorry about Annique.'

'Me too. But I feel relieved that I can't disappoint her or hurt her any more. She deserves better.'

I nod, only now realising that Annique could end up being my mother-in-law. But I'm getting ahead of myself . . .

'I got some great shots of you in the race!' he perks up.

'You did? I wondered if you'd even realise it was me. You know, seeing as I was going by so fast!'

'You were fast!'

I smile back at him. 'I'm glad there's proof because no one back home would believe I did that.'

And then I get a queasy pang. I said 'back home', but it doesn't feel like I'll be going back 'home' at all; it feels like I'll be leaving it.

'You don't want to go back, do you?' Gilles tilts his head at me.

'No,' I admit, so glad to be postponing my exit even by a day, even if it's going to make it harder. 'When do you leave?' I ask him.

'Couple of hours.'

'Back to Montreal?'

'Actually I'm going up to the mountains for a few days – I want to work on my action shots, I thought I'd go to one of the local ski resorts and experiment.'

'That's a great idea.'

'Plus I need to practise taking pictures of people without kissing them.'

'I don't know . . . every photographer needs their signature style . . .'

He smiles and then slides an envelope across the table.

'I wanted to give you this.'

It's a picture of Jacques hugging me at the finishing line. Obviously I knew how smitten my face looked, but seeing his expression sends my heart swirling skyward.

'You said before that you don't much believe in love, but I think you should believe in him.'

I look back at this twenty-three-year-old man, sounding so prophetic.

'Why are you being so nice?' I ask.

'To show my gratitude.'

'For what?'

'For the way that you showed me just how dull perfection can be.'

My brow furrows. 'I don't quite know how to take that.'

'I mean perfection in fashion, the kind of pictures I was creating before. There was no room for real emotion. I want to feel more now. And that's because of you.'

I purse my lips. 'I really want to hug you now but I can't.'

'We've had our hug,' he winks as he gets to his feet. 'It was a pleasure working with you Krista. Perhaps our paths will cross again?'

'I want to visit the polar bears in Manitoba, if you're game?'

'White animals on a white backdrop?' He groans. 'Of course.'

I sit there for a few moments after he's gone. Again I feel a pang of sentimentality. One by one, everyone is moving on. The adventure is drawing to a close. And try as I might to cling on to it, it's just the natural progression of life. Nothing ever stays the same . . .

I'm even sentimental about my darling patchwork-quilted room when I go up to shower and pack. But as I zip my case closed, a smile begins a-creeping. I am not going to the airport. I'm going home with Jacques.

Now that sounds right. And feels right, deep inside me.

33

It's a good couple of hours before we are alone.

We travel back with Sebastien and Mr Dufour, who is pleased as punch on account of having dinner plans with Annique and Coco – he's just coming back to the ranch to shower and change and then he's off out again. Which means Sebastien will now head back to Montreal on his own. Along with all his worldly goods. Or at least the things he brought with him when he came to stay.

'You don't have to take everything,' Jacques tells him, perhaps a little sorry to be seeing him go after all.

'I feel like there are pieces of me scattered all over the province,' Sebastien explains. 'It's time to consolidate.'

'Just know you are welcome back any time. Just not for such a long period.'

Sebastien laughs and pulls his brother into a hug. I turn away to give them some privacy but then feel his arms around me.

'You did good today, Krista.'

'Th-thank you!' I breathe into his shoulder, feeling a rush of emotion.

But then he pulls away, hoiks his bag onto his shoulder and raises his hand as he heads to the car. 'You take good care of each other.'

'One last thing,' I call after him. 'Do I have your permission to save him now?'

Sebastien stalls and looks back at me. 'You already did.'

*   *   *

And then everything goes to the dogs.

All our attention and several tonnes of raw meat. I'm happy to get stuck in alongside Jacques. Making so many furry tummies happy is a kick. They've certainly earned it. And even if I'm getting a bit peckish now myself, my heart is full – it's hard to look into all these grinning, lip-smacking faces and not feel brimming over with love.

'Is there something wrong with your foot?' I ask one dog who doesn't even look up from cleaning his paw when I come by. 'Let me take a peek . . .'

I find a spiky burr hooked between his toes and take off my glove to remove it.

'All better now!' I say as I tuck the prickles into my pocket, out of harm's way.

'Good instinct,' Jacques commends me.

'Oh well,' I shrug. 'I remember when that used to happen with my own dog. They can't always ask for help – you just notice a change in their demeanour.'

He nods and smiles.

'What?'

'Nothing.' He grins. 'It's just nice having you here.'

Chores complete, we head inside to get cleaned up. For me it's just a question of giving my hands a good scrub, but Jacques heads off for a shower, leaving me with a large glass of wine and a comfy chair. But I can't settle, knowing his nakedness is but a few feet away . . .

I move around the kitchen trying to guess what might be on the menu tonight. Eggs, some kind of pâté, a bar of white chocolate . . . I don't see any cheese curds . . .

'You look hungry enough to eat the chopping board,' Jacques observes when he returns to me, all relaxed, damp of hair and mis-buttoned of shirt. 'I think I must cook something *plus vite* . . .'

'Whatever you make, I love it already!' I cheer, and then accept his invitation to hop up onto a stool beside the breakfast bar.

What a nice collarbone he has, I think, as he leans down to the bottom cupboard to pull out a flat pan. What nice forearms I see when he rolls back his shirt-sleeves. And a very alluring hip bone as he reaches up to the tippety-top shelf to grab a pie tin.

'For dessert,' he explains.

And then he starts to dice and slice and simmer and stir. All the while chatting to me and smiling and occasionally coming over to lean close and tantalise me all the more.

I don't know of a better feeling than being with someone you like and it becoming more and more apparent just how much they like you. Deep down you know there is a kiss coming but there's no need to rush it because, in this state, you have all the time in the world. Of course we don't at all. But it feels that way. Tucked in this candlelit nook we can exhale and meander in our conversation and not worry about future logistics. For now anything seems possible. Maybe because we've just shared a glass of Caribou . . .

'I wonder, if you really have to go back tomorrow . . .' He squints mischievously at me.

'Well, I would love to stay, indefinitely actually, but my friend Laurie is moving to New York and I only have a few days to be with her before she leaves.'

'You know New York is only an hour and a half flight from here.'

'Really?' Now that is interesting.

'Mmm-hmm. You can drive to Boston in under seven. Have you been there for your website?'

'Not yet.'

'I think your readers would like it. Not that I can pretend to know what women want.'

You are what women want, I think to myself as he invites me to take a seat at the table. Aside from the fact that you cook, you're kind and honourable and tousled-sexy, with just the right amount of wolf-whispering to maintain the intrigue.

I think about what his dad said, that he doesn't have a mean bone in his body. I love that. I love the idea that I don't have to be wary of him. That he wouldn't turn on me or shake me up with his temper like Andrew used to. And he already knows the worst of me – that I can't have children. Only with him it's not a defect, it's just something we have in common.

'Jacques, this is delicious!' I exclaim as I take my first bite of crêpe.

Up until now I was convinced that the only place that could do a crêpe right was the van parked outside the King William IV pub on Hampstead High Street, but Jacques has matched their bronzed exterior and warm, gooey interior. Cheese, ham and soft asparagus merge with a piquant herb. It's a simple dish but couldn't be going to a happier home.

'You want another one?'

I'm torn. I can smell the freshly baked dessert pie . . .

'We could share one?'

'Perfect!' I jump up, this time joining him by the counter. 'What can I do to help?'

He hands me the cheese grater while continuing to chat about his diet on the last Yukon Quest, and as he does so his hand reaches to the back of my neck and he's entwining his fingers in my hair as if he's done it a thousand times before. It's all I can do to keep my eyes from flickering closed in bliss.

Then he stops talking. And moves closer. I can feel his breath on my cheek. Oh-so-slowly I set down the grater and turn my body towards him. He looks at me. Into me.

And then a siren-alarm starts wailing.

'What is it?' I panic as he rushes to his computer.

'We have to go!'

'What?!' Talk about caribou interruptus!

'Grab an extra coat and blanket!' He instructs while he gathers his things – great, bulky, unidentified objects.

'Where are we going?'

'You'll see when we get there!'

'Are we on some kind of rescue mission? Is someone in trouble?' I ask as he reaches for the brandy and then calls for Sibérie to join us.

'No, but time is of the essence.'

Within minutes we're in the truck. Heading deeper and deeper, darker and darker, into the Middle of Nowhere.

'Is this the point at which I find out you're a serial killer?'

'Serial? Don't be silly,' he laughs. 'You'll be my first.'

Great.

I drum my fingers. 'Is there any way we can get the dismembering over and done with now? The suspense is killing me!'

'You need to relax,' he soothes. 'Like Sibérie.'

I look back and find him flat as a rug on the back seat, lip splayed, emitting a light snore. That is relaxed.

'Not long now,' Jacques assures me, though the opposite is true.

So much so that I'm starting to worry about missing tomorrow's flight.

When we do arrive, I'm none the wiser – we appear to have driven for hours to reach a snowy plain and a cluster of trees, and there were plenty of snowy plains and clustery trees beside the ranch.

'Stay in the warm,' he instructs as he jumps out of the truck. 'I'll come and get you when we're ready.'

'Ready for what?'

'You to join us,' he replies, rather confoundingly.

Whistling for Sibérie, he treks off, carrying the bulky bags rucksack style, one over each arm.

I shift in my seat, trying to get comfortable, trying not to fixate on the caramelised apple pie Jacques had promised me for dessert. If I'd known this was going to be such a long-winded emergency dash, I would have packed a couple of slices.

Tiredness creeps up on me and I give my jaw full rein to yawn. Perhaps I should grab forty winks? I pull my fleecy hat down low and close my eyes. Only to be frightened out of my skin when Jacques comes rapping on the window.

'We're ready for you now . . .'

'Here we go!' I try to psyche myself up as I wade through the snow, following him to a clearing.

But when I see what he has been working on I find myself muttering: 'And I thought being hacked to pieces would be a bad way to end the night.'

A tent. He's erected a tent!

I suppose in a way it's appropriate – I spent my first night freezing my face off at the ice hotel, now we've come full circle. Full artic-flipping-circle, I think, as the wind slices through me.

'So we're camping?' I ask, shoulders up by my ears.

'Not exactly,' he smiles. 'It's just to keep us warm.'

But we were warm! I want to protest. I for one was feeling extremely toasty back at the farmhouse with your hand on the back on my neck . . .

'Come on, let's get cosy.'

Okay. Well. Maybe this isn't so bad. The tent is really small, just one of those little domes, so we have to get really close, into the same two-person sleeping bag, in fact. There are plenty of extra blankets nesting around us, and when he puts his arm around me and I snug into his shoulder, I can't think of anywhere else I'd rather be. For a second I even forget to wonder why the hell we're here.

And then Sibérie gives a little bark, prompting Jacques to reach up and unzip a large panel in the top of the tent.

'We have a skylight!' I marvel.

'The stars are so bright out here – no electricity for miles.'

So this is why – we've come to lie beneath the stars. That's nice. Not quite sure we needed a siren alert but still . . .

And then the light show begins. Just a vapour at first. A mere mist of luminescent green, a wand-like streak across the sky.

My heart starts to tremble. Is this . . . ? Could this be . . . ?

I watch as the green infuses with a ghostly white, shape-shifting and moving like sands blowing across the blackness.

'Jacques,' I grope for his arm as the vista glows ultraviolet. 'Am I seeing what I think I'm seeing?'

He nods.

'*Say it!*'

'Krista, for your viewing pleasure, allow me to present, the aurora borealis . . .'

I flash back to the imitation light show I saw with Mal from the hotel window. But this is so much better. This is *real* . . .

And Jacques is real. And I'm really here with him right now watching nature's ethereal fireworks flare across the sky!

When I turn to face him, he is already looking at me, gazing so fondly, so open-heartedly . . .

His lashes lower, his mouth meets mine . . .

And when he kisses me I feel as if my heart has taken flight, swirling now amid those mystical swathes of silk. I can almost see Sebastien and Julie floating up there, moving with the drift and sway.

'This is heavenly,' I whisper as we pause for breath. And

then I burrow into Jacques' warm neck. 'I can't believe this is my last night!'

'It's not our last. It's our first,' he says, gently lifting my face to meet his. 'This is where we begin . . .'

ACKNOWLEDGEMENTS

I have never begun my acknowledgements with a *place* before but I have to thank 'the province of Quebec' for offering such sparkling inspiration for *Winter Wonderland* – this has been my all-time favourite book to write!

Now to the *people*: firstly Erin Levi at DQMPR who led me to Magalie Boutin who in turn introduced me to Paule Bergeron and Nathalie Guay at Quebec City Tourism. To Carnival media maestro Patrick Lemaire and Sarah Matthews at the Hotel de Glace, Jean Gaudreau at Hôtel-Musée Première Nations, Véronique Dufour at Hotel Clarendon and Geneviève Parent and Santol the dog at the Chateau Frontenac! Such toasty-warm hospitality amid the chill!

To my fellow press trippers: Glenn, David, Adam, Adrian & Julia and Marie-Julie! How I love the company of journos!

And the delightful duo staying at the Auberge Place D'Armes who joined me to coo over husky puppies – darnit, I've misplaced your details but if you know a Doris Day lookalike with a wise-cracking doctor side-kick, say a maple syrup pie hi from me!

In Montreal, many 'mercis' go to Hugo Leclerc for his itinerary suggestions and for arranging such a vibrant tour guide in the stylish form of Annique Dufour.

And so to London! Ah Isobel! Though you are soaring in a new direction I have to say I would like to read a book from you one day, such wonderful thoughts you have! And Harriet with your genius for diplomacy and making me feel you have my best interests at heart – so very much appreciated! To Jaime in publicity, Anneka in design, Penny the copy-editor and the Hodder family as a whole. Thank you for such joyful support! Also in the Big Smoke, the lovely Claudia Webb – my shiny new agent at William Morris Endeavour.

Nick Wechsler – thank you for being my muse for the character of Jacques, albeit just from watching your tousled self on American TV!

And finally, as ever, to my dreamy mother, Pamela, and handsome husband, Jonathan.

Further reading and connections

www.carnaval.qc.ca/en/

www.quebecregion.com/en

www.belindajones.com

Twitter: @vidabelinda

Facebook: Belinda Jones Travel Club

Email the author: writerbelinda@me.com

KRISTA'S TOP TEN TRAVEL
DOS & DON'TS

DO . . .

1. Start with the lightest possible suitcase. Such advance-ments have been made in this area it is well worth considering retiring your old back-buckler in favour of the new ultra-lites, allowing you to pack those extra pair of wedges you know you'll probably only wear once but will totally make the outfit.

I still take my black patent glam-case on roadtrips and week-ends away, but it's long-haul flight days are over. Not least because the airlines are getting stingier with their allowances. Which brings me to . . .

2. Double-check your baggage allowance online (airlines vary greatly) *and weigh your suitcase before you leave home.* Obvious but not to be ignored! I'm all for packing as much as you want (see *DO NOT* worry about 'packing light'), but I am morally opposed to paying airlines' excessive fees for being a pound or two overweight. There's nothing worse than feeling ripped off before you've even left the country.

3. Try and match each outfit you pack to a scenario on your vacation. It's all too easy to load in all your favourite items without stopping to ask, 'Will I really need a red linen jacket (with polyester lining) in Bali?' Think back to what you wore over and over the last time you went on a similar trip (be it beach or city) and pack those items first, only topping-off with the more questionable choices. (Better yet, leave a gap for on-location purchases.)

4. **Bring a pashmina or cosy cashmere scarf / cardi combo for the flight.** You may be jetting off to hundred-degree humidity but chances are you'll get Hôtel de Glace-style frozen on the plane and it's far harder to drift off to sleep when you are hunched and shivering. And you can't even count on being offered a static-electricity-conducting airline blanket any more.

5. **Watch what you spend at the airport.** What with the obligatory farewell fry-up, the glittering bracelets and sarongs at Accessorize and the lure of Duty Free, it's easy to drop £100 while you are milling around waiting for your gate to be announced. You may think that 'travel exclusive' set of lipglosses looks so pretty lined up together, but really, would you wear all five shades?

6. **Research your destination way ahead of time.** I really believe that guidebooks should be read weeks in advance of your trip as opposed to at the breakfast table before you head out on your first day. Not only does this extend the life of your holiday (anticipation is half the pleasure!), but you will also know that the Metropolitan Museum of Modern Art in NYC (and virtually every other museum around the world) is closed on a Monday. Same goes for Broadway shows. More research, less regret!

7. **Book any show tickets as far in advance as possible.** Especially if you are going for the cheaper seats. Rows M–Z may be the same price band but wouldn't you rather be M as opposed to 13 rows back in Z because that's all that's available last-minute?

That said, it's always worth checking for returns on the day itself. There's never been a Sold Out show I haven't got into.

8. Try the lingo. With the possible exception of France, your butchering of the native language will only endear you to the locals. (It's also fun to get so into the habit of saying, 'Gracias!' that you say it to your local newsagent when you get home.)

9. Invest in noise-cancelling headphones. This may seem like a luxury item but the difference they will make to your flight is worth its weight in gold. The leather padding is so soft and snug around your ears, you will immediately get a sense of pampered well-being, but more importantly you can hear every word of the movie, as opposed to only catching the gist. (Which in turn makes the time pass quicker because you are far more absorbed.) You can tune out Chatty Cathy neighbours, crying babies and the feeling that you are travelling in Economy – this may be the most affordable upgrade on the market!

10. Take a carry-on case with wheels. It's just not worth the indentations in your shoulders to lug a carry-on bag with a strap, especially if you're taking a laptop. It may not seem that heavy when you give it a test-jiggle at home, but once you've walked the ten miles to the gate and loaded up on magazines and water bottles and a family-size pack of wine gums, you'll start to feel the burden. Better to be free-wheeling and channel your inner Pan-Am hostess as you walk.

DO NOT ...
1. Forget to boost your immune system prior to travelling. Get into the habit of having daily Vitamin C and echinacea tea a good month before your trip, and with any luck the on-plane lurgies will attack the weaker specimens, leaving your health intact.

2. **Worry about 'packing light'.** There seems to be some ridiculous competitiveness over who can have the smallest suitcase, as if it somehow makes you a better person, and anyone with a bumper load is shamed into feeling somehow 'greedy' or indulgent. Do you really want to be wearing the same outfit in every holiday snap? Besides, for some of us, being on holiday is our only real chance to dress up and play with accessories. I say, go for it!

3. **Wear big boots to the airport.** Aside from being a palaver to remove as you pass through security, they will take up too much room when you want to kick them off during your flight. If there's no getting around it (say you're flying to Quebec and your suitcase is already chockablock), take an extra plastic bag to put them in once you have boarded and store them in the overhead locker for the duration.

4. **Pick an airplane seat close to the toilets.** It may initially seem a 'convenience', but this will be the point of the most coming and going (disturbing your sleep) and you always risk basking in some foul odour. Equally, a window seat is not always the most desirable, unless you're a sleeper. If you're a fidget and hate to feel hemmed in, go for the aisle. Even if you begrudge getting up to let out the other passenger / s, the movement will be good for your circulation.

5. **Have ice with your drink on the flight.** Multiple studies have shown airplane ice contains way too much nasty bacteria. Just say no! (And have a nice glass of red wine.)

6. **Use your mobile phone abroad without checking all the charges first,** especially the data roaming ones, or you could end up spending more than the cost of your holiday on one lousy Internet search. Best to switch to wifi and stay there.

7. Hesitate to talk to the locals. Even if you are not fluent in their language, even if you have to mime out most of the words, even if all you can do is share a drink or dance together, these are the interactions that will make your trip.

8. Expect things to go perfectly. Every new place with its native quirks and customs has a new way to throw you off your game. Even tried-and-tested destinations can have power-outages or insane new 'resort fees' to rack up your bill. But letting a few niggles (however outrageously unjust) ruin your whole trip only serves the Gods of Vexation & Regret. Besides, it's often the 'disasters' that make for your funniest dinner stories. You just might have to practise the phrase 'It's only money' a few times before it ceases to stick in your throat. Alternatively just remind yourself, 'It could be worse, I could be at work.'

9. Miss out on the local cuisine. Worst-case scenario you spit it into your napkin. Best-case scenario, your tastebuds get to feel like they are on holiday too, revelling in a host of new flavours. Really, just because it doesn't look like anything you've ever encountered before doesn't mean it won't be delicious! I could never stand the smell of Indian food until I took my first bite and now I can't get enough of it. (If only I'd known peshwari naan tastes like a pastry sooner!)

10. Be afraid to travel alone. Some of the most rewarding experiences will come when you leave your home alter ego behind, and the best way to do that is not to travel with anyone reminding you of who you normally are and how you normally behave. Given carte blanche to be whoever you want to be, who knows what incredible adventures you will have!

KRISTA'S BEST OF THE WORLD

Best beach-life

Bronte Beach (just twenty miles north of Sydney) has an amazing fifty-metre rock pool built into the ocean with surf crashing over the side and the occasional fish swimming alongside you!

There are so many great sandy shores around the world where you can splay and suntan, but in terms of great add-ons like barbecues and surfer dudes, Australia is in a league of its sunny, friendly, energetic own.

Best-presented food

The French may create clever abstract art with their nouveau cuisine, but for sheer, intricate beauty you can't beat Thailand. Even a humble carrot becomes a blossoming rose. And you should see what they can do with a watermelon . . .

Best avoided

The sex shows of Bangkok. You hear so much about those native girls expelling ping-pong balls, you want to see the phenomenon for yourself. But the fact is, it's just yukky and sad. I don't know if it was because my friend and I left mid-performance or under-tipped, but the girl on stage turned and aimed her ping-pong ball at me as we were heading for the door, making a direct hit on my shoulder. The good news is that I was wearing a jacket. The bad news is that it was suede. Try explaining that to your local dry-cleaner . . .

Best place to have the time of your life

The Mountain Lake Hotel in Virginia, USA, is the real-deal Kellerman's, as featured in Dirty Dancing. From the minute you pull up at the resort, it feels like you are stepping into the movie set: everywhere you look you're reminded of another scene – the gazebo dance class, the staff cabins, that moving lakeside moment with Baby and her dad – so many photo opps! The hotel has plenty of memorabilia and souvenirs in the gift shop and you can even attend special Dirty Dancing themed weekends from May to November. Go swivel like Swayze!

Best place to stroke a cheetah

When I visited South Africa a few years back, Cheetah Outreach was housed at the gorgeous Spier wine estate in Stellenbosch, but it has relocated to Somerset West, just half an hour from Cape Town city centre. Just don't wear dangly earrings or you may experience a 'playful' swipe!

Best sauna

It has to be Finland. Especially since they encourage you to drink chilled Kulta beer (brewed by women in the Arctic circle) and splash some of it on the hot coals to diffuse a woodsy-malty scent while you sit and sweat.

Best hotel suite

Jade Mountain Resort in Saint Lucia. An entire ocean-view wall is missing, offering you unobstructed panoramas of the green-velvet-clad Piton mountains and a gentle sea breeze as you swim in the suite's infinity pool. Your sanctuary also offers a lounge area, a full-size dining table for your fit-for-a-movie-star room-service breakfast and an open-air shower akin to bathing in a waterfall. Even if you stay only one night, the memory will last all eternity – the ultimate Caribbean honeymoon destination.

Best way to time-travel
Get lost in Venice. Step away from St Mark's Square and weave around the backstreets of the Cannaregio district and you will find it's just you, the dreamy canals and ancient palazzos whispering secrets from the past . . .

Best weight-loss programme
A dance holiday in Havana, Cuba. Salsa classes in the morning, exploring the 'decaying splendour' of the city in the afternoon, dancing al fresco till sunrise, coupled with high humidity and food you'd rather skip, means your waist will whittle in a week. Expect your heart to expand, though: Cuban joy is contagious.

Best 'originated here' cocktail
The Singapore Sling as served at the historic Raffles Hotel Long Bar in, you guessed it, Singapore! (The well-to-do island located between Malaysia and Indonesia, where chewing gum is banned and tailors abound.)

Best riverboat cruise
Amsterdam. Touring the city canals and gazing up at the higgledy-piggledy merchants' houses is one of the most relaxing and pleasurable ways to spend your day. The Dutch people are especially wonderful (so smart and easy-going) and they too offer a twist on how to eat your chips – with a big dollop of mayonnaise! (Like poutine, it tastes better than it sounds.)

Best port café
Dubrovnik. Sip a *bijela kava* (latte) in one of the many pavement cafés while enjoying those ruggedly-rumbly Croatian accents in surround-sound before cooling off in the jewel-blue Adriatic.

Best place to blend in if you have a mullet
Utah. You can also wear a rainbow tie-dyed T-shirt, oil-slick sunglasses and a trucker cap. But you don't have to wear any of those things (except maybe the trucker cap) to retrace Thelma & Louise's tyre-tracks around the red rocky desert of Canyonlands National Park. This really is the ultimate road-trip country.

Best Winter Carnival
Quebec. *Naturellement!*

Best cup of tea
Wherever Laurie is brewing up. I'm going to miss you, cupcake . . .

THE TRAVELLING TEA SHOP

If you like the idea of having Laurie as a best friend, you're in luck! Krista is passing the leading-lady baton over to her in the next novel – or should that be battenburg? For this is a cake- themed caper, taking you all around New England on a mission to discover the secret recipes of America's classic treats – to Boston for the Cream Pie, Manhattan for New York Cheesecake, Maine for Whoopie Pie and Cape Cod for all manner of cranberry-flavoured delights. She's travelling with a group of friends, all with their own secrets (recipes and otherwise!) and heartaches to heal.

As well as a grand appreciation of cupcakes, there's also the chance for romance but can making whoopie lead to love?

Find out in autumn 2013 when The Travelling Tea Shop
comes to your town!

HODDER

Escape with Belinda Jones's other wonderful novels . . .

CALIFORNIA DREAMERS

Ever wished you could make-over your life? Make-up artist
Stella is an expert at helping other people change their images,
but when it comes to transforming herself, she doesn't even
know where to start. So when her new friend, glamorous
Hollywood actress Marina Ray, summons her to a movie set
in California, Stella can't resist the chance to start afresh – it
is the land of sunshine and opportunity after all! But are they
really friends or does Marina have an ulterior motive? What is
the secret that both women are hiding about the nautical (but
nice) men in their lives? And what will it take to really make
both of their California dreams come true?

LIVING LA VIDA LOCA

Carmen has been feeling the need to break free for Too Darn
Long. So when her equally frustrated friend Beth suggests
the ultimate escape – dancing their way through a series of
scorchingly-hot countries – she can't resist! There's just one
catch . . . they can only go on this adventure if they partici-
pate in a reality TV show, one intent on teaching them the
mournful tango in Argentina, the feisty flamenco in Spain
and the sassy, celebratory salsa in Cuba! Each dance has a
profound effect on the girls – and indeed the sexy gauchos,
matadors and dirty dancers who partner them . . . But, when
the sun goes down, do they have what it takes to go beyond
the steps and free their hearts for love?

HODDER

We love a happy ending. But, almost more
than that, we love the promise of a new beginning.

Join us at www.hodder.co.uk, or follow us on Twitter
@hodderbooks, and be part of a community of escapists
who enjoy nothing more than curling up with a good book.

Whether you want to find out more about this book,
or a particular author, watch trailers and interviews, have
the chance to win early limited editions, or simply browse
our expert readers' selection of the very best books,
we think you'll find what you're looking for.

And if you don't, that's the place to tell us what's missing.

We love what we do, and we'd love you to be part of it.

www.hodder.co.uk

@hodderbooks

HodderBooks

HodderBooks